GODDESS OF THE ANCIENTS

ROAN ROSSER

Rainbow Dog

RAINBOW DOG BOOKS

Your free ebook is waiting

Sign up for my newsletter to get Jack's prequel story for free. Available at
https://bit.ly/3J1twim

CONTENTS

Chapter One

PRISONERS

THE SMELL OF HOT grease and pizza woke me. I sat up in alarm. When I'd fainted, an ancient vampire had been bearing down on me with murder in her eyes. I seemed unharmed; my wounds healed when I'd shifted from jackal form back to human at dawn. One benefit of shapeshifter powers at least, but there was no sign of Everett. I hoped he was alive, he'd been so terrified when I'd tried to rescue him. I didn't see any sign of the other vampires either. Or Goddess. I'd done my best to fight off the vampire named Goddess, but I'd failed and we were still her captives. If the mages had gotten us back, we'd be at the PCA office. Somewhere safe. Familiar.

I didn't know where I was, but I wasn't at the mage house, the place Goddess had taken us in order to retrieve her amulet. An unfamiliar woman knelt in front of me, holding out a pizza box yet studiously avoiding looking at me. Only when I took the box, moving to sit cross-legged and intending to set it on my lap, did I realize the reason for her blush. I was totally nude.

A cold, heavy handcuff around my ankle pressed into my leg, chaining me to a piece of equipment bolted to the floor. I was in what seemed to be a re-purposed exercise room, sitting on a carpet remnant. A prisoner.

I should be terrified, but I was too hungry. So many form shifts last night had left me ready to chew off my arm. I flipped the box open, almost fainting at the warm blast of steam hitting my face, and my stomach growled angrily. Ignoring the hot cheese burning my tongue, I scarfed down a piece while the woman watched.

"Thank you for the pizza," I said in a rush around the last bite. Now that my initial wave of hunger had been dealt with, I had so many questions for her. "Where are the others?"

Her brow furrowed, she glanced quickly at and then away from one of the two doors. "Goddess and the others are sleeping right now."

With that, she turned and began walking briskly away from me towards the other door.

"Wait," I called after her. "There would've been a man with them, short with dark hair?"

She stopped and turned to face me, crossing her arms and frowning. "Yes. A new one I didn't recognize."

I sagged in relief. I still didn't know where I was, but at least Everett was here as well. "Was he hurt?"

The woman bit her lip and shook her head. "I don't know. They got here just before dawn. Goddess carried him in, but I didn't get a good look."

My stomach growled at me, protesting me sitting there with an open pizza box and not eating more. I gave her my best innocent puppy dog look. "Could you unchain me so I can check on him?"

Her hands tightened on her arms and she tossed her head. "I wouldn't dare. Goddess gave strict orders."

Vampire bites covered her neck and arms. I didn't press; after that much venom her loyalty would be to the vampires. I sighed. "Can you bring him out here, then? I need to check on him. Make sure he isn't hurt."

The woman pursed her lips and considered for a moment. "I'll think about it. In the meantime, I'm going to go see if I have something that might fit you." She turned and left, exiting out the far door. I glimpsed stairs on the other side before she shut it behind her.

While I waited for the woman to return, I finished the rest of the pizza. I was still hungry; too many changes last night, but at least my stomach had stopped growling.

I closed my eyes and concentrated, trying to change. My skin prickled, but nothing else happened. Still daylight then, although this room didn't have any way for me to confirm. They'd covered the windows over with thick black curtains that blocked all the light, so no way to judge the passage of time.

The woman returned eventually, carrying a bucket and a folded pair of sweatpants with her.

I grabbed the pants and turned my back to the lady, intending to put them on, but as I lifted my leg the chain pulled me up short. Shit. This wouldn't work. Holding the pants in front of me I turned back around and pointed to the chain, raising one eyebrow at the woman. "I can't put these on like this."

She blushed and shook her head. "I can't. I don't even have a key."

I grimaced, then just sat back down, holding the pants over me strategically. "What's this for?" I said, tapping the bucket with a foot.

She turned bright red again and stammered, "For your needs..."

"Oh." I wrinkled my nose in disgust, but tried to force my voice to be friendly. "Thank you. My name's Jack, by the way. What's yours?"

She frowned. "Yvonne."

"What about my other request?" I gave her a hard look and folded my arms.

She looked torn, shifting from foot to foot. Giving an enormous sigh, she went over and knocked lightly.

To my surprise, the door opened a few seconds later, and Goddess herself blinked out at us. She'd changed into a tight red dress that hugged her curves.

The sight of her sent my heart racing with fear, and I instinctively tried to shapeshift again. Last time I'd seen her, she'd been trying to kill me. I swallowed hard and stood up, feeling too vulnerable sitting on the floor.

Goddess said nothing and stared at Yvonne.

Yvonne squirmed under Goddess' gaze and gestured to me. "He wanted to check on the new one..."

Goddess's eyes snapped over to me and she slipped past Yvonne to come over to me. She looked me up and down and gave a satisfied nod. "You look much better now."

I didn't react other than a stiffening of my hands holding the sweatpants over my crotch. "Where's Everett? What did you do to him?"

"He's fine. Sleeping." She gestured over her shoulder, back towards the room she'd come out of.

"What happened after—"

She put a hand on her hip and gave me a wide smile. "I brought you and Everett back here, along with my remaining worshipers, to rest and regroup. You should do the same, jackal."

"Wait," I said as she turned to go, forcing myself not to reach for her. "I'd like to take the glass out of him while he's asleep. It'll be painful, and I'd rather do it while he can't feel it."

"Glass?" Her eyes widened in surprise, like she had no idea what I was talking about.

"His back and feet had glass shards in them." I glared at her. Did she care so little for him? Why go to all that trouble to find and kidnap him then? "If vampire healing works like shapeshifter healing, he'll heal around the shards and then cut himself again when he moves."

"I'll bring him out." She disappeared from view between one blink and the next.

I jumped back, startled. She was faster than Everett – much faster.

She emerged from the bedroom a moment later, dragging Everett face-down and by one foot behind her. Goddess dropped him in front of me.

"Be careful. The pain might wake him up." Then she vanished again, and the door slammed.

"Wait," I called after her, wanting to ask about undoing the chain at least long enough to put on the pants, but the lock clicked. Whatever. The pants were more for Yvonne's benefit than mine. At first it had embarrassed me to be nude in front of the others when we stripped to shift, but after over a year of having my shifter powers, I hardly thought about it anymore.

Besides, I needed to focus my attention on Everett. I dropped the pants and knelt next to him. He was paler than I'd ever seen him, ghost white against the beige of the carpet piece. Dried blood tracks and shards of glass crisscrossed his back, legs, and feet, glittering in the harsh overhead light. I buckled down and got to work, carefully picking glass out of my boyfriend's skin.

BONE DEEP COLD STABBED at me, cold so fierce I couldn't do anything but moan as I opened my eyes. My head lay on something warm, but it didn't even touch the chill. As things came into focus, I looked up into Jack's worried face hovering over me.

His bare stomach rested inches from my cheek. My fangs ached for me to turn and sink them in. I resisted the urge although I was so thirsty that I wasn't sure I could even talk. I felt like something was missing, but the dual sensations of thirst and cold made it hard to think.

"Ev!" Jack reached down and cupped my chin, then bit his lip. "How d'you feel?"

"Cold," I tried to say, but all that came out was "Cu-cu-cu." My tongue scrapped my dry mouth when I tried to make the L sound and got stuck.

Jack sighed, eyebrows drawing together in anger, although I could tell it wasn't me he was angry with. "You're white as a ghost. Here." The warmth of his fingers withdrew from my chin as he moved his wrist in front of my mouth. "Bite me. Don't take much though, I haven't recovered from yesterday."

I parted my lips and bit down hard on Jack's wrist. He jerked as my fangs penetrated, so I grabbed his arm with both hands as I greedily sucked down mouthfuls of blood.

"Everett, that's enough."

Jack's words barely had meaning; the pleasant warmth running down my throat and spreading through me consumed my thoughts. I couldn't parse the meaning behind the noise. Jack tugged at his arm, but my hands were vices, pinning him to my mouth, and he couldn't move me.

"Everett, stop feeding and let him go!" A woman's voice stopped me cold.

My fangs retracted, and my hands loosened. Jack jerked his arm back and clutched it to his chest, frowning. I sat up and scooted back away from Jack until my back hit a wall, shaking with a combination of pleasure and shame even as I licked my lips to make sure I didn't waste a drop.

The bone-deep cold had retreated, but I could feel it close by. I hadn't had enough to get fully warmed up. I pulled my knees to my chest, wrapped my arms around them, and hid my face so I didn't have to see the betrayal in Jack's eyes any longer. My chest burned with shame at feeding on my boyfriend yet again.

"I warned you." She sounded amused. "But I do admire your dedication to your vampire. Your jackal instincts are powerful."

"You did warn me," Jack said.

I risked a peek at him over my knees. He had his other hand clenched tightly around his wrist, but he didn't look angry. More... hurt, I'd guess. His eyes were wide as he stared at me.

A hand touched my head, then ruffled my shaggy hair. The Goddess, although I didn't hear her move.

"I thought... I mean, he has controlled himself before," Jack said to Goddess. His eyes cut back to me, but his smile didn't reach his eyes. "But I should have realized how parched he was. Your color looks better at least, Ev. Now you just look like death warmed over instead of death."

I swallowed hard and nodded at him. "I feel a lot better too, thank you." Then I frowned. "Why didn't you change?"

"I tried. It's night, I can feel it, yet something's blocking me." He shook his head. "But I don't see or smell any wolfsbane."

Goddess gently stroked the top of my head. I shuddered at her touch, but didn't dare move away. Instead, I stared at Jack with wide eyes as Goddess talked. From the tightness of his muscles and the way his gaze never left Goddess, I had a feeling she terrified him, too, although he was better at hiding it.

"I had Yvonne sprinkle wolfsbane on your meal. Had to make sure you didn't run off before we talked." She paused and her fingers clasped my head, forcing me to look up at her. She considered me for a moment, then released me and stepped away. "Though given your dedication, you probably would not have left him."

Free of Goddess's touch and attention, I scooted towards Jack, not daring to take my eyes off the capricious ancient vampire until I hit his warm skin with my back.

Kurt—big, black, and imposing—came out of the door to my left, followed by a short white man with mousy brown hair and a sallow face whose name I didn't know, the only two of Goddess's followers that had escaped the carnage at the mage house. Goddess smiled at them. Both vampires dropped to their knees, bowed their heads to her, and held out an arm wrist-up.

Remembering the mage house, my thoughts turned to the amulet. She'd been willing to sacrifice all her pawns to get her hands on it? Why?

Suddenly, I realized I couldn't feel the warm pulse of the amulet anywhere around me. My eyes widened. "The amulet! I can't feel it!"

Goddess turned from the two vampires, who both looked disappointed when her attention shifted. "Do not worry, High Priest. It's somewhere safe." She considered me for a moment, hand on a thrust-out hip. "Jack's right. You look better, but not great. Are you still thirsty?"

I swallowed, dry tongue scraping at the roof of my mouth.

Her mouth curved in a smile. "Come, drink your fill from our congregation. Once you're feeling satiated, we'll get you cleaned up and into fresh clothes."

She stepped to the side and swept an arm out at the two groveling vampires, who both thrust their wrists in my direction with renewed vigor, although neither moved towards me.

I just stared at her. The words didn't have the weight of an order, unlike her earlier demand. We both knew I couldn't refuse a direct command from her, so I wasn't sure why she was being so sugar sweet and not ordering me to feed.

Behind me, I felt Jack shift and touch my arm. I glanced back at him and he shook his head, frowning. He mouthed something, but

I wasn't sure what he was trying to say. Yet it was clear he didn't trust her either. Still, I was so thirsty, my fangs ached and pressed into my lips.

And what harm could it do? Goddess had already bitten both these vampires. They were already in her thrall.

I pushed away from Jack and tried to stand, but stumbled and fell into the wall. Bracing against it, I lurched towards the two vampires, eyes fixed on the pale one's wrist where I could see a dark blue vein stark against the white of his skin. I knew vaguely that I was still naked except for my briefs, and they looked significantly worse for wear, but I was more interested in a meal than covering up.

The blood from the two vampires was like mana on my tongue, a spicy tang that had been missing from Jack's blood. I moaned with pleasure as I sucked, taking as much as I could from each before Goddess stopped me.

My head spun with how much vampire blood I'd taken, and my skin tingled as if little sparks were jumping about on me. It stung, but wasn't unpleasant. I lay down between them, rolling on my back to stare at the ceiling in bliss, until the Goddess's face popped into view. She flashed me a wicked smile. "Excellent. Now, Yvonne will take you upstairs so you can shower."

A door creaked behind me. I blinked at the unfamiliar name, but rolled up to one elbow to see a well-dressed woman come in through the door on the far wall.

"May I take Jack with me?" I asked as Yvonne helped me to my feet. Her fingers were warm on my arm. I stumbled, but she was a good deal taller than me and caught me easily, hauling me up. I felt drunk.

"No, Jack and I need to have a little talk about his duties." Goddess gently pushed me a few stumbling steps towards the stairs that I could see now through the open door.

"Duties?" I frowned and exchanged a look with Jack, who looked as puzzled as me.

"As your jackal guardian," she said, as if that explained anything. "Now go upstairs and shower."

This last bit was an order. The compulsion settled over me, lifting my feet against my will out of the room, Yvonne hovering at my side.

Chapter Two

THE GODDESS PLANS

Once Everett left with Yvonne, Goddess flicked her eyes to me and smiled. I shrunk back at the intensity burning there.

Not taking her eyes from me, Goddess crouched down between the two vampires. "Boys," she said, stroking Kurt's broad back. He groaned, but twisted his head to smile up at her. "Go take Miles and find something to eat while I talk to Everett's jackal."

"Yes, Goddess," Kurt slurred. He staggered to his feet, pulling the other smaller vampire, Miles, up with him, and left the basement. His heavy steps tromped up the stairs.

One hand on her hip, the Goddess tugged on her necklace, revealing a small handcuff key dangling from the end. She twirled the key around one finger and gave me a coy smile. "We're going to have a little talk. Up to you if we have it with you free... or chained up like an animal."

I sighed and lifted my leg. "Free. I don't understand what hold you have over Everett, but I just want to help him."

One of her eyebrows rose. "A sign from the heavens that my apprentice found such a loyal guardian jackal so soon after being turned. And one that can take the half-form as well. Rare...or it was. Is that still the case?"

She cocked her head, eyes going distant, and then nodded. "Yes, I see it is. Wonderful. Such a strong jackal my apprentice found. The signs are clear."

Her smile widened as she came over and unchained me.

"Apprentice? To what?" I asked her, before reaching down to massage the sore red skin where the bracelet had been rubbing my ankle raw.

"My legacy, of course," she said, straightening. "Let's go talk upstairs, where it's more comfortable." She turned and left without waiting for my response.

Not that I had any choice in the matter but to follow her. Without my powers, I was helpless as any human before her. I took a moment to pull on the sweat pants before following her upstairs.

The stairs opened into a gorgeous hallway. All the floors were solid wood parquet, beautiful and expensive. Original framed artwork lined the walls. The kitchen was visible through an open doorway as we went down the hall and I glanced inside. It was huge, with solid marble counter tops and gleaming silver appliances.

"Is this Yvonne's house?" I asked.

Goddess shrugged and tossed her hair, shooting me a smile over her shoulder. "It's my house."

I raised my eyebrows, but didn't argue with her.

The sitting room she led me to had pure white wall to wall carpet covered with handwoven rugs and solid wood furniture. Goddess settled onto the blood-red couch and patted the cushion next to her.

Like that was happening.

I sat on the matching loveseat across from her. The plush pillows that had looked so inviting were not comfortable. Clearly, the furniture had been chosen for its looks.

Goddess smoothed down her tight skirt. "Don't worry, I'm not offended," she said, looking significantly at the couch cushion next to her.

Honestly, I didn't care that I'd offended her; I was not sitting any closer than I had to.

I crossed my arms across my bare chest, wishing I had a shirt. Dirt and blood crusted my hair and body from the run through the woods and my fight with Goddess. Compared to the Goddess's designer dress, perfect makeup, and styled hair, I distinctly felt the gulf in power between us. I leveled a look at her and stayed silent. This was probably part of her psychological manipulation. If she was even half as old as I suspected, Everett and I were far outclassed in more ways than one.

Now that I had time to look at her more closely, I could see the age lines on her face hidden beneath the expertly applied makeup. Yesterday I would have judged her age to be mid-thirties, but looking closer now in the bright overhead lights, I would have guessed her closer to fifty or older.

"Did Yvonne get you dinner yet?" Goddess smiled at me.

I blinked in surprise, caught a bit off guard. I thought she'd want to talk about my role here, or Everett. My stomach growled at the mention of food. "No, she didn't," I said.

"I'll have Kurt order you something when he returns." She pulled a cell phone out of thin air and sent a quick text before setting the phone aside on the couch next to her. Where had she been keeping that thing? "There. I also asked him to find you some clothing. Anything else you require before we get down to business?"

That she knew how to use a cell phone impressed me. Stacy had said a lot of the older vampires struggled with new technology. Even Stacy didn't like to use a newer smart phone, sticking with a simple flip Nokia.

"You were the mummy in London. The one that disappeared at the same time as Kurt and his girlfriend," I said without thinking.

Her eyes widened briefly before her expression smoothed out. "Yes, that was me."

She leaned back on the couch, throwing her arms out along the back. Goddess looked relaxed, but the predator in me recognized the increased intensity of her focus on me.

"How does one go from a mummy to looking like that?" I paused, and added. "How does a vampire even survive not eating for that long?"

Stacy had told me that vampires could, and did, starve to death if they slept too long. Too long being a relative term for a vampire, but I knew it was a lot less than the couple of thousand years she had to have been sleeping for a museum to have labeled her as an ancient Egyptian mummy.

The Goddess just fluttered her eyelashes at me and blew me a kiss. "Now, now, I don't share beauty tips. A girl's got to have some secrets."

I grimaced and tried, and failed, not to roll my eyes. But I was tired, starving, worried about my boyfriend, and not in the mood for her games. "Why did you call me a jackal guardian downstairs?"

"That's what you are. Jackals are the guardians of the dead."

"Like Anubis," I said without inflection.

"Yes!" Goddess brightened, smiling so wide it showed her teeth. "I was so delighted to find out some things have survived the long passage of time."

I huffed.

"Don't be like that," Goddess purred. "The death dogs are sacred in my church. Revered. You will be worshiped almost as much as me, and Everett."

While I didn't believe in what she was saying, she clearly did. At least one benefit was that she was obviously intent on keeping me around, which meant Everett wouldn't be stuck here alone. But she terrified me. My skin prickled as she examined me. I nodded and licked my lips, unable to think of what to say.

"Let's get to business then," she said. "Here are my expectations while you are here. When Everett is training with me, you are not to interrupt no matter what. Otherwise, you will support Everett in whatever he needs while he is awake. You will also protect the congregation."

I furrowed my brow at her referring to her assembled humans and vampires with that word. Stacy and the other vampires used different words, most often I heard coven or family to refer to the groups of humans and vampires that lived together.

She paused. "You look confused. Do you have a question?"

"No, just thinking. Is that all?" Nothing about her demands bothered me. I wanted to keep a close eye on Everett while we were here, anyway. I was concerned about what she might be training him to do, exactly, but I could already tell from the flash in her eyes while telling me my duties that I would not get an answer from her.

"There is one other thing." Her eyes bored into me. "I need a favor from you."

"What?" I whispered and froze, hardly daring to breathe. The look in her eyes frightened me. I was very glad indeed that I hadn't sat right next to her.

"I lost my jackal while I was sleeping." A flash of sorrow crossed her face, gone as quickly as it had come.

"That's too bad." I kept my voice neutral. It had to be hard, waking up to find everyone you ever loved dead and gone for thousands of years. I wondered what Everett would do when I was gone...

"Would you tell me the names of any other jackals in the city?" Goddess smiled sweetly at me, her eyes wide and her lips slightly parted.

Things clicked into place. A bead of sweat formed on my brow and I swallowed hard and shook my head. I was fairly certain she wouldn't hurt me, not her jackal guardian, but my voice still shook. "No."

Goddess suddenly loomed over me; I hadn't even seen her move. I twitched back, but her hands shot out and grabbed my arms, pinning me to the couch. Her eyes blazed red and a single fang descended on the left side of her mouth, marring her otherwise symmetrical face.

"Tell me the names of any other jackals in the city," she hissed.

Teeth chattering, I stammered out. "I said no."

My fists clenched on the cushions. The hairs on my chest and arms stood straight up, and my skin rippled as my body reacted to her presence by trying to change. But the wolfsbane I'd unwittingly consumed earlier stopped me cold. The failed change hurt, seizing up my muscles like I'd just run ten miles.

Her skin was like ice and her fingers hard as rock where they dug into my muscles. Goddess's stale breath stung my nose as she took a breath to talk. "Then you leave me no choice."

She lunged forward, burying her fang into my neck.

DESPITE MY FRUSTRATION AT being separated from Jack, the shower was just what I needed. Heavenly. Steam billowed around me as I stepped out. The shower enclosure was one of those stone walk in deals with shower heads that sprayed on you from multiple angles. Easily large enough to fit two, and I entertained fantasies of using this together with Jack later. Then remembering the Goddess dashed that thought from my mind.

Towel safely wrapped around my waist, I left the bathroom to find a small pile of clothes on the bed. Sweatpants and a t-shirt, both too large for me, but better than nothing. I tied the laces of the sweats tightly to get them to stay up, but just let the baggy shirt hang around me.

Yvonne waited for me outside the bedroom when I came out. "You should stay here," she said.

I ignored her and headed down the hall towards the basement, when a noise from the living room caught my attention. I detoured that direction and then stopped, frozen in shock.

Goddess had Jack pinned to the couch, her mouth on his throat. Jack struggled under the Goddess, but the most he could do pinned under her greater strength was weakly kick his legs.

"Jack!" I screamed. My voice echoing in my ears unfroze my legs. I dashed at vampire speed into the living room.

Goddess glanced at me across Jack's face, her red eyes flashing. A voice echoed in my head, *STOP. SILENT.* My legs stopped working. I pitched forward, barely catching myself with my hands as I landed face first on the carpet.

Her order kept me locked to the floor, watching helplessly as she continued feeding. Inside, I raged. I tried screaming and yelling, fighting against the command holding me still and silent on the floor, but my body refused to obey me. My vision turned red and all I could focus on was Goddess' face pressed to Jack's neck.

"I didn't expect you back so soon." She leaned back, resting her weight on Jack's knees and keeping pressure on his arms.

Unable to answer, I just glared at her. I hadn't lingered in the shower, too worried about leaving Jack alone with her to enjoy the luxury of the accommodations.

"You may speak now," Goddess said.

"You said you wouldn't hurt him." I wanted to push her off of him, but clasped my arms and restrained myself.

"I said no such thing. I said we needed to talk, and we did."

Licking her lips, she slid backwards off of Jack and then straightened her dress and smoothed down her hair while she stared down at me.

Groaning, Jack sat up and clutched at his bleeding neck.

"Everett." Goddess reached behind herself and pulled out a set of handcuffs. She tossed them onto the carpet in front of me. "Cuff Jack to yourself. You are not to let him out of your sight," she ordered.

Hands shaking as I tried to resist, I picked up the cuffs and snapped one around my right wrist, then crawled up to Jack, and attached the other one to his left.

"Sorry," I whispered, regaining control of myself.

Jack gave me a weak smile back. "It's alright," he whispered. Louder, to Goddess he said, "I thought you trusted me as a loyal jackal."

"Oh, I do." She raised an eyebrow as she glanced at him. "I trust you to be loyal to him." She turned her attention back to me. "Everett, sit. I have some questions for you."

Jack laced his fingers with mine and pulled me up onto the couch with him, although he kept his other hand on his neck. Our clasped hands rested in my lap, and I could feel him shaking where his leg pressed up against mine. I leaned into his side and rested my head against his shoulder.

Goddess sat down on my other side, squeezing us together on the small love seat. "Tell me about..." she trailed off and her eyes unfocused. Her expression smoothed out, blank. After a moment she said, "Montana."

Jack jumped. I glanced at him, frowning. He furrowed his brows, but shook his head at my look.

"Why do you want to know about Montana?" Jack asked.

"I didn't ask you," Goddess hissed.

In a sweeter voice she said, "Everett, tell me about Montana." She put force into the statement, making it an order.

My mouth started moving before I registered what I was going to say. "It's a state. Farther north and east of here. Big empty plains, lots of snow in the winter. I've never been there."

Goddess hummed thoughtfully and wrinkled her nose. "Doesn't sound like much of a place for a vampire."

"Probably not," I said.

"How about Minneapolis?" Goddess said.

Jack jumped even higher than he had before. "Shit," he muttered.

"I don't know anything about that city," I said truthfully, looking at Jack sideways, wondering what was up with him. Why was Goddess asking about such random places?

"Alright." Goddess went silent again, staring at nothing. I stared at her curiously. "Las Vegas," she said, her eyes snapping back into focus. Jack squeezed my hand and went stiff.

"Let's see, it's in the desert. Hot. Dry. Lots of sand. There's twenty-four-hour gambling... it's a party city."

"Oh my!" Goddess squeezed my hand and brought it up to her lips to kiss it. "It sounds lovely." She let go of my hands and stood, walking over to the couch to grab her phone. I used the opportunity to take Jack's arm and press closer to him before Goddess came back.

Wrapping one arm around my neck, she cuddled up to me and held out the phone so we could both see the screen. I squeezed Jack nervously.

She tapped Las Vegas into the search and started scrolling through the pictures. Every few seconds she squealed happily. Abruptly she stopped strolling and stabbed a finger at the outline of the Luxor's giant pyramid in the distance of a picture of the strip. "What's that?"

"That's the Luxor Hotel."

She tapped that into the search, bringing up pictures of the inside.

"Wow, that's tacky," I said.

"No," Goddess breathed, eyes widening. "This is amazing. So ostentatious! I love it! The Pharaohs themselves would be jealous of such luxury!" She pulled the phone to her chest and sighed dramatically. "You said this is a hotel?"

I nodded.

"Here. We're going to Las Vegas and staying here. Apropos that it is a pyramid. A grand tomb for the grandest of the pharaohs, me." She kissed my cheek suddenly, making me flinch. "And a fitting sleeping place and base to rebuild my church."

Chapter Three

ESCAPE

Yvonne brought me takeout Chinese. Forewarned, I examined it carefully, and she'd stirred little purple specks into the noodles. I mean, they could have been innocent, but I was being a little paranoid. Besides, wolfsbane was poisonous to humans. Being a were-jackal, it hadn't killed me, only stopped my change, but who knew what would happen long term if I kept consuming it. I pretended to eat and threw the food out when Yvonne wasn't looking.

Goddess finally let us go to bed near dawn, but left us hand-cuffed together. It was awkward trying to get ready for bed that way, but we eventually figured it out.

"Why were you flinching at all her questions about places in the US?" Everett asked once we'd laid down together under the covers.

"Those were all places where I know jackal shifters live." I stared up at the dark ceiling.

"Like you?" I could hear the frown in his voice.

"Yeah, like me. She asked me about other jackal shifters. I refused to tell her."

"And that's when she bit you," Everett finished for me.

"Yes, but why..." It clicked. "Like you took my memory of the first night I changed. She bit me to steal my memories."

Our handcuff chain jingled softly as Everett reached over and squeezed my hand.

"We need to get out of here," I said, intertwining my fingers with Everett's. I wanted to cuddle with him, but the way our hands were cuffed together made it impossible.

"We—" Another yawn cut him off. "She'll just come find me again. Besides, we can't leave without the amulet. It has to be the key, otherwise why would she go to such trouble to get it back and then hide it from me?"

"So, we'll get the help of the PCA." I rolled on my side and reached over to touch his cheek.

He shook his head against my hand. "What can they do? She tore through the mages... and any vampire that comes near her doesn't stand a chance."

"The shifters..." But I knew that was probably a non-starter. They'd consider this a vampire issue to solve. Although we worked together at the PCA, usually the vampire employees covered the vampire problems, the shapeshifter employees covered the shifter problems, and the mages covered the mage problems. When investigating the vampire murders last month, I'd gotten a lot of pushback from the vampires.

"Besides, if she called me back, I'd have to go." A tear rolled down Everett's cheek, and I brushed it away.

"What do you mean?" I asked.

"The sleepwalking that I told you about, and the other incidents. That was her." He rolled over so that we both lay face to face. "When I'm further away from her, I can fight it a bit, but as soon as she gets close, I'm her puppet."

Sighing, I pulled him close and kissed him. "We'll figure something out," I said when I pulled back. He sighed and closed his eyes, flopping back to the pillow.

"What?" He threw up his non-cuffed hand.

"Look, we don't leave for Vegas until tonight. The amulet has to be somewhere in the house, right?" I asked.

He nodded, not opening his eyes.

"We'll wait a bit for everyone to fall asleep and then search for it."

"Alright." Everett sighed, breathing steady. Probably out of habit. His breath tickled my neck.

Now the trick would be keeping me awake. My stomach growled. Actually, maybe it wouldn't be that hard. I was so hungry I wasn't sure I could sleep.

I WAITED UNTIL THE house had been still and quiet for a while. Faint sunlight was visible around the thick drapes. Judging it safe enough, I touched Everett's still and unmoving body. Shit, when had he stopped breathing? He must have fallen asleep.

No reaction. I shook him. No reaction. Goddamn it, this is not what I needed right now.

"Wake up," I growled, unwilling to yell.

For all I knew, Goddess could be sleeping anywhere in the house. Or, if she was anything like her progeny, she might even still be awake. Everett didn't respond, even when I dragged him over to my side of the bed and practically jumped up and down on him.

With some maneuvering, I got Everett into a firefighter's carry draped across my shoulders. He was so small, so how the hell did he weigh so much?

The enormous grandfather clock bonged the hour. Nine AM. Not seeing any sign of movement in the hallway, I hefted Everett higher and stepped out. My back already ached.

I could get Everett out of here... but he was right. The amulet was probably our only shot of stopping the Goddess. If we left without it now, we might never have another chance at it.

Where to start looking? The basement... probably full of vampires, so no go.

I tried to step lightly as I went by Yvonne's door. I wondered if we were sleeping in her former room, but I'd been too embarrassed to ask.

With having to continuously rebalance Everett on my shoulder, it took me almost five minutes to search the first room. Nothing.

A strange smell led me to the garage where I found dead bodies moldering in the corner. I wanted to search the tool rack there for a tool to break the handcuffs, but the appalling smell drove me back out immediately.

Going around the first floor, I checked under every painting looking for a safe, but found nothing.

The grandfather clock bonged noon. I ground my teeth in frustration. I was no closer to finding the amulet, I was exhausted and starving, and my patience was about gone.

Sunset happened at nine during summer, so I had roughly nine more hours to find the amulet and escape before Goddess whisked away us to Vegas.

But... What if Everett was wrong about the amulet? I chewed on my lip and glanced at his still face. While I debated, I was wasting daylight.

Instead, maybe we should escape while the Goddess slept, take Everett to the Paranormal Creature Alliance offices. Maybe I'd been wrong about them not being able to protect us. We could at least try. The longer I stuck around here looking for this amulet, the less time I had to escape and put some distance between us.

Everett had survived sunlight before with nothing but a bedsheet. Burned, but alive. I'd only have to run him from the front door to the car.

But first I'd need a phone to call for a cab. And a way to figure out our address.

Before leaving the bedroom I'd been searching, I wrapped Everett in the covers from the bed. Then I hefted him back up and headed to the kitchen, the best place I judged might have what I needed.

A landline phone sat on the wall by the back door. I started pulling out the drawers and found one full of takeout menus. I rifled through them until I found one that had been mailed with an address still on it. Bingo.

Some sun came in through the back door window, but wrapped in the thick blanket Everett didn't react as I stepped into the light to use the phone.

"Dave, don't hang up, it's Jack!" I hissed into the phone when it got answered.

"Jack, what the shit? Where have you been?" Dave yelled back.

"Shh, don't." I leaned against the wall to relieve some of the weight on my shoulders. "We need help. We're with the Goddess."

"Jack, oh my god." Shuffling and then the sound of typing. "I don't know how long it'll take us to send anyone. Almost everyone's still at the mage house doing triage—"

I shuddered, remembering the dead bodies I'd seen scattered around the house and the blood painting the walls.

"No, no time!" I whispered. "Just... send someone to pick us up." I read him the address. "Goddess is sleeping, and we can sneak out. I'll explain everything when we get there."

Keys clicked in the background. "A cab will be there in ten minutes. Be ready."

"Thank you." I hung up. That was a weight off my mind. We'd hole up there, protected, until we could figure out what to do and how to defeat her without the amulet.

Although, I might take care of that before we left. I could burn her in her sleep. I didn't want to go into the garage, but I was in the kitchen, a notorious source of most house fires. There was an oversized jug of cooking oil in the cupboard and a book of matches in the same drawer as the menus. I poured the oil across the floor, trailing it through the first floor of the house. I emptied the last bit as I backed up to the front door, and reached for the matches.

The basement door opened. I stumbled, hitting the door with my back, barely keeping Everett in place as Goddess stepped into the hallway. She had her arms crossed, eyes narrowed, staring me down. All the hairs on the back of my neck stood up. I stammered, mind racing, as I stared at her.

"I see Everett is still asleep. Does he know about this plan of yours to drag him away from me?"

"No," I admitted. "I couldn't wake him up."

She pointed at the oil and moved it up to the matches in my hand. "Planning to burn the house down? I'm not sure why you think that would hurt me."

Goddess smiled sweetly at me and took a step closer, holding out her hand. I sighed and dropped the packet of matches in her palm. The matches disappeared into a pocket of her dress.

"Set him down," Goddess ordered with steel in her voice, dropping her smile.

Shaking, I did as she asked, sitting down and laying Everett across my lap, his arm wrapped around his chest to connect to the handcuff and my arm. I unwrapped the blanket from his face. He was still dead asleep, stiff and unmoving. "Well?" I glanced up at her.

Her eyes blazed red. Everett jerked in my arms and sat straight up, pulling me with him and digging the handcuff band painfully into my wrist. His eyes snapped open, but his gaze skidded past my face and focused on Goddess.

"Everett, your jackal was trying to take you away from me." Goddess flashed a sad smile my way and I stiffened, hackles raising. Despite the daylight, my jackal pushed close to the surface. The wolfsbane had worn off, finally. I could feel it.

"I know he means well. He only wants to protect you, but you need to *tell him you want to stay with me*," Goddess continued.

Was I wrong, or had I felt an extra emphasis on the last part? My skin prickled.

Everett nodded and craned his head back to look up at me. "Jack, I want to stay with Goddess," he said, his voice an odd monotone.

I remembered what he'd said about feeling like a puppet around her. But I had no chance against her on my own. Pretending I believed his words, I sighed and hugged Everett close to my chest. "Fine. If that's your wish." I kissed the top of his head. "I'll take Everett back to our room and rest until nightfall," I said with a glance up at Goddess hovering over us.

"Perfect." Goddess smiled and twirled. "Las Vegas, here we come."

Chapter Four

FLIGHT

Goddess herded us into the car as soon as nightfall hit. Kurt drove with Goddess in the passenger seat, and the rest of us stuffed in the back seat together, with Everett sitting in my lap. She'd taken off the handcuffs, and my wrist was red and raw where it'd rubbed me all day.

"To the airport," Kurt said, putting the car into gear.

"No, first my house!" I called. "I need my ID, and both Everett and I need clothing."

When we got there, my porch light was on, my front door was shut, and the inside lights off. Not how I'd left it. Kurt pulled into the driveway behind my car, still parked in the carport, and shut off the engine. I opened the door and got out, bringing Everett with me. Kurt followed me out.

"Kurt will accompany you two," Goddess yelled after us. "Everett, come right back after you've changed clothes."

Everett stuck out his tongue. "Yes, Goddess."

I grimaced and turned, hurrying up the walk with Kurt and Everett right on my heels. My door was shut... I tried the door, locked. I frowned.

"Mr. Smith, Mr. Smith!" a quavering voice called. I plastered on a smile and turned to see my white-haired neighbor, Miss Hudson, a retired school-teacher and neighborhood busy-body, waving to me from the walk. "I saw your door was open and locked up for you."

"Thank you. I had to leave in a hurry and must have left it open." I walked down the steps and across the grass to meet her.

"Your spare key." She smiled and handed it to me. She must have still had one from the previous owner, an old lady that had probably been friends with her. Since she'd died before I bought the house, I hadn't thought to change all the locks.

"I have to go out of town for a bit." I held up the key. "I'll bring this right back to you. Can you monitor my house for a few, uh, weeks? "

She raised a white eyebrow at me, but nodded. Her eyes darted to my red wrist where I'd been rubbed raw after being cuffed to Everett all day, and she whispered, "Did you get arrested?"

I clasped her hands and leaned close, shaking my head ever so slightly. "I'll explain later, but we're in a hurry to catch a plane."

"Of course, deary."

"You're the best." I grinned at her and ran back up my steps and unlocked the front door, then tossed the key back to her. She caught it in a surprising display of dexterity, waved at me, and tottered away back up to her house next door. I hoped the promise of future gossip would tide her over for at least a bit, keep her from gossiping about my handcuff mark.

Inside, I wrinkled my nose at the sour scent that greeted me. The mug of blood that Everett had only half drank sat abandoned on the coffee table, now coagulated into a soupy disgusting mess.

"Oops." Everett giggled. "That's gross."

"I'll get it. You grab your clothes and get changed."

Wrinkling my nose at the stench, I scooped up the mug and dumped it out in the kitchen sink, then rinsed it out. I glanced at the fridge, but Kurt's glare told me he wouldn't wait for me to empty it. I'd just have to ask Miss Hudson to clean it out for me.

I brushed past Kurt back into the living room, where I gathered up all the discarded clothing from the couch and floor, along with my wallet and cell phone. I glanced at the screen and saw I had over twenty missed calls.

"Give me that." Kurt ripped the phone from my hands before I could unlock it. When I stood to protest, he growled, "Goddess' orders. Now hurry."

I clenched my teeth, but didn't argue with him. I should have been more careful about hiding it.

"I know," I snapped back, and rushed into the bedroom rather than punch him.

The bathroom door was closed and the light on. While Everett changed, I started packing. My small suitcase still sat half-unpacked in the closet from my last trip. I dumped the brand-new bag of Everett's still tagged clothing into it, along with a few random outfits of my own, barely looking at what I grabbed. That done, I shut the bedroom door to change myself, but Kurt's palm caught it, pushing it back open.

"Keep it open."

The door to the bathroom clicked open, and Everett came out fully dressed. "Jack, there's..." He jerked his thumb at the bathroom but trailed off when he saw Kurt. "Um, Jack, you can change in there," he finished lamely.

"Are you going to follow me into the bathroom, too?" I crossed my arms and glared at Kurt.

Kurt rolled his eyes. "Fine, I'll wait here. Just don't try anything funny."

"I have to head back to the car." Everett stopped next to me and got up on his tippy toes to kiss me on the cheek.

I pulled him close and rubbed his back. "Be right there."

"Thanks," he whispered. He leaned into me a moment longer, then pulled away and left.

I grabbed an outfit and stomped to the bathroom, slamming the door shut behind me and locked it before turning on the lights and looking around. The bathroom was empty except for a letter sized brown envelope with my name on it sitting on top of the closed toilet. Interesting.

I flushed the toilet to hide the sound of me opening the enve-lope. It was heavy, and when I dumped it out into my hands a small rechargeable cell phone and charger slid out, along with a pre-paid minutes card and a letter.

Jack,

You missed your ride. Left this here in case you find a way home. Text the saved number in the phone for further instructions.

Stacy

Well, that was cryptic. I quickly dressed before stuffing the phone down into my pocket. The charger was too bulky to hide, but hopefully Kurt would think it went to the phone he'd confis-cated.

When I emerged from the bathroom, Kurt sat on my bed staring at the bathroom door. His eyes bored into me as I strolled past him and dropped the charger in the suitcase. I crouched, rearranging and folding clothes in the bag. Discretely as I could, I pulled the phone from my pocket and dropped it in. I zipped it up, but then stopped and cast about.

"Shit. Everett's ID. He lost it in the fire..." I said, turning to Kurt. "Guess we'll have to drive."

Kurt barked out a laugh. "That's a good one. You done?"

"Just need my shoes. And what do you mean?"

"You'll see, now—"

"I know, hurry." I carried the suitcase to the living room and slipped on my shoes, ushered Kurt out of the house, and made sure I locked the door before heading back to the car. The hidden phone felt like it was burning a hole in my suitcase. I wondered what Stacy had planned. It had better be brilliant, because I was scared out of my mind.

I KEPT MY HAND laced with Jack's, trying to keep from panicking while Yvonne checked us in and printed our boarding passes. Our group traveled light; we didn't have any bags to check and only one carry-on suitcase between the six of us. All in all, we looked like quite the group, I was sure. This late at night, only one security line was open. The lineup to the counter where the agent was checking IDs moved quickly.

"Goddess," I whispered, reaching for her but pulling back at the last moment. "I lost my wallet in the fire. I don't have ID to get on the plane."

Goddess dropped back and linked her arm through mine. She glanced at Jack. "You. Go on ahead."

Jack squeezed my hand and moved in front of us in line.

"Do you think I have one of those modern things?" Goddess said to me in a low voice, leaning close to me. "Of course not. Kurt can hypnotize us through security."

I frowned. "You've flown before?"

She squeezed my arm and ran the fingers of her other hand along my arm. "Yes, short flies at night to get across America. This land is so vast. They told me it would take weeks or even months just driving at night. And I was too impatient to get to you."

"The word is 'flights', not flies," I told her, trying not to shudder as her hair brushed my neck.

A few minutes later, we were at the head of the line. Jack handed over his ID and boarding pass, glancing back at me with a frown. I shrugged.

"Next," the agent said.

Kurt joined Goddess and me as we walked up, still arm in arm.

"One at a time," the agent snapped. I halted, stopping Goddess with me as another agent at the conveyor belt noticed and glanced our way.

Kurt caught the eye of the agent and said, "When you examine our boarding passes, you'll also see matching ID."

"Yes. Next!" she called; her eyes blank.

Goddess patted my hand and gently pushed me forward. I stumbled up and handed the agent my boarding pass. Her eyes flicked over it and she handed it back to me. "Next."

Dang. I needed to learn that trick, but if Goddess was relying on Kurt to do it, there was little hope that I'd be able to do it either.

Goddess passed through right after me, and we all joined Jack and the others at the line for the x-ray machine.

I slipped off my tennis shoes and dumped them on the conveyor. I figured we were probably past the worst of it. However, one thing I hadn't counted on was my status as a trans man going through airport security.

Ahead of me, Jack went into the full body scanner. They scanned him, cleared him, waved him on, and then called me up next.

The scanner was shaped like a giant cylinder. I stepped inside, let them scan me, and waited. It had only taken them a few seconds to clear Jack, but they left me standing there for several long minutes until the TSA Agent standing in front of the bubble said, "Ma'am, you'll have to come with me for a full pat down."

Figured. I was too poor to have ever flown myself, but I'd read about this happening online. Any discrepancies between your appearance and the gender the agent assigned you would flag you for additional screening, and of course trans people almost always did. I followed her, but said, "I'm not a ma'am, I'm a sir. I'm trans."

She glanced at me over her shoulder and I caught the end of an eye roll from her. "Would you prefer a male or female agent then?"

I hesitated, unsure.

Behind me I heard Goddess's raised voice. "Where are they taking him?" and an agent saying, "Ma'am, you need to go through screening before you can go over there."

I called back to her, "I'm fine. I'll be right back after we're done." Even that delay had the agent glaring at me, so I hoped it was enough to calm Goddess down. If she did too much to attract securities attention, we'd be in trouble. I wasn't worried about her safety or my own, but I was worried about the human gate agents.

When we got over to the screened-off area, the agent stopped and looked at me with arms crossed, still waiting for an answer.

"Female, I guess," I said. I didn't really want a strange man putting his hands between my legs.

"I'll do it then," she said. "Stand like this." She pointed to a poster on the wall and I mimicked it while she ran her hands up and down my chest and back, then down my legs and grabbed my crotch. I bit my lip to keep from crying while she did, wishing I knew how to mind control the agent, like Kurt had done earlier, so I could have skipped this.

Finally, she was done. She walked me back to the security area, where the rest of my party was waiting. Jack held my shoes. I sat down to put them on, discreetly wiping my eyes when I bent over to tie the laces.

After I stood back up, Goddess took my arm again, and we strolled as a group towards the gate.

"Shall I kill that woman for you?" she asked me casually as we went down the endless airport hallway, as blandly as if she was asking if I wanted sugar in my coffee.

"What!" I hissed back, halting. Goddess yanked my arm to get me going again. "Absolutely not!" I said back to her under my breath.

She shrugged. "She upset you, but I'll respect your wishes."

"Thank you." Goddess terrified me. My voice quaked, but I hoped she attributed it to me still being upset about the pat down.

In the waiting area, boarding hadn't yet started, so Goddess pulled me down into a seat next to her. Jack sat down on my other side. Yvonne stood at attention nearby.

"Everett, sit here until I return." Goddess squeezed my hand, infusing the words with an order.

Smiling, Goddess stood, gestured to Kurt and Miles, and moved off a little way with them. They had a quick whispered conversation, then Kurt and Miles left, walking at a brisk pace back the way we'd come from.

I reached over and took Jack's hand. He stroked his thumb around on the back of my hand as Goddess strolled back to us.

"Where are Kurt and Miles going?" Jack asked. "Boarding starts in ten minutes."

"I sent them to get something to eat." Goddess grinned and sat back down next to me. "Speaking of that, Yvonne, go get something for you and Jack."

Yvonne's eyes widened, and she nodded. "Yes, Goddess." She whirled and ran off.

I took a deep breath. This was as good a time as any since we were alone with her. "I've been thinking," I said, drawing out the last word until she turned towards me. "After we get to Vegas and find your were-jackal—"

"You figured it out." She smiled slowly. "No matter."

"Yes, well, after, if I help you find a new apprentice, will you release me from the contract?"

A roll of energy came from Goddess. I squeezed Jack's hand tighter. "Everett, even if that were possible, which it's not, the signs are clear that you were Chosen."

I bit my lip. "What do you mean it's not possible? You could just make another vampire—"

"I cannot, even if I wanted to," she hissed, making a fist and staring at it. "I'm too weak. Maybe after another decade. But even then, you'd still be bound by the contract."

Jack clapped his other hand over mine and drew in a deep breath. I could feel his pulse speed up, pounding gently against my arm. It frightened me too, to think that this was her at her weakest.

She lowered her fist and touched my arm. "Besides, I'm happy with you and your jackal. You'll make a marvelous apprentice."

"But—"

"The contract's spell is not so easily broken. You're tied to my amulet." She raised an eyebrow and leaned closer. "Until death."

Chapter Five

A Grand Tomb

Everything came back to the amulet. It was all I could think about during the plane ride from Portland to Las Vegas while stuck in first class with Goddess. She'd had Yvonne book us in first while everyone else rode in coach. When I'd woken, Jack had told me in a quick whisper about his fruitless search of the house for the amulet. It didn't surprise me that he couldn't find it; something that important Goddess probably carried on herself, although I was at a loss how she prevented me from sensing its location.

After we landed, we took a shuttle van from the airport to the Luxor. The Pyramid gleamed black in the moonlight, the edges lit with blue LED lights, looming over us as we got close. Goddess squealed with delight as she peered out the windows, so excited that she made the cabbie circle the block so she could see everything before having him drop us off at the hotel entrance.

On the sidewalk, I closed my eyes and smiled, enjoying the warmth. I hadn't fed yet today and the heat still radiating off the asphalt warmed me almost as much as fresh blood. Jack stank of sweat already and he tugged at the front of his shirt, panting.

"How can it still be this fucking hot at three in the morning?" he growled as we headed for the doors.

A blast of cold air hit me as the automatic doors whooshed open for us. Jack gasped in relief, but I shivered and took his hand, pressing close to him for warmth.

Despite the late hour, or early hour depending on your point of view, there were still people wandering the lobby and a clerk manning the reception desk. Everything in the lobby was made of gleaming white marble, so bright it hurt my eyes, and I had to cling to Jack's arm, blind and stumbling up to the counter behind Goddess.

"You alright?" Jack whispered to me.

"Fine." I rubbed at my eyes and cracked them open. My vision was adjusting, but it still stung. "Just bright in here."

Goddess's imperative commands to the clerk were unmistakable. "We require your nicest suite, and it must have an eastern facing balcony."

Things swam into blurry view. Yvonne, Miles, Jack and I stood near the check-in counter desk with the only clerk. Goddess leaned against the counter smiling at the clerk, and Kurt stood at her elbow.

The clerk, a tall, thin, pale man with sandy brown hair, looked up at Goddess and adjusted his glasses. "And what name is your reservation under?"

Kurt snapped his fingers, causing the clerk to glance at him. Kurt caught and held his gaze. "You will assign us the requested suite, and comp us the room."

The effect on the clerk was electric, but not in a good way. His polite customer service smile dropped away, and he scowled at Kurt with red eyes, then bared his fangs. "Tourists. Think you can come in here and get whatever you want." As fast as they'd come, his fangs vanished and his eyes went back to their light green, but his smile didn't return. He crossed his arms and glared at Kurt. "I take it you don't have a reservation."

"Oh, but we do," Goddess purred, leaning over the desk to display her cleavage. Even this far away, I could see the hungry look on her face.

His customer service smile returned, albeit more plastered on than before. "Let's start over then. What name is your reservation under?"

Goddess rolled up and over the counter, her loose skirt twirling around her legs, so fast that I could barely follow it. She landed on the employee, driving him to the floor behind the counter out of my sight.

Next to me, Jack jumped. "Where'd they go?" he hissed, twisting his head this way and that.

"She jumped over the counter and tackled him," I said.

Goddess stood up, straightening her hair and then smoothing it away from her face. The way she grabbed it... was it a wig? I frowned.

Huh. That might be a clever hiding spot for the amulet, actually.

Goddess leaned down and gave a hand up to the now dazed-looking employee. His eyes were out of focus and he had to lean on Goddess to stay upright. A tiny spot of blood marred the collar of his white shirt, but of course being a vampire the actual wound where Goddess had bitten him had already closed.

"Now Gray, darling," Goddess said, putting her hands on the employee's keyboard, "a suite, facing east." Her eyes went distant, and she started typing rapidly on Gray's computer.

"Miss, miss, you can't be back behind the counter," a woman said, rushing out of a door behind the two. Given the ruddiness of her skin and the tan lines, I guessed she wasn't a vampire.

Goddess put one hand on Gray's side and wrapped her other around his back, turning around with him leaning on her. "Of course, I'm sorry. Mr. Gray here fell and hit his head and I came over the counter to make sure he was alright."

"Oh!" the woman stopped and cast a critical glance over Gray. Her eyes widened. "You're right. He looks out of it. Nevertheless, miss, you'll need to go back around to the other side of the counter. I'll help you."

She stepped forward, but Gray waved her off. "I'm fine, Dorothy."

Smiling, Goddess walked around the counter to join Kurt back in front of Gray's desk. Gray put a hand to his head, but with his other tapped at his computer while Dorothy looked on, chewing the side of her lip pensively. "Are you sure you're alright, Gray? You look, well, even paler than usual."

"Fine. Just a little lightheaded from hunger. If it's alright with you, I'll take my lunch break after I get this group checked in."

"Why is she so insistent on the room facing east?" Jack leaned over to whisper to me.

I shrugged and shook my head, joking, "Maybe she likes to watch the sunrise."

Jack lightly punched my arm. "Very funny."

"Here are your keys." Gray slid two packets of keycards across the counter to Goddess.

"Two rooms?" Kurt asked, picking up the keys.

"There are too many of you for one, I'm sorry." Gray swayed and grabbed the counter to steady himself. "I did give you adjoining rooms, so you won't be too far apart."

"Thank you." Goddess purred.

We moved off, Goddess in the lead, striding purposefully like she knew exactly where she was going. I glanced back at the counter, but Gray had gone and Dorothy stood where he had been.

The entrance to the casino yawned open on our right, flanked by giant statues of Pharaohs. Marble sphinx statues of a variety of animals lined the walkway up to the casino entrance in the lobby. The clangs and chimes were audible even from here. Goddess stopped to look over the statues and even went over and climbed onto the base of the closest sphinx to pat its head.

When she got back, Goddess said, "In my day the statues were painted. These white ones are so cold and impersonal. I don't understand why they are so plain."

"By the time European explorers and archaeologist found them, the paint had all worn off," I told her. "Early archaeologists thought they were supposed to be white."

We'd learned about this in school. Some of the old archaeologists had even scrubbed off the remains of paint they found on them. The white was a lie. "But now with ultraviolet light," I continued, "we can figure out what color the old statues had been and recreate that color. It's fascinating—" I stopped talking abruptly, realizing everyone was staring at me.

"Sorry, I thought it was interesting," I muttered, looking away.

"Don't apologize, Everett." Jack laced his fingers with mine and bumped me gently with his body. "It *is* interesting."

Goddess hummed and led the group the rest of the way to the elevator.

The elevator ride up was swift and quiet. It ran up the inside of the pyramid at an angle, and I marveled at the movement and at the view of the casino below us. The interior of the pyramid was hollow, and the glass elevator let you see everything.

When we got to our rooms, Goddess took the key to the larger corner suite and beeped the door open, then handed the key to the other room to Yvonne.

"Goddess," I spoke up, clutching at Jack's hand, "can Jack and I have the other room to ourselves?"

Goddess narrowed her eyes at me, then flicked her gaze to Jack. Her expression smoothed out into a knowing smile. "I'll think about it."

I sighed and my shoulders slumped. That was parental code for no way.

"Kurt, Miles, go hunt, but return before dawn for the Sun Ceremony." She turned back and threw the door to her suite open but then stopped short, clenching her hands. "Wait. What is this?"

The suite was tiny. The two outside corner walls angled in sharply above the bed, making the room feel claustrophobic.

Yvonne keyed open the other door. I looked over her shoulder. This room was even smaller and had two beds crammed inside.

"Two beds..." I said out loud and groaned. There went our private room, unless Goddess was willing to give up the bigger corner suite. Bigger being relative, of course, with these tiny rooms.

"Where is my balcony?" Goddess stamped one foot. "We cannot have the Sun Ceremony here. Not unless we want to fry all our congregation."

"It's the pyramid shape," Jack said, rolling his eyes. "Didn't you notice outside? The balconies are inside, overlooking the casino floor," he said, pointing at the railing outside the door.

"Yes, I see now." Goddess cut him off with a slash of her hand.

"Goddess," Kurt knelt down in front of her and kissed her wrist. "One of the hotels next door. They overlook the pyramid and the sphinx, but look like they may have more traditional rooms."

"Thank you for the suggestion, Kurt." Goddess placed her hand on the top of Kurt's head like he was a dog. "But we will make this work for now. The energy of the pyramid will assist. But we may have to rearrange..." she said, glancing at her corner room with a grimace. "Everett, you and Jack sleep here with me. No way to cover these corner windows enough to keep the boys safe from the sun. Yvonne, you have that room with Miles and Kurt. Now, you two go hunt."

Goddamn it all. I crossed my arms and scowled.

"What's this Sun Ceremony?" Jack asked, following Goddess into our new room and setting his suitcase in the closet.

"You'll see..." she glanced at the windows and grimaced, "in a few days once we have prepared and spread the word."

MY HEAD POUNDED, AND my ankle ached. I rubbed at my skin, still bloody from where the handcuff had been. I needed to change to heal, but I was leery of doing so in front of the vampires. And especially Goddess.

My stomach rumbled. All I'd had to eat was a bag of pretzels on the flight and the substandard sandwich Yvonne had bought from the coffee shop in the terminal.

Everett flopped backwards back onto the King size bed with a groan. He had to be as thirsty as I was hungry.

"Goddess, perhaps I should take Everett down to the casino to hunt," I said, sitting down next to Everett and putting a hand on his knee.

"Nonsense." Goddess crossed her arms and glanced at us. "Kurt and Miles will be more than happy to feed Everett when they return."

I sighed when my stomach growled again. "How about me? Don't tell me I have to wait for Yvonne to bring something back when there's an all you can eat buffet down there calling my name." Not that I'd seen it, but it was Vegas. I'd heard the stories.

She glanced at Everett and raised an eyebrow. "Very well. I trust your loyalty to your vampire will bring you back far more effectively than chains."

I jumped to my feet. Everett sat up, grabbing my hand, his eyes wide. "Don't leave me alone with her, Jack, please," he hissed.

"Everett, you do not need to be frightened of me." Goddess crawled across the bed and reached for Everett's back, but he twisted away, clinging tighter to my arm.

Goddess frowned and settled onto her stomach, head in her hands. "Jack, go get your meal and return. Your vampire will be safe here with me. I'll start teaching him some of what's required of him while we wait."

I hesitated, looking between Everett and Goddess. I actually believed she wouldn't *physically* harm him. She seemed to care about him in her own way. Sighing, I pried Everett's hands off. I couldn't be with him every second of the day and night. "Everett, I promise, I'll be back shortly."

He let go of me and swallowed, obviously coming to the same conclusion I had. "All right," he whispered.

"Just going to freshen up before I go." I grabbed the suitcase and took it into the bathroom with me. Goddess had fixated on Everett, but I still didn't want to chance her seeing the phone.

Opening it reminded me that in my haste I'd forgotten to pack bathroom supplies. Hopefully Las Vegas was as much a 24-hour city as advertised. When I emerged, I replaced the suitcase in the closet and went over to Everett, planting a kiss on his forehead. "I'll be back soon."

He gave me a wan smile.

The buffet was heavenly. I spent far too long there, getting seconds and then thirds before going on a hunt for a gift shop to buy us toiletries.

While eating I'd texted the number saved in the phone with our new location in Las Vegas and warning them that Goddess was after jackal shifters here. Whoever was on the other end of the number texted me back a time and a place to meet them. I just hoped I'd be able to make the appointment.

When I got back to the room close to dawn, Kurt opened the door before I could swipe my key. While I'd been gone, the vampires had been busy. They'd clipped all the blinds closed with binder clips, and Goddess had changed into a pair of Everett's pajamas. I suppressed an angry response at her having gone through my luggage. Stay cool. No need to chance angering the ancient vampire over something so trivial.

"Sleep well boys." Goddess waved to Kurt and Miles who filed out past me on their way out.

"How you doing, Everett?" I asked, shutting the door behind me.

Everett lay on the bed, his eyes closed, still wearing his jeans and T-shirt. He cracked them open to look at me then sighed and closed them again. "I'm fine," he said dreamily, a goofy smile on his face. He slurred his words, and sounded drunk.

"It can't be healthy to eat nothing but vampires," I said, setting my shopping on top of my suitcase.

"It's fine." Goddess waved a hand at herself. "Look at me, after all."

"Yeah, look at you." I frowned at her and crossed my arms.

She focused on me. "Oh, yes, one more thing in case you try something like you did yesterday. Everett." Goddess touched his leg. "You are not to leave this room without my permission, and if you wake up outside it, you are to return immediately."

Everett stiffened, the smile sliding off his face. He didn't say anything, but rolled onto his side and curled up into a fetal position. From Everett's reaction, she'd just given him another order.

I kicked off my shoes, went around the bed, and lay down facing Everett. My butt hung slightly off the edge, but I fit. I pulled him to my chest and rubbed his back. He gradually relaxed into me, at least until Goddess lay down behind him and he stiffened up again.

My hackles raised, and I growled. My jackal was close to the surface, and if it wasn't for the coming sunrise, I would have been tempted to give in to it. Goddess huffed and rolled her eyes, but she must have seen something in my face because she moved over a few inches away from us. If I didn't have somewhere to be later, I would have moved to the middle and spooned Everett's back to put myself between them. But I couldn't risk waking her when I left.

Eventually, Everett's shallow breathing ceased entirely. I opened my eyes and peeked over him at Goddess. She'd taken off her wig and lay on her back with her hands crossed on her chest. Her head had an inch or so of growth of jet-black hair. I watched her for a moment, but I couldn't tell if she was awake or not; unlike Everett, she didn't normally breathe except to talk.

At least from here I could see the nightstand clock on her other side, lighting up the side of Goddess's face an eerie red. I'd be worried about falling asleep except that her presence in the room left me so on edge.

I lay there, watching the clock, until fifteen minutes before my meeting time with my contact from the Las Vegas PCA. Moving slowly, I pulled my arm out from underneath Everett's cold and limp torso and slid backwards out of bed, then tiptoed out of the suite, grabbing a keycard from the table on the way out.

This early in the morning, the hallways of the hotel were quiet. I was alone for the elevator ride down to the casino on the bottom floor.

Once there, I exchanged a twenty for a gambling card, then headed over to the designated meeting area my contact had given me and sat down at a machine in an empty aisle. I put my card in the game and gambled while I waited.

After about five minutes, a woman sat down at the machine next to me. I glanced at her and then pushed the button for a minimum bet. The machine began beeping and playing music as pictures flashed by.

"Good betting today?" the woman said, her words almost drowned out by the machine's jingle.

I didn't look at her when I responded with the other half of the code. "You win some, you lose some." I hadn't known the identity of who I'd be meeting, so she'd suggested this system.

"How you holding up?" the woman asked. Her machine lit up with a win, but she didn't react.

"Just fine," I said, pushing for another spin. The noise of the machines would hopefully make it so no one could overhear our conversation. "She got a suite right here at the Luxor."

"Did you find out any more about her plans?"

"Nothing more than I already texted." I shook my head, forgetting that she wouldn't be looking at me.

"They murdered a TSA agent in the Portland airport yesterday," the women said, starting another bet. "Do you know why?"

"A woman?" My contact nodded. I paused, hand hovering over the screen, and closed my eyes, my gut churning. It had to have been when she sent Kurt and Miles to feed. "They selected Everett for additional screening and the pat down upset him... He asked Goddess not to retaliate. Guess she doesn't listen." My stomach twisted at the thought of telling Everett, but he deserved to know the truth.

"Try to text me next time something happens."

I opened my eyes and continued gambling. "Of course." I looked at her out of the corner of my eyes. "She's also going to be hunting for more vampires for her church, so try to spread the word for vampires to be on the lookout for Everett or Goddess and avoid them if they can."

"I'll do what I can, but vampires that eat other vampires are an old wives' tale. A fairy tale. Most will not take the threat seriously." She got up from her machine.

"Wait," I hissed, and she paused at me. "How long until the PCA gets a team together to take Goddess out?"

The woman folded her arms and stuck out one hip, looking down her nose at me. "We'll put together something, but we need to keep the element of surprise. You will not be informed; the risk of you revealing info to her is too great. In the meantime, you can help by gathering more intel. Weaknesses, anything."

"Fine. I'll text you the moment I find anything else out."

She gave me a nod and strode away.

"You forgot your card!" I called after her, but she ignored me, disappearing around the corner.

Sighing, I let the machine finish my last pull, and then collected my card and leaned over to get hers before standing. Maybe the card was my pay.

I still felt bad lying to Everett what I was doing, but as he'd pointed out he wouldn't be able to lie to her if she pressed him.

Better for him not to know. So why did I feel so conflicted about it as I rode the elevator back up to our rooms?

Chapter Six

Another Jackal

"Why did I have to come again?" I whispered under my breath. I also wondered why Goddess had been so adamant that Everett not come with us.

Walking ahead of me, Goddess turned and skipped backwards like a little girl, hands behind her back. "Because your memories in my head are fading. I can't remember what this were-jackal looks like. I'd either need to bite you again—"

"No!" I growled at the suggestion and my jackal pushed at my skin, demanding to be let out to attack this threat. I wrestled back control before any change started, but it was a near thing. Something about the ancient vampire frayed at my nerves. I'd gotten very little sleep after I returned to the hotel room earlier, which also didn't help.

Goddess giggled. "That's what I thought." She twirled back around, throwing out her arms and dancing even further ahead of me. I frowned at her back.

When I'd first met her, I'd have put her age at late thirties or early forties, but now she struck me as much younger than that, twenty at the most. Maybe it was her makeup, or the airy peach sundress she wore today.

The first floor of the Bellagio casino was packed. Slot machines spread out from us in wave after wave of aisles, most of the seats occupied. More people clogged the surrounding aisles. Scattered around the floor were tables of card games. To my eye, it looked a lot like the Luxor, only with different carpeting and less Egyptian themed decorations. I even recognized a lot of the same machines that I'd seen walking through the Luxor.

"Where to?" Goddess asked when we came to the center of the floor, stopping to look around at the swirling crowds around us.

I shrugged and crossed my arms. "How should I know?" I cursed myself that I'd ever been curious enough to look up other were-jackals in the PCA's system.

The vast majority of shifters in the United States were wolves, with various other predator species making up the rest. Jackals were on the rarer side, at least here in the states. I'd been the only known one in first Maryland and then Oregon, which had made me curious enough to look up others. But that had been over a year ago, soon after I'd first changed and moved to Oregon. I hoped against hope that the Las Vegas jackal no longer worked at the Bellagio, or if they still did, that the PCA had warned them in time.

"Fine. Guess I'll have to do this myself." Goddess flipped her hair over her shoulder and put a hand on her hip. She swayed over to a guard standing at the end of the one of the nearby rows of slot machines. "Excuse me, sir?"

The guard turned to look at her, meeting her eyes. "Yes, ma'am, how can I help you?"

She swayed, batting her eyelashes at him. No vampire powers behind it, my jackal told me, just seduction. "We're looking for Brun."

The security guard shrugged and grinned, hooking his hands on his belt. "If you don't mind me saying, you're not really Brun's type. But I get off in an hour."

Goddess smiled at him. "We have other business to discuss. But after... well," she pulled out her phone and held it out to him, "I'll text you?"

The guard's eyes widened. He took Goddess's phone with shaking hands and put in his contact number.

I grimaced, but didn't intervene. I couldn't save everyone from being eaten by Goddess and her crew, especially not someone who was willing throwing themselves at her. That guy was doomed, and there was nothing I could do for him.

Goddess took her phone back and batted her eyes. "Now, point me in Brun's direction, sweet man."

He chuckled and pointed further inside. "Head back and to the left, can't miss them."

Goddess winked at the guy and sauntered off. I trailed after her with my hands stuffed in my pockets.

"I'll see you later," the guard called after her. Goddess didn't turn around but raised her hand and waved at him. I just shook my head.

Brun was easy to spot. My heart sunk. I'd warned the PCA, so why were they at work?

Brun stood with their hands on their hips, casually watching the passing traffic. Their long black hair was tied back against their neck in a low ponytail. Built like a football player, tall and wide, they towered over almost everyone. They looked familiar, and I wondered if they maybe had played in college.

Lots of shifters played professional sports. Not that being a shifter made you any stronger or faster than a human while not changed, but the ability to heal instantly with a shift after a game was a massive advantage. I rubbed my sore red wrist and then reached up to touch the crusted over tooth mark where Goddess had bitten me. Even if I couldn't find somewhere isolated to go for a run, I should at least change in the room tonight after we got back to heal those.

Goddess zeroed in on Brun while I was thinking. Hips swaying, she sauntered up to them. She gave them a big smile, craning her neck back to look up at them. "Just who I was looking for."

Brun looked down at her impassively. "Can I help you, ma'am?"

"Oh, a big boy. My favorite." Goddess purred and put a hand on Brun's arm.

Brun's eyebrows drew together, and they jerked their arm back, almost hitting the door behind them with their elbow. "No touching."

Goddess's smile stayed plastered on, increasing in intensity and she clasped her hands under her bosom, pushing it up to strain against the light fabric of her sundress. Brun and I exchanged an eye roll over her head. "I'm so sorry. I was just so excited to meet you."

Brun rumbled something under their breath that I didn't catch. I drifted closer. This was my chance. I needed to play this carefully, though.

I draped my arm across Goddess's shoulder.

"Hey babe." I tried to imitate all the straight guys I'd ever known, emphasizing the word babe. "I don't like him." I eyed Brun while gently trying to tug Goddess back a step. Like trying to move a boulder. I didn't even shift her, but I ended up almost falling backwards and having to cling to her shoulder for support.

"I told you, I'm not a *him*," Brun snapped and tapped their name tag, which had They/Them written in smaller letters under their name. I'd been trying to push their buttons and looked like I succeeded.

Goddess scowled at me but didn't move my arm. "Jack, I do not care what you think." Her attention shifted back to Brun, her scowl replaced again by a wide smile. "I have a proposal for you."

I hated to do this, because the animosity between vampires and shifters was, at least in my view, a bunch of racist crap, but I played the cards I had. I leaned down to whisper, loudly, so that Brun was sure to overhear, into her ear. I almost gagged as I forced the words out. "Goddess, a powerful vampire such as yourself could find a better shifter to serve you."

Brun chuckled, glancing between Goddess and me, their eyes lingering on my neck as I straightened. "A vampire, huh? Look lady, go bug some other shifter to get your threesome rocks off. I'm not interested."

"That's not what I'm proposing at all," Goddess snapped. She shook my arm off, and then shot a hand out, hitting me square in the chest. It was like being hit by a truck. I flew back a good five feet and crashed into the side of a slot machine, the back of my head cracking painfully against the metal.

The woman sitting at it stared down at me, her fangs coming down briefly before she shook her head and pulled them back up. Then she went right back to gambling, not giving me a second glance.

I sat up, reaching to touch the back of my head. My fingertips came away red with blood. "Fuck."

My body pushed at me to change, to fight back, but I had enough control to suppress it. Although if Goddess came at me again with more warning, I probably would change from pure adrenaline.

Brun glared down at Goddess, crossing his massive arms. "If you were smart, you'd leave my casino right now."

Goddess put her hands on her hips and glared right back up at him. "That one," Goddess pointed an accusing finger back at me, "does not speak for me. I already have all the male companionship I could ever need." She framed her face with one hand, then dropped it back down to her hip. "I seek friendship and, perhaps, a guardian, if one is found worthy. Think about it. We'll be in the Lily Bar for a bit if you're interested."

"That's in my casino," Brun growled.

Despite the throbbing pain at the back of my head and the sharp pain in my ribs, I suppressed a smile and turned my back to her as I climbed to my feet so that she wouldn't see the satisfaction in my eyes. I clutched my side and leaned on the vampire woman's machine. She'd broken a rib at least, just from that one hit.

Goddess pouted, a cute thing that I was betting she practiced. Too bad, judging from Brun's non-reaction to her, that they didn't like women. Or vampires. Or perhaps both. She pouted at him a second more, then glanced back at me. "Jack, darling, where would you like to go to eat?"

I blinked at her for a moment. "What?"

"Food, darling. An apology." She swayed over to me, one hand on her hip, and laced her arm through my free one.

Whatever. I tried not to shudder at her touch, mind whirling. What had we passed on the way here that would still be open?

"We passed a Denny's..." I hazarded. They were always open 24 hours, and they served large enough plates to satisfy even a hungry shifter. Since now I'd definitely need to shift after we got back to our rooms.

Over her shoulder she said to Brun, "We'll be at Denny's then, if you'd like to join us."

The radio at Brun's hip crackled. They reached down to fiddle with the dial with one hand and lifted the cord that ran to their ear with the other. "Be right there," they said into the tiny microphone. Then they trundled off without another word to Goddess, although their lip twitched in a lopsided smile as they lumbered past us.

GODDESS HUNG ONTO MY arm the entire walk from the Bellagio to the Denny's diner down the block.

After being startled by the woman vampire at the machine in the Bellagio, I tried to play spot-the-vampire in the crowd on the sidewalk. After fifty, I gave up and stopped counting, and those were just the ones I could spot with my untrained eye.

Goddess hadn't been joking about this sounding like a vampire haven. This was bad. If she could recruit even a fraction of the vampires in this town... I made myself stop that line of thinking. We wouldn't let it get that far. We couldn't.

"I did not appreciate your comments back there, Jack." Goddess said suddenly. "I would have had them on my own."

"Why are you so sure of that?" I snorted. "Brun clearly isn't into women."

"Do not interrupt me again, Jack. That is the last warning you will get. I went easy on you because you are my High Priest's jackal, but you need to learn respect." Goddess' hand tightened on my arm.

That was easy on me? My rib ached with every step I took and I could feel blood crusting up the back of my head where I'd slammed into the slot machine. I pressed my lips together in an effort not to reply with something scathing.

Inside, the Denny's was moderately empty. Late enough that the dinner crowd was gone, but not so late that the place had filled up with drunks from the nearby bars.

Goddess requested a four-seater table at the window overlooking the sidewalk. Not wanting to sit next to her, I sat across and kitty-corner from her, although my back itched at having it towards the doors.

While I perused the menu, Goddess texted someone on her phone.

"If we're going to eat," I said when Goddess put down her phone, "why not invite the others to join us. Or at least Yvonne... and Everett."

"No," Goddess snapped. "Brun will not set eyes on Everett until after I bond them to me."

I raised my eyebrows. She was jealous. Interesting information. Instead, I said, "Brun uses they pronouns. Besides which, you really think they're coming?"

Goddess frowned. "Who could resist me?"

I lifted the menu higher to hide the roll of my eyes. The server came over with some waters and I ordered dinner. Goddess ordered an appetizer plate, which I didn't comment on.

"There are other were-jackals, you know," I said after the server left.

Goddess took a sip of her water. "I remember enough of what I got from you to know how rare jackals have gotten. I'm not ready to give up yet. Besides, I rather like this Las Vegas already." She gestured out the window at the crowds visible on the sidewalk below. "So many vampires."

I sighed and picked up the dessert menu for something to do. They all looked good, but I should wait and see if Goddess expected me to eat the appetizers she'd ordered.

"How long do we stay if Brun doesn't show up?" I asked eventually as I replaced the menu into the holder in the table's center.

Goddess smoothed her hair. "They will."

"Don't we need to be getting back to meet that guy you picked up?" My ribs ached and I really didn't want to sit here all night waiting when I could be back at the suite healing and spending time with Everett.

Goddess threw back her head in a full-throated laugh. "No, no. He's not for me. In fact, I was texting Kurt to let him know to be expecting him."

My stomach twisted. Goddess took out a compact mirror to check her makeup.

A server came by with a tray, dropping off my hamburger and Goddess' appetizer platter. He winked at me as he set down the food. I ordered a beer, and he swept off again.

I had just taken my first bite when Goddess stood up, her eyes sparkling, and started waving at someone behind me. "The universe provides," she said softly to me.

I twisted around to see Brun making their way past the host booth towards our table.

"How did you plan this?" I hissed to Goddess. She gave me a lopsided smile and settled back in her chair.

"Brun, welcome!" Goddess pulled out the chair next to me, ushering them into it.

Brun sat down, then gave me a hesitant nod as Goddess moved back to her seat.

"I ordered you some appetizers, but you're welcome to get a meal or something else if these aren't to your taste," Goddess continued, pushing the plate across the table to Brun.

Had she planned this, or did she just get lucky? I took another bite of my burger and watched Brun from the corner of my eye. They dug into the appetizer platter with gusto.

"I'm not sure why I'm here," they said after they'd cleared half the plate.

Goddess smiled and sat forward, her long black hair brushing the table. "Well, I'm not sure either. But let's start with introductions. You've met Jack." Goddess waved her hand at me. "And you may call me Tawaret."

I almost choked on my hamburger. What in the world? She hadn't even told Everett her name.

"Nice to meet you both." Brun nodded to me and Goddess.

"I need to go to the bathroom." I stood abruptly. "Brun?"

"What?"

I gave them a wide-eyed look then jerked my head and eyes in the direction of the toilet.

"I guess I need to go too." Brun stood and followed me. Goddess, or Tawaret, narrowed her at eyes at us but stayed where she was.

The men's bathroom was empty. I pulled Brun into the handicap stall with me, locking the door behind us before rounding on them. Not the most pleasant place to have a conversation, but it would not be a pleasant talk, regardless.

"Relax, I'm not after your girlfriend." Brun folded their arms.

"She's not my girlfriend. I'm gay." I threw up my hands. "I was trying to scare you off. Plus, I told the PCA to warn you. So *why* are you here?" I pointed at them to emphasize my point.

"To be honest, the PCA actually asked me to spy on her for them. They said it's too dangerous to send vampires after her. But I said no. What do I care about one more vampire in my city?"

"No?" I frowned. "So, what changed?"

"You did." Brun shrugged. "A shifter, your arm around the leech, whispering in her ear. Acting cozy with her."

"Leech?" I stared at him, my hands balling into fists.

"Yeah. You're way too comfortable with that blood-sucker. I wondered if maybe there's a reason those PCA folks are worried about this vampire. So here I am." They threw back their shoulders, puffing out their chest, and moved forward into my space.

Shit. "How'd you know I was a shifter?" I backed up, but Brun crowded me into the corner.

"Your eyes, after she punched you into next week. They flashed yellow, just for a moment. Enough to keep you from getting crunched up too bad. I don't know if a human would have survived that." Brun leaned down into my personal space, eyes flashing amber as they sniffed me. "What are you doing with that leech, anyway?"

"Trying to save my boyfriend." I sighed and touched the bite on my neck, deciding to gloss over the fact that my boyfriend was one of the 'leeches,' and at least try to be pleasant. "If you really want to help, I'll be grateful for it. But I'll give you warning. Do not let her taste your blood. She can read memories from you if she does."

"Thanks." Brun grinned and backed away. They unlocked the stall door and left. I lingered, taking a few moments to freshen myself up in the sink and clean some of the blood from the back of my head before rejoining them.

Chapter Seven

Sleeping with the Enemy

I WOKE UP TO Jack's arm draped over me and him snoring. The sound was music to my ears. I rolled onto my side and snuggled up to him. Jack sighed in his sleep and pulled me closer to his chest, enveloping me in his warmth. The hair on his chest tickled my bare back, and the pajama bottoms we both wore were a frustrating barrier between us.

Somewhere further into the suite, I heard dishes rattling around and the slamming of cupboards. The microwave beeped and the smell of something cooking wafted over me. Yvonne. I groaned and glared at the doorway, holding my breath at the smell.

At least Jack and I had our own bed today, although the adjoining door between the rooms was open. Which meant besides the fact that we could hear anyone else moving around in the space, that I was still sexually frustrated. But at least now I got cuddles, which was better than being at the vampire house.

Faint late evening sunlight came in around the edges of the floor-to-ceiling curtains that covered two of the walls. Part of the reason Jack and I had been given this room, with the vampires and Goddess taking the other room with the two queen beds.

I couldn't wait to get away from her, but I'd searched through all the vampire's things last night while she was gone, and hadn't seen any sign of the amulet. So frustrating. I knew it was the key tying me to Goddess.

Goddess poked her head in. "Good, you're awake. I have a job for you and Kurt tonight."

I groaned and pulled the covers over both our heads. Jack jerked awake at the movement. The overhead light flicked on, half blinding me, even through the light blanket. Then suddenly the blanket was stripped all the way down off the end of the bed. Goddess stood over us, and I was very glad we both wore pajama pants now.

Jack rolled onto his back and threw an arm over his eyes. "Bright," he mumbled.

"Everett, come with me." Goddess put command behind her words, forcing me up out of bed as much as I wanted to stay where I was.

Sighing, I followed her out into the sitting area. My arms and legs moved against my conscious thought, dragging me along behind Goddess.

Yvonne sat at the table eating. I'd only been a vampire for a few months, but I was already repulsed by the sight and smell of human food. Averting my eyes, I hurried after Goddess.

Goddess strode over and yanked open the curtains, letting in weak sunlight through the eastern facing glass. "We need to recruit vampires to come to our ceremonies."

"The Sunrise Ceremony," I said. The weak sunlight tickled my exposed chest and face, making me wince, although Goddess didn't seem to even notice. Her skin didn't even react, but my chest was already reddening with a sunburn.

She'd been teaching me the words to the ceremony, a chant in ancient Egyptian, but she still hadn't explained what the ceremony was.

"Exactly." Goddess leaned into the glass and looked out over the city. Neon lights were already on, flashing and blinking in the growing twilight. "Tonight at sunrise, we'll perform it for the first time on this continent. But I need an audience, you understand?" She glanced back at me.

In the kitchen area of the suite, the coffee maker beeped and I glanced over my shoulder to see a yawning Jack pouring himself a cup of coffee. I knew exactly what she implied; I was supposed to bring back vampires for her to bite, and she would force them to worship her. But I was going to make her say it. As much as I despised her orders, I wanted to make this as difficult as possible for her.

Goddess fully turned to put her back to the window, narrowing her eyes at me. "You will go out with Kurt and bring me back a local vampire. None of those casino addicts." She waved a hand, scowling, while pushing that awful compulsion into her words. "Someone off the strip, with lots of friends. No drinking from anyone but the vampire you are bringing me, and then only enough to make them pliable."

I nodded, shivering. Her words crawled on my skin, already pushing me to leave, to go do what she ordered. "Can Jack come with us?" I asked.

Goddess glanced from me to Jack, who sat at the table next to Yvonne munching on cereal and drinking his coffee. "Not tonight." I opened my mouth to protest, and she gave me a silent order to not interrupt her. "He's far too fond of you and might prevent you from doing what you might need to do to lure a vampire to me."

"Tawaret, that's—"

Her eyes widened, turning red as her fang dropped. Talons grew from her fingers and I shrunk back from the palpable anger pulsing from her. "You will not call me that!" she roared.

Jack jumped to his feet, fur sprouting from his face and hands. Yvonne yelped and dove behind the counter.

"You will forget that name, Everett," Goddess snarled, leaping at me. She hit me in the chest and drove me to the carpet. I landed on my back with her on top. "You will refer to me only as your Goddess. You will think of me only as your Goddess. Understood?"

The force of the compulsion crowded out all other thoughts for a moment. All I could see were her red eyes, spittle-flecked lips, and single fang. Her long, dark hair brushed my cheeks. "Yes, Goddess," I gasped, struggling to get a breath in with her entire weight resting on my chest.

There was a flash of tawny fur, and then suddenly the weight was gone. Jack stood next to me, looking like an amalgam of a man and jackal, all golden fur, muscles, and teeth. Goddess rolled to the side and sprang to her feet, smoothing back her hair, her eyes and hands back to their everyday appearance like nothing had happened.

I sat up, gasping, and buried my face in the fur of Jack's leg where his pajama bottoms had ridden up.

"This is why I do not want Jack going with you tonight, Everett. Now get up and prepare to go as soon as Kurt wakes." Goddess whirled and strode away, disappearing into the adjoining room where Miles and Kurt still slept.

Jack snorted, and his form shrank. I let go of him and scooted away, watching as he turned fully into a jackal. He shook himself, kicking to remove the loose pants, and growled, "What the hell happened?"

I blinked at him; my mind still cloudy from the force of my Goddess' recent orders on me. What orders had those been? What had happened? Confused, I shook my head and shifted to sit with crossed legs. "I don't know. I asked her if you could come with me tonight. She said no, and then..." I trailed off. "I can't remember what I said to her. Did you hear what it was?"

Jack padded forward and sniffed at me. "No, I didn't. I was eating cereal. You know how crunchy that stuff can be. You alright?"

"Fine." I leaned over and hugged him, then ruffled the fur between his ears. "I need to go hop in the shower. Goddess ordered me to go out hunting for her tonight."

He whined, but nodded his long head into me. "I met that other shifter last night. Going to try talking to them about meeting some other shifters in the area."

I sighed, wanting to stay there holding him all night, but duty to Goddess pulled me to my feet.

My hackles rose as Tawaret sauntered by, and my instincts urged me to shift again to better protect myself. I pushed down the change as I finished eating my bowl of cereal that had gone soggy while I'd been in jackal form. I worried a lot about Everett, and that he hadn't even been able to tell me what he'd said to Goddess that had pushed her into attacking him.

Combined with the change I'd done last night to heal my broken ribs from where Tawaret had hit me, I was still ravenous and cereal would not cut it. After Everett left with Kurt, I showered and changed. I had my hand on the doorknob to leave when Tawaret stopped me.

"Where do you think you're going?" she said in a sharp tone.

I glanced over my shoulder at her. She had one hand propped on her hip, glaring at me. "I'm going to go hit the gym and then the buffet." I was tempted to add a sarcastic, 'if that's okay with you' to the end, but bit it back, afraid she'd take me seriously.

"Stay here and get room service."

"I can't work out in the room," I countered, putting my back to the door and crossing my arms. "And room service isn't exactly all you can eat. I'm sure you remember how much food shifters need."

Her eyes narrowed.

"If you don't trust me, Miles is welcome to come with me." Really, that was a bluff. The last thing I wanted was a nosy vampire spying on me for Tawaret. Besides, that would leave her here alone, and one thing I'd noticed already is that she always had at least one vampire at her side. I added one more trump card as her eyes narrowed still further. "You've bitten me. You know I'm loyal to Everett."

Her lips curved, and her eyes crinkled up in a genuine smile. "Too true. Alright, jackal, but try to be back before your master, hmm?"

I gave her a stiff nod and ducked out. Master? She seriously misunderstood our relationship. Could I use that to my advantage? I pondered that as I rode the elevator down to the gym. I hadn't been lying about my destination, just in case she had other people or spies watching me that I didn't know about.

I bought an insanely expensive pair of shorts and shirt from the gift shop, having packed no workout clothes in my haste. Maybe the PCA would reimburse me. I hoped so. Between this trip and the beating my wardrobe had taken with all these changes, my finances were seriously drained.

While in the locker room, I pulled out my hidden phone and texted Brun; they hadn't given me their number, but I'm memorized it when they'd given it to Tawaret. *"Hey, this is Jack. Can we talk?"*

I waited a few minutes, but no response, so I went out and hopped on the treadmill.

The workout was just what I needed to clear my head. Brun texted me back as I finished up. "I'm on my lunch break. What do you want?"

"I was hoping you could introduce me to some of the local shifters. Living with the vampires has me going a little nuts."

"You're LIVING with them?"

I paused and bit my lip. Oops. I should have known not to tell them that. *"My boyfriend is too. I gotta be there for him."*

"Hanging out at night is one thing, but during the day you're as helpless as any human."

"I KNOW." I lost my temper a bit. I stared at my text and cursed, then sent, "Tawaret thinks jackal shifters are sacred. She'd gut anyone of them if they tried to touch me."

"But not your boyfriend," Brun texted back.

I couldn't tell them my boyfriend was a vampire, not with his prejudices. They'd find out eventually, but I wanted to keep that day far off in the future.

"Look, if you ask me, your boyfriend's a lost cause. He's been bitten. Even if you get him out, he's an addict now," Brun texted while I tried to figure out how to respond.

A moment later, Brun added, "If you wanna bounce, you're welcome to stay at my place."

"I'm not giving up on my boyfriend." I probably could have been a little nicer, but Brun was rubbing me the wrong way. "Can you at least tell me when and where the next run is?"

"No. I don't trust you. You're entirely too tight with vampires for my taste."

Well shit. I threw the phone in my locker and went to take a shower. I had no other way to contact the local shifters. Going directly to the local PCA office was too dangerous, just in case Tawaret had someone following me. I didn't want her to think I was betraying them. But I didn't know any other shifters it the city.

When I got out of the shower, there was another text waiting for me.

"You ever wonder why shifters can only shift at night? It's to protect us from vampires. You're sleeping with the enemy."

Brun was more right than they knew. But I wasn't going to give up on Everett that easily.

CHAPTER EIGHT

TAKE-OUT MEAL

I COULD FEEL THE bass rattling my teeth before we even got to the club. Kurt, walking next to me, had been quiet during the trip to the clothing store. He'd gotten an outfit as well, stylish gray slacks and a royal blue button down that complimented his dark skin and eyes. The clothing Kurt had picked out for me was a bit more... outrageous. I currently had my arms clasped across my chest, trying, and failing, to cover my bare abs and pecs with the open-style jacket.

Kurt saw and stopped us both, putting a hand on my shoulder. "The style works better if you keep your hands at your sides or in your pockets."

Blushing furiously, I stuffed my hands in the pockets of the black silk pants and scuffed the bottom of my new black boots on the sidewalk. The pink shimmery jacket hung open without my hands holding it in place and the mesh tank underneath did little to cover my chest. Sure, I'd had top surgery now, but I still wasn't used to the sensation of other people's eyes on me. Having my nipples hang out was an unfamiliar experience.

"I feel ridiculous," I told him.

"Nonsense, you look great. Any vampire in the club will be drawn to you in this." He gently pushed on my back to get me going again towards the club's entrance.

I didn't resist, and let him guide me to the door. With all the excitement, I wasn't sure what day of the week it was, but from the crowd of people around the doorway, I guessed it must be a weekend night. Or maybe not. Vegas was weird.

I had a brief flash of panic as I saw the bouncer check the ID of the straight couple ahead of us in line. The bored-looking bouncer waved the couple in. Kurt wrapped his arm around my shoulder and surged forward.

"ID?" The bouncer held out his hand, barely glancing at us.

Kurt leaned towards the man and caught his eyes. "Here's our ID's. We are good to go in," he said in his London drawl. The girls in the club were going to be swooning over him. He held up a palm like he was showing the man something, but his hands were empty.

"Of course, thanks." The bouncer got a glazed look in his eyes and waved us inside.

Music and a wall of heat blasted us when Kurt opened the door. My fangs ached with thirst at all the warm, nearly naked bodies writhing on the dance floor. In my mesh shirt and open jacket, I was practically overdressed compared to this crowd, and Kurt even more so. Clenching my jaw against the urge to lower my fangs, I pressed on inside with Kurt on my heels.

"I'm so thirsty," I yelled up to him over the music as I took an empty spot overlooking the dance floor to scope out the room for any vampires.

He crossed his arms and shrugged. "Best hurry then." I could barely hear his low rumble over the pulsing bass of the music.

"What if there aren't any here?" I yelled back.

Another shrug of his wide shoulders. "Then we go to the next club."

I huffed and turned my attention back to the dance floor. Honestly, I had no idea what to look for. That guy at the bar wore a paisley shirt with wide-winged collar, but it could be ironic and not a hopelessly out-of-fashion vampire from the seventies.

Closing my eyes, I took a deep breath, looking for the spicy tang of vampire, but all I could smell besides stale sweat was Kurt's appalling body spray.

I opened my eyes and elbowed him gently. "Move away. No one will approach me with you looming over me like that."

"Fine." He handed me a hundred. "Text me if you need more. I'll go mingle. We'll give this place an hour and then move on to the next club."

I took the money and nodded. Kurt had gotten me a cheap pre-pay cell phone after the clothes shopping spree.

With Kurt gone, I went the other direction, weaving along the edge of the dance floor, eyes half-closed to better focus on catching a whiff of another vampire. About halfway around the room a tantalizing scent hit me, the spicy tang of a vampire from somewhere in the crowd. I stopped and glanced around, hoping I hadn't accidentally wandered towards Kurt. He was so tall, he would be easy to spot, but I didn't see any sign of him.

However, I did see a pale couple of white guys dancing together on the dance floor. One had blond hair frosted white at the tips and a lean surfer's body. His partner was taller with dark hair, and a portly furry bear body. The blond one ground and swayed against the taller man's front.

I hesitated, although I was certain they were vampires. While her orders hadn't explicitly said I couldn't bring back more than one, I couldn't bite one without the other noticing. Still, they were both hot and very gay, and I stopped to watch them appreciatively. I wished Jack had come with me. I fantasized about dancing with him like that someday.

I must have been very obvious about my staring, because a moment later the blond man grinned at me, winked, and waved me over. My mouth moved, but no sound came out; I really wasn't used to being hit on by anyone, let alone one half of a very hot gay couple. The man stopped grinding on his partner and danced over to me at the edge of the floor.

"Hey cutie," he yelled over the music. "Wanna join us?" The tangy smell of him made my knees weak. Well, weaker than they already had been.

He'd tied his shirt around his waist, and his bare chest kept drawing my eyes away from his face and dimpled smile.

I flushed, or at least would have if I'd been fed, although I could still feel the tips of my ears getting hot. "I don't want to interrupt. Besides, I'm looking for someone... single," I said, giving him a toothy grin although I didn't show fang.

He laughed. "You're new here."

I nodded, flashing back to Vanessa's words about parties for the newcomers and all the vampires knowing each other. "Just moved here, yeah. I'm Everett." As soon as the words left my mouth, I winced. I was supposed to be Evan now. Oh well. Less of a chance of them recognizing me here in Vegas.

His grin widened further, deepening his adorable dimples. "Wild. I'm Oakley."

Oh my god. Even his name screamed surfer boy. I wondered what he was doing in Vegas, where there was a distinct lack of ocean. I tried and failed, to blush again. Swaying a bit on my feet, I turned to move off into the crowd when Oakley grabbed my arm. I stopped and gave him a raised eyebrow over my shoulder.

"Hold on, meet my boyfriend before you go," he said, then gestured over his shoulder to the dark-haired guy he'd been grinding on.

I nodded and shifted from foot to foot, trying to hold my fangs in. Being this close to him, and knowing he was safe to bite quickly wore down my willpower. The boyfriend danced his way over, still swaying a bit with the beat even as Oakley threw his arm around the taller man's back. "Nate, this is Everett. He just moved here. Everett, Nate."

I nodded politely. Oakley was more my type. Nate was older, or at least had been when he died, and had a full dark-brown bushy beard and mustache. His ruddy face was lined and weathered, but kindness sparkled in his brown eyes. Muscles shifted under his mesh shirt; I'd have guessed he'd been a fisherman or some other career that had him outdoors and doing manual labor before he'd become a vampire.

"Well, what a cutie," Nate said, giving me a wink and a broad smile that showed teeth under his beard.

"Thanks."

"You here alone?" Nate asked, his smile turning down at the corners. "You look a bit parched. Need help finding a likely target? Oakley and I know the scene, if you need some help."

I shook my head. Last thing I needed was two helpful vampires trailing me as I hunted. "Not alone; my friend Kurt's here somewhere. And I can manage on my own, thanks."

Oakley nodded, but Nate's smile faded.

"You sure? We know people here. We can get you fed in ten minutes, tops," Nate said.

I backed away a step. "Yes, I'm sure." I decided to be straight with them. Nate had a look in his eyes that said he wasn't going to drop it. "I have... orders." I paused here, trying to figure out how to word this. "I need to bring back someone for the Matriarch of the house before I can feed."

Suddenly, Nate now stood on one side of me, Oakley on the other. I'd seen a flash as they moved, but was too thirsty to escape from their sudden pincher move.

"No, no, no, honey," Nate said, placing a firm hand on my back and guiding me away from the dance floor. I tried to duck away to the other side, but suddenly Oakley was there, pinning me between them.

"This just won't do." Nate tutted as they guided me out the back door to the smoking area. There was a little fenced in patio back here where smokers could smoke without having to leave the club. The two vampires walked me to the far end, away from the group of smokers congregated at one end of the patio. As soon as Nate took his hand off my back, I tried to make a break for it, but Oakley moved between me and the door.

"Look, we just want to talk for a moment before you go back to hunting," Oakley said, holding up his hands against his chest, palm out in a calming gesture.

I hugged myself and scowled, leaning my butt back against the picnic table that had been shoved into the corner. "Fine," I snapped. "I'm listening."

Oakley and Nate exchanged a look, then Nate spoke. "Look, we won't ask why. We have a place you can stay as long as you need. No need to go back to this woman's place."

"Thanks for the offer, but I'm a bit stuck right now." Tears started gathering at the edges of my vision. I dashed them away with my sleeve and swallowed down my emotions.

They both looked skeptical, and I wasn't sure they'd believe me about being forced to follow her orders. From what Stacy had said, this wasn't how it worked. I suspected it had something to do with the magic attached to the missing amulet.

"My boyfriend is still there," I said instead, hugging myself. "If we try to leave..." I started tearing up again. The bit of kindness these two vampires were showing me seemed to have torn down the bulwark I'd built up around my emotions.

Nate's frown turned into a scowl. He exchanged a look with Oakley. "Damn it. Who is this vampire? I'm going to go give her a piece of my mind."

"She goes by Goddess," I said. "But I wouldn't. She's scary powerful."

Oakley snorted. "I've never heard of her. And Nate and I are both older than we look. How about we take you back, pick up your boyfriend, and you both come back to our place?"

Shit. These guys were too nice. Why couldn't they be jerks so I wouldn't feel bad about feeding them to Goddess? I shook my head. "Thank you for the offer, but we can handle it on our own."

I tried to push past them, but Nate crossed his arms and stared me down. "Look, we won't force you to go, but we *are* coming with you to set this woman straight. How did you meet her?"

The order from Goddess to bring a vampire home was pushing me to accept their offer; I got a stab of pain in my forehead when I considered leaving them behind. "She's my maker. I'm stuck with her for a while."

Oakley frowned at me. "Wait, how long have you been a vampire?"

"Not that long," I hedged. Nate and Oakley exchanged a glance.

"She should be teaching you, not sitting home on her ass." Oakley's face twisted up.

"How about this," Nate said. "We both fed well, and I could pass for human at first glance."

Oh shit. Bring someone back for her. They thought I was looking for a human. But the Goddess's compulsion latched onto Nate's words. I wouldn't be able to turn him down, but I tried to take one last-ditch effort to warn him away. "If you insist, but Goddess is not someone you want to mess with."

Nate waved a hand. "You're young. Every old vampire thinks they're something special, but they never are. No skin off my nose until they try to bully the newbies."

I didn't respond other than to shake my head as I got out my phone to text Kurt to meet me at the exit.

"Trust me, Everett," Nate said, putting a hand on my arm. I tried to smile at him, but I think it came out more as a grimace.

KURT SAID NOTHING WHEN I turned up with a pair of vampires. He had a human woman that at first, I thought was plastered until I noticed a trickle of blood on her neck.

We took a cab back to the hotel. I sat between Nate and Oakley in the back seat, watching their profiles flash in and out of shadow. My guts twisted as I imagined what Goddess would do to them.

Nate mistook my guilt for nervousness, and grabbed my hand, giving it a squeeze and leaning over me to whisper, "Don't worry. I won't let her hurt you. I'll tell her the deception was all my idea, and that you had no idea."

I nodded and squeezed his hand back before he went back to watching out the window.

The keycard beeped us into the suite. I led Nate and Oakley in first, and Kurt carried his human in after us, slamming the door shut with his foot. He brushed past me and disappeared into the adjoining room.

Goddess waited for us. She lounged back on the bed while Gray from the front desk and Miles massaged her feet. She gave us a lazy smile. No sign of Yvonne or Jack. Good. I didn't want him to see what might come next.

The sharp tang of blood came from the other room and my fangs came down before I realized what I was smelling.

"Boys, go." She waved them away. Both darted out of the room, fangs down.

Goddess stood and stretched, thrusting out her chest at the three of us. "Oh, Everett. Two at once? Divine." She posed and flashed us a dazzling smile. I glanced back at Oakley and Nate. Both were unmoved and stony faced.

Oakley stepped forward first and put a hand on my shoulder, giving it a little squeeze before Nate moved up to flank me.

"It was absolutely reckless to send this one out hunting by himself. Look," Oakley snarled, dropping his own fangs and pointing to mine. I put a hand over my mouth, blushing. I hadn't even realized they'd come down. "He's so thirsty he can't even keep his fangs up at the scent of blood."

Goddess merely held her pose. If anything, her smile widened.

"Caught me by surprise, that's all, see?" I muttered, dropping my hand to show my fangs were back where they belonged, but Nate talked over me.

"Progeny are not slaves to do you bidding," Nate snapped, stepping between me and Goddess. "And then keeping his boyfriend hostage! The nerve. We're taking both of them home with us and then I'm reporting you to the PCA."

Goddess listened impassively, then let out a peal of laughter at his ultimatum. "Oh no, the toothless PCA." She put a hand to her chest. "Whatever will I do?"

Nate bared his teeth at her, his fangs coming down. "Don't make light of this."

Goddess grinned at him. "Besides, whoever said I sent him hunting for me?"

"What?" Nate's fangs went back up and he looked confused.

"Everett, dinner time," Goddess called, pushing an order into the words to bite whichever vampire I desired.

Both Oakley and Nate whirled toward me as my fangs dropped again. I had a split second to decide, and settled on Oakley, mostly because he was shorter and easier for me to reach. I lunged for him, latching onto the crook of his arm at the elbow. At the same time, Goddess hit Nate from the other direction, driving him to the floor with a thud.

Oakley smelled like mint and body wash. He let out a low scream as I sunk my fangs in. My fingers dug into his skin, holding his arm tight to my face as I drank. With his free hand, he laced his fingers in my hair and tried to pull me off, but with the vampire blood pumping through me, I was the stronger of us and he didn't even budge me.

His pushes got weaker and weaker as I gulped down his blood. I loved the taste of him; spicy and sharp with a sweet aftertaste.

"Everett, what the fuck?" Jack's voice pulled me out of my near trance. My eyes snapped open, and I opened my mouth, pulling back my fangs. Oakley slumped senseless to the floor, moaning softly. Still alive, at least.

The room spun around me as I sat up to look at Jack. Everything felt far away, like I was floating.

Jack stood in the doorway, staring at me with wide eyes. He shut the door behind him, but didn't move farther inside.

Beside me, Oakley's fangs came down, and he slurred, "Thirsty," as he rolled over and started crawling towards Jack with a blank expression.

I sighed and grabbed the waistband of Oakley's pants, sliding him roughly back along the carpet away from Jack. Licking my lips, I looked back at Goddess. She lay draped across Nate's stomach, nuzzling at his neck.

"Who are they?" Jack asked, his eyes going hard. He crossed his arms and glared down at me.

"This is Oakley," I said, gesturing with my free hand at the blond vampire, who still feebly struggled to crawl to Jack. "And that's Nate." I bobbed my head at Goddess and her meal. I lowered my head, not wanting to meet Jack's disapproving gaze. "I didn't have a choice, Jack," I whispered.

I heard him sigh. "I'll come back later." The door opened, then shut, and I heard his heavy footsteps in the hall.

I turned to Goddess. "What now?" I growled.

Goddess pulled away with a pout, resting her elbows on Nate's stomach to prop her head up. "Now we invite their friends to our party. Get out his phone."

I rolled Oakley over roughly and dug it out of his pocket, then showed the locked screen to Goddess. "I don't know his passcode..."

The phone started ringing in my hands, a woman singing about "So you're a really tough guy," and I almost dropped it. I rejected the call.

"Of course, you do. You just drank him nearly dry. His memories are yours now, at least some of them. And something as recent as this," she snapped her fingers, "should be easy to retrieve."

"Like the dreams," I mumbled. "But I can't access them consciously."

"Just concentrate on what you need to know." Goddess crossed her arms, lay her head down, and twisted one finger along Nate's side down to his pocket. "I imagine myself as the person whose memories I'm accessing."

I stared at the phone screen, squinting at the lock screen and the prompt for a code number. I felt a fingerprint reader on the back, and briefly thought about suggesting just using his finger to unlock it. But then again, I'd been wanting to find someone to teach me my powers. No use wasting the opportunity.

Imagine I'm Oakley. I glanced at him, squelching down a stab of jealousy, and tried to picture myself as him, dancing with Nate at the club the way I'd first seen them. Without conscious thought, I found my fingers taping in a string of numbers and then the lock screen was gone, and I was treated to two dozen missed text messages. Geez Oakley.

"Now what?" I glanced up at Goddess, who was already tapping away at Nate's phone.

She grinned and spoke without looking at me. "Message all his vampire contacts and invite them to meet you here just before dawn. I want as many vampires as possible to witness our first ceremony."

I hesitated, my head rolling with Oakley's memories and still lightheaded from his blood. "We're not going to bite them all, are we? I don't know that I could drink much more tonight."

"No, only those that volunteer. And from them only a sip. This is more about the ritual. I want to get a buzz going."

That explained why Gray was here as well. "Why not invite them one at time? Like this?" I pointed at Oakley.

Goddess grimaced and lowered Nate's phone. "As you've seen with Kurt, it tends to blast away much of the mind. Some of the others liked that, loyal and mindless servants, but I never did. They make horrid conversationalists, for one." She slid off Nate and reached out to brush some of my shaggy hair away from my ear. I froze, not even daring to breathe, heart in my throat. "Not like you, so eager to learn and quick with the questions. Just what I want in a lover."

My mind stuttered, unable to think or come up with a response. "I'm flattered, but..." I finally got out.

She let out a throaty laugh. "Your boyfriend, yes. So adamantly gay. Adorable." Goddess laughed again and stood up, tugging her skirt back into place. "But I'm patient."

EVERETT STUMBLED INTO THE doorway with a thud. I sat up and stared at him as he walked a meandering line towards me.

"Are you..." I trailed off. His expression when he'd looked at me, blood dripping from his fangs... My stomach twisted. His eyes had been empty, the same look I'd seen on Tawaret's face when she'd fed from me. I'd never see Everett like that before.

"Are they...?" I didn't want to say dead.

Everett flopped next to me on the bed and rolled his head to look at me. "Totally brainwashed to worship Goddess like a god?" He wrinkled his nose.

Not what I'd expected.

Everett sighed and flipped over to his back, staring up at the ceiling. I got up, walked around the bed, and grabbed Everett's hands, pulling him up and into my arms. He relaxed against my chest with a deep sigh.

"How did it go with the shifters?" he asked into my shirt.

"It didn't," I whispered, rubbing his back. "Brun doesn't trust me, and refused to help me out. I just ended up going out to eat by myself." And called the PCA office to urge them, again, to stop Goddess before she gained more power, but I'd gotten no response.

I pushed Everett out to arm's length, one side of my mouth quirking into a smile. My nether regions stirred at the flashes of bare chest that flashed through the fishnet shirt. It would have been sexier, though, if Everett didn't look so uncomfortable. "Love the outfit, by the way."

He blushed and pulled the jacket as closed as it would go. "Kurt picked it out."

I moved to the side and pointed to the bed. "That too?" A white robe had been laid out on the end of the bed.

"I've never seen it before," Everett told me. "It's probably for the ceremony Goddess is doing at dawn."

"Everett, you need to be careful," I whispered, pulling him back into a hug.

"I told you, I can't disobey her." Everett wrapped his arms around me, resting his cheek on my chest. "I hate it too."

"For how long?" I asked in a low voice.

"I don't know." Everett shifted in my arms. "When you were a jackal, did you catch any scent of the amulet anywhere?"

I didn't blame him for the abrupt change of subject. If we didn't find a way out soon... I'd seen how she could dance him around like a puppet. At first, he'd obey her out of fear, but vampires lived a long time. How long before he grew to love wielding power over people and Goddess no longer had to order him to do it?

I shook my head. "The place reeks too much of vampire." I paused, realizing what I'd said. "No offense."

"None taken. Can't be as bad as wet jackal fur, anyway," Everett teased back, lifting his face up to mine with a grin, his eyes sparkling.

"Oh, and while I was out, I went to an internet cafe and looked up Tawaret's name," I said to change the subject. At least if he could joke, he was feeling better.

"What name?" Everett pushed away and looked up at me, cocking his head to the side.

I frowned down at him. "What? I told you last night, remember? Goddess introduced herself to Brun. It's Tawaret."

Everett stared up at me blankly. "Well, what is it? Why'd you cut off like that?"

"Fuck." I closed my eyes and ran a hand through my hair, scowling. Had that been what happened earlier when he made her mad? "Look, Ev, it's nothing. Doesn't matter, it's an alias, anyway. Wife of the God of Evil in ancient Egyptian mythology. Also, the Goddess of the home."

"Figures." He snorted. "God of Evil."

"Wife of," I corrected him.

He shrugged. "Same difference."

Chapter Nine

THE SUNRISE CEREMONY

The robe did turn out to be for the ceremony. An hour before dawn Goddess poked her head in the room and told me to change. She wanted me naked under the robe, but I held firm on not losing my underwear. She eventually conceded after I explained, again, about being trans. So far, I was mostly stealth, with only her and Kurt knowing my secret, and I wanted to keep it that way.

As I changed, I heard knocks at the neighboring door in the adjoining suite and the murmur of conversation out in the hall.

My hands holding the robe shut shook. "I can't do this, Jack," I whispered to him.

He hugged me from behind. "Do you want me there?"

Goddess hadn't specifically invited him, but she hadn't uninvited him either.

"If you feel safe enough to come..."

Jack nodded into my neck and then let me go, stepping back and shucking off his clothes. A moment later he was growing fur and shrinking down to his jackal form. He gave a head-to-tail shake, sneezed, and then trotted up next to me. I smiled down at him, already feeling better knowing he'd be there.

Even with Goddess's ruse with Gray, Oakley, and Nate I'd thought that at most we'd get one or two vampires. I guess I hadn't counted on the power of curiosity, because when I entered the hallway, I found it filled with unfamiliar faces. Some I knew from Oakley's memories, but at least half were complete strangers.

The curtains were tightly closed with clips except for the far east window of the main room. Goddess mingled with the strangers in the middle of the adjoining room. She wore a white robe identical to mine, although she held hers shut with a sash around her middle.

The chatter died down as I came in. I froze in the doorway, eyes going wide, and clutched my robe tighter around me, fighting back a blush. Jack was a warm, comforting weight against my leg and I reached down to stroke him between the ears.

"High Priest." Kurt bowed to me and then turned to the guests, raising his hands until everyone was silent and looking at us. "We'll be beginning soon. Form a semi-circle around the door. Stay back behind the tape lines or you'll risk a burn when the sun comes up."

One of the newcomers, a tall dark-haired woman who looked to be in her late teens at most, giggled and leaned into her companion to whisper something. They both laughed and moved to the side.

Most of the vampires gathered on the balcony that overlooked the casino floor below, although a few curious ones were closer.

"Where are they all going to sleep?" I hissed, gesturing with one hand at the crowd. My other hand I kept on Jack's head, like a good luck talisman.

Kurt shrugged. "If they want to stay, they can sleep on the floor after we're done. Although I suspect most will go back down to the casino."

I'd noticed the lack of windows inside the two casinos I'd been in so far. I nodded in understanding. Jack had told me that was purposeful, to keep people gambling without realizing how much time had passed. Conveniently, it also suited vampires just fine. I half wondered if that was also intentional. How much of Vegas was built for vampires and how much to make money on the gamblers?

Goddess swept out of the crowd and up to the closed door. I knew my cue and rushed forward to join her. Jack hung back; ears perked.

The vampires we'd bitten already all knelt at the new tape lines by the doors. The rest were frowning at their friend's eagerness to be so close to potential sunlight.

A teenage-looking vampire held a phone up. Judging from the glowing light, she was recording us. She smirked at me when she saw me looking at her. Probably thought she was going to get a video like the one Stacy had shown me of two stupid vampires burning to death in the sunlight.

I followed Goddess's lead in the ceremony. She began chanting the song she'd been teaching me, and I followed along with her as best I could. A few lines in, Goddess untied her sash and shrugged off her robe, leaving herself fully nude. I followed suit, blushing at so many eyes on me. At least I had my underwear on.

Gasps came from the back of the room when Goddess and I threw open the doors to the smaller corner suite. The eastern drapes I'd opened made a stripe of bright sunlight on the carpet. With the door blocking the light, the stripe angled across the floor away from the vampires kneeling behind the taped line.

More gasps came when Goddess walked out into the sunshine with me at her heels. I closed my eyes tightly against the glare, but the light still speared my head. I wished I had polarized sunglasses... The sun tingled on my skin, quickly turning to an agonizing burn. I gritted my teeth, but couldn't stop my fangs from descending.

As we turned our backs on the sun to come back to the hall, I risked cracking my eyes open. My skin was dark brown, like a deeply tanned surfer, but no black burns like I'd seen back in Oregon.

One curious vampire from the back of the room drifted forward, almost past the taped line on my side of the door. I couldn't see him well as he stood in the shadows and I was still sun-blinded.

"It's a trick," he shouted as he stepped out to block our way back inside. The shadow from me and Goddess protected his body, but sunlight fell fully on his face. He fell back screaming and clawing at his eyes, as his face burst into flame.

Goddess dashed forward, hitting him in a tackle that any linebacker would be proud of, driving him back out of the sun. I hurried after her, blinking sunspots from my vision as I shut the door behind us, cutting off the bright glare of the morning sun. Right before the door closed, a naked Jack dashed inside.

The vampire continued to scream as Goddess straddled him, her eyes blazing red as her fang dropped. Barely hesitating at the flames licking out from under the vampire's palms, she drove her fang into the side of his neck and started drinking deeply. More gasps came from the back of the room, but all the kneeling vampires, ones that we'd already bitten, leaned forward eagerly, their eyes wide.

Unsure what to do, I grabbed my robe from the floor and shrugged it back on. The vampire's screams and thrashing stilled slightly, replaced by a low whimper.

Goddess rolled her head to look up at me, and pointed to the vampire's arm. Her voice echoed in my head. "Drink."

Unable to resist her order, I dropped to my knees and grabbed his arm, sinking my teeth in. His blood tasted different, like it had been burned in an oven. I gagged and wanted to spit it out, but her order held me fast. I drank deeply for several moments, choking with each swallow.

"Stop." Her voice sounded in my head. I spat his wrist out, not bothering to lick at the last few drops of vampire blood.

Goddess helped the vampire sit up and then gently pulled his hands from his face. His eyes were red, the skin around them blackened, but the flames I'd seen were gone. And he was still alive.

Dead silence from all the onlookers. The vampire we'd been feeding on stood and hugged himself. "Thank you," he mumbled.

"How did you do that?" I wasn't sure who'd spoken at first, but then the girl vampire, her phone still held out in front of her like a shield, took a step towards us.

"That's the benefit of the blessing of the dawn." Goddess stood, hooking her arm through the burned vampire's and cuddled up to him.

I bit my lip and shuffled to the side, unsure of what the big deal was.

The crowd murmured. A rifle cracked somewhere nearby, echoing in the enclosed space.

Goddess fell back, blood spraying out from a giant hole her chest. Vampires stared in stunned silence. I whirled, looking for the attacker. The space inside the pyramid was hollow, with the room's balconies looking out over the casino floor.

A man on a balcony opposite us was darting back inside one of the rooms.

I started to run around the hallway when I was stopped by Goddess's voice. "Everett, don't bother."

I paused and looked back at her. She was already sitting up, aided by Kurt. None of the other vampires had moved.

"But you were shot..."

"With silver," Miles hissed, jerking his arm back from Goddess's chest.

A smashed bullet tumbled free of Goddess's bloodstained robes and landed on the carpet. It glinted in the overhead light. The vampire with the phone, still recording, knelt down and touched it with one finger, then she too jerked back with a hiss. Smoke curled up from her blackened index finger.

"How did you survive?" she asked in a hushed whisper, turning the phone camera on Goddess. "It looked like a heart shot."

I put a hand to my collarbone, remembering how much pain I'd been in when shot with silver. How my skin had blackened. Then my hand went to my chest, remembering when I'd been shot through the heart with a high-powered rifle. So much pain. I hadn't even been able to speak until Stacy gave me blood. But Goddess had sat right back up like nothing had happened. And silver through the heart... shouldn't that have killed her?

"I'm a Goddess. Eternal. Immortal." She waved Kurt back and opened her robes. Her skin had already healed back to a milky brown. A small sliver of black around where the bullet had entered disappeared as we watched. "Now who'd like a blessing?" Goddess said, putting her free hand on her hip.

Kurt, Nate, Oakley, Miles, and Gray all pushed forward. The newcomers hung back, exchanging long confused glances while Goddess and I moved down the line, biting each of the volunteers.

THE LAS VEGAS PCA office hid in plain sight in the back of one of the casinos fronting as a coffee shop, serving a steady stream of walk-up customers. I ignored the line and the counter, going around the side and through a side door labeled "Employees only."

Inside, the office was a noisy overlapping jumble of conversations. Four people pacing the lobby on cell phones. I recognized one of them and did a double take.

"Stacy?" I said, stopping dead in my tracks. Her red hair and figure were unmistakable. "It's almost noon. What are you doing awake, and in Vegas?"

Scowling, Stacy pulled her cell phone away from her ear and pierced me with a glare. Her eyes flashed red and her fangs peeked out bone white against the pale pink of her lipstick. "Trying to clean up this mess is what I'm doing."

"You mean the failed assassination attempt." I ran a hand through my hair.

Stacy nodded. "Right. Can you tell us what happened?"

"I wasn't there. I was nervous being around so many vampires in my human form, but Everett told me what happened. That's why I'm here."

"I'll call you back," Stacy said into her cell phone and then put it away. "Jack, come with me."

She led me out of the lobby, her heels clacking on the tile. From down the hall, I heard a man shout, "She survived a silver bullet through the heart! Beheading is the next obvious thing to try!"

We came to an open door and behind it a long conference room filled with people shouting at each other. There were papers stacked on every available surface. They quieted down as Stacy and I came in.

A white board on one end of the table had a bullet point list written on it of ways to kill a vampire. Silver bullets was crossed out.

"Ah, our man on the inside." This was said by the man I'd heard shouting. He was sitting down, but even so, it was obvious from his long limbs how tall he'd be if he stood.

Then everyone was yelling questions at me all at once about what had happened and how to kill her.

Stacy glared at them until everyone settled back down. Then she turned to me. "Jack, we all saw the video. That shot was perfect, but she got right back up."

I nodded and spread my hands. "I heard from Everett. So, what's the plan now?"

"We were hoping you could tell us." This came from one of the people I didn't recognize. A pale gentleman with blond hair so light it was almost white.

"Ah, introductions." Stacy nodded her head at the speaker. "That's Rowan. He's the oldest vampire in Vegas, and basically controls the city." Then she gestured at the lean vampire. "This is Pembroke, from Oregon. He's the head of the Pacific Northwest coven. We flew in together last night."

I recognized the name, and nodded to him, trying to keep my hackles down and my voice even. "Everett told me about you."

He'd cried while doing so. I couldn't entirely keep the growl out of my voice. Pembroke just gave me a knowing smile.

She gestured to the final person at the other end of the conference table. "Annabelle. She's here representing the city's mages." I recognized her as the woman who'd met me at the slot machines.

"What about the shifters?" I asked, glancing around.

"They refused to get involved. Claim it's a vampire matter." Stacy sat down at the table next to Pembroke.

"So, you've been living with her, yet you can't tell us anything?" Annabelle glared at me. "Suspicious."

I glared back at her. "If she does have a weakness, it's not like she's going to go about advertising it. But Everett is convinced that if she has one, it's the amulet. I'm inclined to agree."

"You said it's missing, though," Stacy said. "Wouldn't she keep it in sight if it's that important?"

"But she did sacrifice all her minions to get it back." Pembroke frowned and drummed his fingers on the table. "I'll have to think on this."

"In the meantime, I think it's our turn to try, since the vampire's plan failed," Annabelle said.

Pembroke snarled at that, and his eyes flashed red for a moment. "What if she truly is immortal, as she claims?"

Rowan's fangs came down. "Impossible. Something obviously stopped her before. We can do it again."

"But even they didn't kill her," I pointed out. "They just put her to sleep."

"Mummified," Pembroke corrected. "They must have thought her dead."

Stacy stood. "We've got researchers on that angle. In the meantime, I'm with Annabelle. We have to try something. Before we go back to planning, I'll escort Jack out."

"Annabelle, when your team makes its move, please make sure you don't hurt Everett."

She shrugged. "We'll do what we can. Goddess is the target, but I can't guarantee anything if he gets in the way."

I sighed and scrubbed my face. "I understand. I'll keep trying to see what I can turn up. Good luck."

"Stacy will see you out," Annabelle said, pointing to the door. "Do not come here again. It's too dangerous. If Goddess finds out you've been working with us..."

"Believe me, I know." The thought terrified me.

Chapter Ten

SUPPORT GROUP

I WOKE UP FEELING hungover, something I hadn't experienced since becoming a vampire. It wasn't something I'd missed, that's for sure. I rolled out of bed and bolted for the bathroom. I landed on my knees in front of the toilet and began spewing my guts out. Jack had left the seat up, which usually annoyed me, but this time I was glad.

My throat and nosed burned and the toilet water turned blackish-red. After I was done, I fell back to the cold tile floor and put a hand over my face to block the bright bathroom light that burned my eyes.

"Everett?" Jack called. I heard footsteps and then felt his warmth as he knelt next to me.

"What happened?" he said, then gagged.

"Too much..." I moaned, curling up in a tight ball. Draining Oakley, followed by biting all the other vampires after the ceremony had been far too much. I'd been queasy going to bed, but now. Gods.

Jack gave another choked gag and then the toilet flushed. "I can tell. C'mon, let's get you back to bed."

Jack put my arm around his neck and I hung off him as I stumbled back into the bedroom. I beelined for the bed and collapsed face first onto it with my legs hanging off the side.

"I hate seeing her do this to you," Jack said softly, sitting down next to me. The bed bounced from his weight. "She's trying to get you addicted to vampire blood, like her, and I'm afraid she's going to succeed."

"I won't let that happen," I said with as much conviction as I could muster, which wasn't much. I knew Jack was right. Even before meeting Goddess, I had already been craving it over human blood. If she had me drinking nothing but that while with her, I wasn't sure I'd ever want to go back. Not that I could right now anyway, with her order preventing me from biting humans.

Jack didn't say anything, just reached over and started rubbing my back in slow circles.

After a few minutes he said, "You aren't burned as much as last time you went in the sun."

I twisted my head to look up at him with one eye. "Yeah, I noticed that too."

"It's the vampire blood." Goddess stood in the doorway to the adjoining room, arms crossed, smirking at us both.

I tensed and buried my head in my crossed arms. Jack's hand on my back stopped moving.

Jack said, "That doesn't make any sense. Vampires burst into flame in the sun. Wouldn't more of their blood do the opposite?"

I sensed more than heard Goddess stride further in. "And humans are fine in the sun. Yet the vampires who feed on them are not. Why? Shifters cannot shift during the day. Why?"

Jack's hand on my back tensed. "I don't know."

"Exactly. Still as much of a mystery now as it was to my people."

A cool hand touched my foot. "Everett, go shower. We have training to do. Your chanting this morning was awful."

I sighed. "Yes, Goddess." There wasn't an order behind her words, but I knew better than to argue with her.

Goddess left and I slunk off to the bathroom. The hot water and steam on my skin helped warm me up, but the cold pit in my stomach remained. I wish I'd never gotten Jack wrapped up in this mess with me. I felt responsible for how upset he was now.

Jack had barely been able to meet my eyes when I left the bedroom. I had a feeling my subservience to her worried him. It worried me, too.

THINGS WERE QUIET FOR the next few days. We'd moved in with Oakley and Nate, who had a large McMansion out on the edge of the city.

Yvonne disappeared the day after we moved in, and I noticed a mound in the shape of a grave in the yard one morning during the ceremony. My stomach twisted, but there wasn't anything I could have done for her.

Nights I spent training with Goddess, perfecting my performance and learning the other religious ceremonies she wanted to do once we had more worshipers.

Each morning at dawn we did the Sunrise Ceremony to a growing contingent of regular attendees.

A few days later, Goddess sat me down on the couch for what I thought was our regular lesson. Instead, she said, "Everett, I'm going out this evening to meet Brun for dinner." She shifted to sit sideways on the couch and put her other hand on my leg as well to lean closer to me. "I'd like to take Jack with me."

I nodded, a quick jerk. "All right, Goddess," I whispered and twisted my hands together in my lap. I didn't really want to let her take him with her, but I couldn't really say no.

Goddess went to stand up. I gathered my courage and spit out, "Goddess, there is somewhere I'd like to go tonight then, if it's okay with you."

She smiled at me and took my hands in hers. "Of course, Everett. Just be sure to take one of the boys with you."

"Of course." I nodded vigorously.

I grabbed Oakley.

"Where we headed?" he asked, as we headed out.

I hugged myself. "A... support meeting I found online. You'll have to wait outside, I'm sorry."

Oakley shrugged. "Suits me. I can go hunting and come back for you after I'm done."

I relaxed a bit. I'd thought he might argue with me.

We took a taxi from the house over to the community center. It was a few blocks away from the strip, but still close enough that we could see the lights twinkling over the buildings.

"What is this meeting?" Oakley asked as we strolled inside.

"Nothing," I muttered, stopping and putting a hand to his chest. He gave me a dazzling smile, his blond hair somehow perfectly styled.

My own hair hadn't been cut since I'd been changed and was getting to that unruly length where nothing could be done to it. I tugged at the hair over my ears as I scowled up at him, self-conscious. Maybe a haircut was in order after the meeting.

"We're here," I waved to the meeting room, where a few other early attendees were milling around already. "Go hunt, and come back in an hour."

Oakley frowned and crossed his arms, muscles flexing under his tank top. "I thought we were going to a casino. I don't feel right leaving you here. I don't know what I'd do if something happened to you, High Priest."

"Don't call me that." I balled my fists, trying to keep my voice low as more people filed past us. "So just hunt around here."

Oakley shook his head. "They're all locals. Better to target tourists." He patted my back and turned me, pushing me towards the meeting. "Go, I'll hang out in the lobby until you're done, High— I mean, sir."

"Fine," I muttered. Sir wasn't much better, but I'd take it. English didn't have a lot of honorifics.

Oakley plopped into a seat in the lobby and fiddled with his phone. I strolled into the meeting room and found an empty seat. It was still ten minutes until it started, but a half-dozen people were already there.

A large man broke off from the group socializing and came over to sit on the chair next to me. He stuck out a hand towards me. "Hey there, I'm Avery. First time here?"

"Yeah. I'm Everett." I hesitated, wondering if I'd be warm enough, but what were the odds that he'd know enough about vampires to be suspicious? I shook his hand.

"Ohh, icy hands." Avery settled back into the chair. "Did you just move here?"

I gripped the edges of the folding chair and looked at the carpet. "Maybe. Not sure yet. But I think the woman I'm..." I stopped, grasping for a word to use and settled on, "working for is talking about staying here permanently."

He lowered his head and looked at me with raised eyebrows. "Is that right?"

I bit my lip and tears sprang into my eyes. I wiped them away, then covered my face.

"Hey, it's alright. Let me get some tissues," Avery said. I didn't feel his warmth move and peeked between my fingers to see someone else carrying over a box of tissues and setting it in my lap.

"Upset about the move?" Avery asked as I dabbed at my eyes. The friendliness he'd exuded when he'd first come to say hello had faded, and now he sounded almost angry with me. I found the sudden change odd, but maybe he was just irritated that a newcomer was making waterworks before the meeting had even started.

"No, I don't care where I live. My family cut me off for being," I gestured at myself and shrugged. "It's kinda just, everything, right now. The woman, she..." I wiped my eyes again.

"Ooh, drama. Juicy." The guy who handed me the tissue box sat down on my other side and slung his arm over the back of the chair to regard me. He had an undercut and wore a jean jacket covered in patches.

"It's not that." I waved him away. "It's just my boyfriend and her keep butting heads. He doesn't like her, but I'm kinda stuck right now."

Avery and jean jacket leaned closer.

"My boyfriend tries to understand the changes I've been going through," I said, knowing they'd think I meant transition and not becoming a vampire, not that it really mattered in the end. "But sometimes he just doesn't get it. I think maybe that's what's been driving the wedge between us."

"Ah well, sorry to cut you off here." Avery pointed to the room, which had filled up as we'd talked. "But it's time to get started."

I smiled at him and dabbed at my eyes again, already feeling better.

"Is that your boyfriend waiting outside in the lobby?" the other guy whispered to me as the Avery stood and began the meeting. That explained why Avery had been so friendly. It was protective, sussing out the new guy before the meeting started.

"No, that's my bodyguard," I whispered back.

"Bodyguard?" he said loudly enough that everyone fell silent and turned to stare at us.

I shrunk down in my seat. "Sorry to interrupt. Please, go on."

Avery chuckled. "No way. I need to hear this. Bodyguard, really?"

My shoulders went up around my ears. "My employer insists. Can we just get on with it?"

Avery shook his head, and we went around for introductions.

The meeting was standard fare. People talked about hormones, family, and other transition issues. I mostly stayed silent and listened, just enjoying being out of the hotel room for a bit. Plus, I didn't want to accidentally say something that could tie me back to my former identity in Portland. I'd already slipped up and used Everett instead of my new ID name of Evan. Really, what were the odds that someone multiple states away would put two-and-two together and connect me to my dead identity? Even so, Stacy and Lin had drilled caution into me enough that I tried to error on the side of being too quiet.

As we stood up after the meeting, jean jacket, or Xander, as I learned during introductions, tapped my arm.

"Hey, we all go for drinks after the meeting. You interested in coming?"

I paused and bit my lip, glancing towards the door where everyone was filing out. "Maybe… I need to check with my bodyguard first."

"We'll be there if you decide to come." Xander gave me directions and a thumbs up before leaving.

Before I could stand up, Avery was suddenly standing directly in front of me, his arms crossed, looking serious. I couldn't stand up without bumping into him. "Everett, I need a word with you before you go."

"Sure, what's up?" I looked up at him from under my bangs. We were the only two left in the room.

He leaned down, putting his hands on my knees to get right up into my face. "Vampire," he hissed. I started back. "I don't know what you think you're playing at, but my meetings are off limits for hunting, got it? Now get out of here and I never want to see you again."

My eyes widened. "What? I wouldn't—"

"Did I stutter?" Avery's eyes flashed yellow. A shifter. Figured.

I growled and shoved him off me, pushing with a little more strength than was strictly necessary. Avery flew back, landing on his back in the middle of the large circle of chairs.

"I'm not here for that!" I yelled. "I'm trans. I came for the same reason as everyone else."

Avery twisted and jumped up in the same fluid motion to land on his feet. "Liar," he growled, his words distorted by the sharp teeth that were filling his jaw. "Never heard of a trans vampire before."

"What's all the yelling?" Oakley strolled in, glancing between Avery and me. He grinned and lowered his fangs, focusing on Avery. "You hurt the —" he glanced at me and grimaced, changing his word, "my friend here and you'll regret it."

"He didn't hurt me," I said, crouching and pressing my face into my legs. I felt lightheaded and tight, like my world was constricting around me. I'd lost my family and all my friends when I became a vampire, then the house burned and I was adrift again, clinging to Jack, but I felt him slipping away from me, and now this. I burst into tears, sobbing into my jeans.

Oakley, by the cool presence and his smell, crouched next to me and rubbed my back.

I stood up, still crying, and wiped my eyes with my sleeve. "I want to go back to the hotel now."

I didn't wait for an answer, but spun and ran out to the street, past a knot of people from the group standing outside smoking. I stopped on the sidewalk and closed my eyes, trying to force myself to stop crying. It wasn't really working, though.

"What's wrong?" One of them asked. I heard the footsteps of more than one person approaching me.

"Avery said I'm not welcome," I said. "I'm sorry for crying, I've just had a bad week and—"

"He said *what!*" a second person said. "Don't apologize for crying over that, Everett."

Sniffing, I nodded, using my palm to rub my cheeks, then opened my eyes. I recognized the second person who'd spoken as Xander in his jean jacket, but not the others. There had been almost twenty people there, and I didn't remember everyone's names.

"I'll talk to him," Xander said, and moved to go, but I stopped him.

"No, it's okay." I hunched my shoulders and hugged myself. "I get his reasoning. It just hurt on top of everything else."

"I called a cab," Oakley called to me as he came out of the community center. He eyed the group of smokers hungrily.

I elbowed him gently. "Don't you dare," I hissed at him under my breath.

Xander looked back at the community center with a frown. "That doesn't sound like Avery. Give me your number. I'm still going to talk to him, see if he'll give you a second chance over," he waved his cigarette in a circle, "whatever his issue is."

"Thanks." I took Xander's phone and put my number in. I had little faith that Avery would change his mind, but I supposed it couldn't hurt. And at the very least, Xander sounded like he could be a friend.

Chapter Eleven

Viral Video

When Oakley and I got back to the house, a small crowd of vampires already waited on the walk up to the front door. I didn't recognize any of them, but they hushed and parted for us.

"Oh my gosh, it's him," a girl whispered.

Okay, not creepy at all. I stopped and checked the time on the phone.

"Not that I'm unhappy to see you all here, but it's not even eleven. The ceremony doesn't start until close to dawn," I told the assembled crowd.

"We know," one of them said. "But we wanted to get here early to make sure we got a spot."

"How did you even hear about this, anyway?" I asked, pausing at the door. The last few nights since our first show, the new attendees had been dragged in by previous ones. Of course, none of the following ceremonies had been as wild as that first night with the fire and the gunshot, but I preferred it that way, anyway.

The first one who'd spoken stepped forward and held out a phone, showing me the screen. A shaky video played on it. I peered closer. It showed Goddess and me coming back in surrounded by sunshine, then the vampire catching fire, finishing with the gunshot, showing her healed chest. That explained how they knew me.

"Wait, this can't be right," I said, glancing at the bottom of the screen. "This has like a million views."

"Yeah, why do you think we got here so early?" The vampire put his phone back in his pocket and leaned against the wall next to the door. "We tried knocking, but no one answered."

"We all went out." I unlocked the door and propped it open with a sigh. I couldn't leave them out here. Didn't want the neighbors to call the cops or something. Well, maybe it wouldn't matter. But still, it felt wrong to leave them all standing in the yard of Oakley and Nate's house. "Come on in."

Grinning, they all filed past me and arranged themselves on the couches and chairs in the living room. Over a dozen of them. It was already crowded. I let the door close after making sure there wasn't anyone else waiting. I walked over and took a seat at the breakfast bar, swiveling the stool to look at the crowd. Oakley hovered near my elbow.

"In the video, you and that lady bit a bunch of vampires," a woman said from the couch.

"Yeah." I folded my arms and met her gaze. She looked like she'd died at maybe nineteen at most, not that that meant anything. Most people put my age at fifteen or sixteen at first glance. The group of them all looked at me expectantly. "Don't worry," I assured them. "You can just watch. We only bite volunteers." I kept myself from glancing over at Oakley. I hoped that it had been a one-time thing.

"That's not –" one began, but he was cut off by another louder question from a different vampire.

"Is it a trick?" The question came from the male vampire that showed me the video. "The sunlight and the silver bullet bit?"

I shook my head. "It's not. My maker…" I stalled, trying to think what to say. "She's an ancient from old Egypt. At least 3000 years old. Vampire blood doesn't harm us. In fact, she claims it's beneficial to those we bite."

The vampire crowd sucked in a breath at the mention of Goddess' age. Next to me, Oakley added, "Very beneficial." He sighed and ran his hands up and down his arms, then thrust a wrist out toward me. "Can you, Everett? I don't want to wait till dawn."

I licked my lips. The offer was tempting. Goddess did not explicitly say I couldn't bite people outside the ceremony. The last few nights when I hadn't eaten until the ceremony had been torture. Self-conscious, I glanced at the crowd with a blush. "Do you mind?"

Most of them shook their head, although one woman looked queasy. Before I could bite, the doorbell rang.

Oakley pulled his arm back. "I'll get it, high priest. You stay here."

"I told you not to call me that!" I growled at his back.

Three more vampires, all guys, were at the door. Oakley let them in and they huddled in the entryway as Oakley came back to join me at the bar. This was getting ridiculous already. I wondered if I should text Goddess to warn her.

"Is that your boyfriend?" one of the newcomers asked me. Made sense with this many vampires in the city that not all of them would know each other.

"No!" I buried my face in my hands. "Is it that obvious I'm gay?"

The newcomer laughed. "You're kidding right?"

"You gonna lose underwear tonight?"

"Yeah, we want to see the goods." The third called.

I could feel myself blushing, so I jumped to my feet and barred my fangs at them. "Absolutely not!" I glared at them and pointed at the door. "If that's what you're here for, show yourselves out."

The door clicked and opened behind them. Goddess had returned with Jack. I sagged with relief. Her eyes widened as she took in the crowd in the room. Shooing the cluster of guys out of the way, Goddess strode inside with Jack behind her, grinning from ear to ear.

"My! Are you all here for the ceremony?" Her eyes sparkled with delight.

"Yes, we are," one of the seated vampires said.

Jack walked over to me, his steps hesitant and his neck stiff. I grabbed his elbow and pulled him close. He looked down at me with an unspoken question, and I shook my head. "Goddess, I'm going to go to my room with Jack." I started gently tugging him in that direction when Goddess stopped me.

"Everett, you cannot abandon our guests." She swept over to me and grabbed my free arm.

"Yeah, you were going to bite him for us." A woman called, pointing at Oakley.

The gaggle of gay guys lingered by the door, giving Jack and me curious looks.

Jack disentangled his arm from my grip, then leaned over to kiss me on the forehead. "I'll be in our room when you're done."

He beat a hasty retreat around the corner and upstairs. I could practically smell the fear on him. I couldn't help but feel a rush of disappointment that he would be scared of vampires. Of course, I'd felt the same when he took me to the shifter picnic, so I knew I was being hypocritical. Still, it stung.

I plastered on a smile and let Goddess pull me farther into the living room.

More and more vampires kept showing up, until the room was standing room only. Kurt and Nate watched the door and had to send vampires away when the crowd grew too large even for Nate and Oakley's house. Goddess kept me with her socializing until nearly dawn, when she let me go back to my room to change into my robes for the ceremony. Jack lay on the bed snoring, so I let him sleep.

Until now, the only vampires who had volunteered to be bitten at the end of the ceremony were the usual crew. Tonight, half a dozen more vampires volunteered out of curiosity. And a desire to get some of the sun-proofing effects Goddess and I had shown in the video.

Kurt, having been around the longest, demonstrated by having me crack a curtain to let in a small strip of light that he stuck his hand into. His skin smoked and blackened, but there were no flames.

"As you see," Goddess called, striking a pose and raising her arms. "The Church of Ra."

She paused, looked around at the crowd to judge their reactions, frowned, and then added, "The Church of the Sun. Bringing sun back to the vampires."

The crowd roared in approval and longing.

My head spun at how fast Goddess' plans were progressing. I thought we would have had years to figure out a way out. I obviously haven't counted on the vampire's obsession with the possibility of seeing the sun again.

"GOOD MORNING." JACK STROKED my side gently and spooned me from behind. I'd actually been awake for a while, but had stayed laying there enjoying Jack's warmth. The worst part of drinking from only vampires was that there was nothing to chase away the constant bone deep cold. "Or I guess I should say good evening instead."

I smiled and stretched against his chest. "I like good morning."

Jack kissed my neck. I wanted him to keep going, but... I had things I needed to tell him. "I have some good and bad news," I told him.

Jack paused after that kiss, mouth hovering over my neck. "Bad first, I guess," he breathed out, breath tickling the hairs on the back of my neck.

I turned away, hugging my legs to my chest. "A video of us saving that burning vampire went viral." I let out a laugh. With Goddess baring it all for the camera, it really wasn't a surprise that the video took off. I didn't even like women and I could see how attractive she was.

"Everyone online thought it was a clip from an upcoming movie or something, but the more internet savvy vampires who saw it put two-and-two together."

"Leading to that chaos we came home to last night," Jack finished for me with a snort. "I had to turn into a jackal after the fifth vampire came in here thinking I was an easy meal."

"I'm sorry."

"Not your fault." Jack sighed. "We need to get out of here."

"We're no closer than we were when she took us prisoner."

"Even if we find the amulet, we don't know how to break whatever spell connects you to it."

"Right." I sighed. "Maybe with the book that Lady Ann had, but that hasn't been seen since the night of the explosion."

"And that would be a longshot, anyway." Jack put his arm around my back and rested his cheek against the top of my head. "I had one other idea, but it involves the shifters. The only shifter I've met here is Brun—"

"You can't contact the PCA?"

I felt his head rub against me as he shook his head, and his hand tightened on my side. He was silent for a moment, then said, "No."

I knew Jack too well by now. That pause, he was lying to me, but I didn't understand why. Well, that was wrong. I shifted, tightening my arms on my legs. I knew why. If Goddess ordered it, I'd have to tell her any secrets Jack told me. It was bad enough I'd already seen that envelope addressed to him in his house, I was just lucky Goddess hadn't pried it from me.

"Let me guess," I said. "That assassination attempt was them."

"Yeah. That was the vampires. The shifters said this was a vampire problem, but I need to convince them otherwise."

"I've met a shifter," I told him.

Jack started against me. "What, you? When? You've hardly left the house."

I put my legs down and twisted my head to glare up at him. "Not like I've had much choice."

"Right, I'm sorry." Jack kissed my forehead and smoothed my hair back.

"But I have once. When you went to dinner with Goddess, I went..." I took another shuddering breath. Not that I needed to breathe, but the habit calmed me. "I went to a trans support group."

"One of the trans guys?" Jack laughed. "Excellent."

"I don't know how to contact him, though. He wasn't exactly happy to see a vampire at his meeting."

"Oh." Jack deflated a bit.

"But I'll see what I can do." I shifted away so I could look at him properly. "What's your plan?"

"Shifters can protect you from the vampires."

"No, they can't!" I tried and failed to keep my voice down. I covered my face with my hands. "They can't keep me safe from myself."

"I know. But if you're restrained, and they can keep her from getting to us." Jack pulled my hands down off my face.

I slumped. I imagined being locked up. Goddess puppeting me, trying to get me out. "That doesn't sound like much of a life," I whispered.

"Just until the PCA can figure out how to untangle you from her influence." Jack squeezed my hands.

"Why can't we just stay here until then?"

"Everett, I'm already seeing her influence on you." He cupped my face with one hand. "When you fed on Oakley. Your expression…" He shuddered.

I shook my head, looking away from him, but he pulled my gaze back.

"When was the last time she even had to give you an order?" Jack asked.

That was easy. "The night she sent me out to get Oakley and Nate."

"That was weeks ago." Jack looked me deep in the eyes, so deep that I looked away, ashamed.

"You don't know how it feels," I said.

"So you said. You avoid doing things that might set her off, or force her to control you. But is it any better to obey her?"

"At least it's my choice."

"It's a slippery slope, Everett." He leaned forward and kissed me. His lips were soft on mine. Gentle. Warm. I opened my mouth and leaned into him, wanting more, but he pulled back.

"Alright, I get it. I'll be careful."

Jack hugged me to his chest. "Thank you."

CHAPTER TWELVE

A MIRACLE

I'D BEEN THINKING ABOUT what Jack had said the other night, but I was still unsure of what I could do about the situation. Without a way to escape from Goddess or destroy her, I was stuck. Goddess had told me she was immortal, and seeing her get shot through the heart with silver weeks ago had only made me more sure she wasn't lying.

This morning's ceremony began as usual. About a dozen vampires crowded around the back of the room where we did the dawn ceremony. Goddess threw off her robe and sang her way outside. I usually would have been right on her heels, but a bullet whizzed by me as I started taking off my robe. I jumped, tripped on the hem of my robe, and fell hard on the tile floor.

None of the watching vampires moved. The silence pounded in my ears until a high-pitched scream from outside shattered the tension. I scrambled to my feet and dashed outside.

A cloud surrounded Goddess, glittering in the morning sunlight and obscuring her form and three more shapes that jumped down from the roof to circle around her. A shaft had pierced Goddess through, pinning her into the grass.

The morning dew wet my feet as I dashed towards her. The sun tingled on my skin, but by now I could ignore the burning, though I still had to squint against the glare. But as soon as I entered the glittery cloud, my eyes and skin smoked, sizzling and popping like I'd just stepped into a fire. I screamed, but that was a mistake. The moment I opened my mouth to suck in a breath, the burning moved inside me, ripping and searing at my throat and nose. Gagging and crying, I fell onto my side on the grass and curled into a fetal position.

A gloved hand grabbed my hair. I swiped a hand limply at them, but every movement sent waves of pain dancing along my skin. The assailant dragged me across the grass out of the cloud and then dropped me. Immediately the burning sensation lessened.

I uncurled and squinted after my savior. My eyes were still dazzled by the sun and the burning cloud, so all I could make out were three black forms running away across the dewy grass. They dashed out the fence that led to the desert and I lost track of them.

The sun seemed to burn me more than usual this morning. I glanced around, but I'd only been able to see the running people because of the movement and by how much their outfits stood out from the bright morning. Nothing else moved. I could smell blood in the air, human and something else, something like vampire, but different.

"Goddess? High Priest?" Kurt called from inside the house.

I tried to respond, but my throat still burned and I couldn't do more than croak. Gasping in pain, I got up on my hands and knees and crawled back inside.

"Everett!" Nate cried as I came got through the door. I crawled towards his voice, my eyes still dazzled by the light. "What happened to you? Where's Goddess?"

I winced when Nate touched my arm. Still unable to speak, I turned and bit down on him and started drinking. I only stopped when Kurt and Oakley dragged me off of him.

"What happened, Everett?" Kurt asked, kneeling in front of me. "Your skin was black. And Goddess still has not come inside."

"Something glittered out there. It burned..." it finally hit me, "Burned like silver." I doubled over coughing and then spat out a blackened glob of spit. My throat felt a lot better now. "Go wake up Jack, and any other humans here while I go back out and look for Goddess."

Only when I stood did I realize I was still naked except for my underwear. My skin was black and burned, flaking off in places to reveal new pink skin beneath. The unhealed portions cracked and bled as I moved, making me wince in pain with every step.

Outside, the sun had moved higher, and the day was already heating up. The glittery cloud of silver dust had fallen, dusting the grass with sparkling silver motes. With my eyes healed, I could now see what I'd missed earlier.

Goddess' head lay by her feet, eyes staring blankly at me. Her body lay on its back in the middle of the lawn. Her arms were spread and her fingers covered in blood. The stump of her neck faced away from me, which made me glad I couldn't see more. Even what I could see made me queasy. Her skin was covered in half-healed patches of black silver burns.

She stared at me as I took hesitant steps across the grass. Then she blinked and her mouth opened. I screamed and jumped back, slipping on the damp grass. I landed on my ass and scrambled backwards until my fingers hit the lintel of the backdoor.

"Are you hurt?" Jack cried, bolting outside. He hopped down the three steps and landed next to me in a crouch, growling low in the back of his throat. If it had been night, I'm sure he would have changed already. He wore only a cut-off pair of sweatpants.

I shook my head and lifted a trembling hand to point at Goddess's body.

He glanced that direction and then started, eyes widening. "They did it!" he said under his breath. "She's dead?" he said louder.

They. So, he'd been in on this plot, and I assumed, the earlier attempt at the Luxor. I swallowed down my hurt, knowing why he hadn't confided in me, and shook my head. "She blinked at me, and her mouth moved. I don't think she's dead."

"Everett, even a vampire as powerful as her can't come back from beheading." Jack pushed up to standing and offered me a hand up, then pulled me to my feet. "Let's go back inside."

"We can't leave her out here!" I hugged myself. Waring emotions of guilt, elation, and disgust with myself for feeling the first two ping-ponged through me, leaving me both giddy and sick to my stomach. The healing had burned away the normal buzz the vampire blood gave me, leaving me still thirsty for more.

Jack grimaced and glanced back at the door, apparently realizing that the listeners inside would agree with me. "Fine. Wait here, I'll go get a sheet— "

As the words came out of his mouth, a folded sheet came flying from inside to hit Jack's chest with a thud. Jack caught it with a scowl. I followed him back across the lawn. Goddess's body was starting to smoke. We had chosen the back door for the ceremony because of a lack of things to block the morning sunlight, which also meant no shade. I averted my eyes from the jagged cut on her neck, focusing my gaze on the curve of Goddess's belly fat and hips.

My skin prickled and burned from being out here for so long. Even the places where the silver burns had cleared up were starting to smoke. Jack shook out the sheet and laid it over her body. "You get her feet, I'll get the arms," he said, crouching to slide his arms under the body's shoulders.

"What about..." I said, stopping to stare at the head. The sheet had missed covering the severed head and it rolled her eyes to stare up at me. Her lips formed words, and the tongue moved, but without the lungs no sound came out. I gagged. From this angle, I don't think Jack could see the face moving.

"Leave it. I'll come back for it after we get this part inside."

I swallowed and stepped over it. The remaining silver dusting the grass burned my feet as I walked up to the body. I was leaning over to grab the body's ankles when something chomped down on my foot. I yelped and kicked; Goddess' severed head tumbled away. Her black wig flung free as it rolled. It came to a stop near the side of the house. Thankfully facing away from me now.

"What was that, Everett?" Jack hissed as I took her ankles.

"She bit me. I don't think she liked her head being left behind."

Jack rolled his eyes. "Hilarious. Now, on three."

We shuffle walked back into the house, her body swinging limply between us.

The vampires all moved away reverently as we carried her into the middle of the room.

A few muttered prayers, and one, I didn't see who, started openly weeping.

We laid her down on the carpet in the aisle between the rows of pillows. Jack darted away, back outside. He came back a moment later with Goddess' head. He held the head outstretched in front of him, holding it facing away from himself. Goddess' eyes had been closed but opened as he came closer. She looked straight at me and I stiffened as she gave me an order. "Re-attach my head."

Jack went to set the head next to the corpse's stomach, but I yanked the sheet back and off her, then pointed.

"No, put her head at her neck."

"Ev— "

Goddess's eyes widened, and she repeated the order. As much as I didn't want to, I darted forward, grabbing the head from him. I took two steps over to her neck, knelt, and set Goddess's head down so that the severed parts of the neck met. Nothing happened.

"Feed her." I stood, grabbed the nearest vampire to me by the arm, and practically threw the startled girl at Goddess' face.

"Everett, she's dead." Kurt came over and draped my torn robe over my shoulders.

The girl screamed, and everyone turned to look. Goddess had latched onto her wrist and was sucking greedily. The girl was flailing, dragging Goddess with her. Goddess's neck had already partially healed, but as the girl pulled it started to tear apart again, the healing seams re-ripping open.

No one moved. Even Jack sucked in a breath and then held it.

The girl didn't get far. A moment later, the venom hit her. She sank to her knees, giggling, and placidly let Goddess feed from her. Goddess's neck snapped back together with a pop.

We all watched in silence as Goddess devoured the girl down to a dried-out husk. Goddess shoved the withered body aside and stood, rubbing her neck and giving me a rueful smile. "It's always so painful when that happens."

Jack cried out and bolted from the room. All the vampires dropped to their knees. One crossed himself, probably out of habit.

"A miracle," Kurt whispered.

THE FRONT DOOR OPENED, spilling a wash of light out onto the porch and a blast of noise, poppers and kazoos.

"Welcome, Goddess!" a chorus of voices yelled.

Everett shook confetti out of his hair. Tawaret left it where it was, giggling. The plastic suns and stars sparkled in her black hair.

"Oh, why thank you!" Tawaret purred, tugging Everett into the house. An adoring group of vampires immediately surrounded them. One of them was probably our host; one of Oakley's friends who'd been attending since the first ceremony where Goddess 'revealed her divinity,' according to the whispers I'd overheard the last few days. This party was to celebrate her great rebirth after she'd been beheaded last week.

I was the last one inside, and I followed the music and lights out of the entryway into the living room. There had to be a hundred vampires there, packed into the large room and spilling out into the open-plan kitchen and dining room. I glimpsed Kurt's bald head over the top of the crowd before dozens of red eyes turned in my direction.

I backpedaled, only to almost back into another vampire that had come up behind me. I let out a yip that had even more vampires turning towards me.

Fur prickled under my skin, but I resisted.

"Everyone," I said, holding up my hands and trying to look harmless. I tried to smile as I backed up against the wall, but I think it came out more as a grimace. "I'm here with Everett. He's my boyfriend." Red-eyed stares looked back at me and one of them licked their lips. "The High Priest—"

A vampire on my side rushed me. The change took me as he tackled me into the wall. I fell to the marble floor with a yelp, clawing my way out of my shirt that had tangled over my head in my smaller jackal form. I tried to be careful, but my claws caught, and there were several loud ripping sounds as I pawed the shirt off. The stink of vampires burned at my nose, strong enough to make my eyes water. A semi-circle of disappointed vampires surrounded me, looking down at me with disgust.

"Who brought the shifter?" One of them turned to call back into the party. "Loser!"

Another opened the front door and started trying to shoo me out of it.

"Hey!" I barked, trying to stand as tall as I could. "I'm here with the Goddess and her High Priest."

"Yeah right," a vampire growled, crouching down to bare his fangs at me. "Now get out of here before I forget the truce, and my buddies and I eat you."

I briefly entertained the idea of leaving, but I couldn't, wouldn't, abandon Everett like that. I bared my teeth right back at him and put my ears back. "No."

His eyes widened at my refusal. Or maybe at the fact I was growing back to human-sized, my claws extending, my jaw widening, and muscles bulging. A moment later, I stood even taller than usual, the tips of my over-sized ears nearly brushing the bottom of the opulent light fixture hanging in the entryway. Now a half-human/half-jackal, I roared in his face and slashed at him with one paw, driving him back.

The chattering hum from the party died down, everyone falling silent and turning in our direction. Even the music cut off with one final thump. The silence echoed in my ears between my heartbeats and ragged breath.

The vampire facing off with me growled and feinted forward again. I dodged easily, but then a line of fire clipped my back. I whirled, snapping my jaws at a second vampire who'd clawed me from behind.

"Stop!"

Everett's voice echoed through the room. Suddenly he was at my back; my tail brushed his legs. "Anyone who hurts my boyfriend will answer to me," Everett growled, his words slurred a bit by his fangs.

"And me." There was a swirl of air, and then Tawaret stood between me and the closest vampires. The circle of vampires that had been tightening backed up a few steps.

"Jack, you're bleeding!" Everett said, touching my back lightly.

"Who hurt him?" Goddess growled, whirling around to scan the crowd. "Jackals are sacred."

I slumped forward onto all fours, letting the change that I'd been fighting pull me the rest of the way to full jackal. My legs shook with exhaustion and I slumped over onto my side, panting. Just those few moments in my half form had left me drained.

Everett dropped to his knees next to me and put a shaking hand on my back. The slashes had healed with the change.

"How was I supposed to know?" Vampires pushed forward the attacker. My blood dripped from the tips of his fingers.

"We were invited as guests into this house." Tawaret pointed at me, other hand on her hip. "Is this how you treat guests?"

"He attacked us," the vampire argued.

"Defended myself," I snarled, climbing to my feet. My claws clicked on the tile as I approached him, ears back, hackles raised.

"Jack, I'll handle this," Tawaret said in a tone that brooked no argument.

I moved back and sat at Everett's side, keeping my ears alert and flicking around to hear the crowd.

"Kneel." Tawaret pointed at the floor in front of her.

Frowning, the vampire looked around at the gathered crowd. "Is she serious?"

About half the crowd muttered something akin to yes. My hackles started rising again. Had so many come over the last week? Once dawn hit, I was helpless, as Brun had so tactlessly pointed out to me, but he was correct. I trusted Everett, but not the rest of them. So, I'd been making myself scarce.

"Has that one attended the ceremony before?" I whispered to Everett, cocking my head to look up at him. Funny how tall he looked when I was a jackal; when I was a human, the top of his head barely came up to my chin.

Everett shook his head, not taking his eyes off the drama unfolding around us.

Only after the crowd's disapproval became louder did my attacker kneel in front of Tawaret. She smiled down at him, then lifted her head to address the crowd. "First rule. Jackals are sacred and any in my church that harm them will face that harm returned threefold."

She gestured Everett and I forward. I stayed pressed against Everett's leg as we shuffled up to stand beside her.

"Second, we observe the rules of hospitality. Which you have *broken.*"

"Look lady—"

"Silence!" Tawaret's voice thundered, so loud my head rang. I flattened my ears to my head and dropped to my belly with a whine, pawing at my ears. Most of the vampires did the same, clapping their hands to their ears and falling to their knees with cries of pain. Everett seemed unaffected, as did two other vampires in the crowd, tall beacons in the otherwise kneeling room. But even their eyes widened at Tawaret's show of power. The dissipating magic made my fur stand on end.

Tawaret stood, smiling sweetly around at everyone cowering on the floor. "Now, Everett. This one is yours to punish as you will." My ears still rung from the blast and at first, I thought I'd misheard.

"Me?" Everett took one step back and glanced down at me. I whined and looked up at him. He crouched and pulled me into a hug. "Jack is fine. See?" He ruffled the fur on my back to show I was uninjured. "No need to do anything."

"He broke the laws of hospitality, High Priest," Tawaret snapped, moving to stand next to Everett. She bent over and grabbed me, ripping me out of his arms, and picking me up. I struggled until she wrapped her arms around my legs, arms like steel, pinning me to her. "And he harmed your jackal, even if he has already healed. The culprit must be punished."

Still crouching, Everett swallowed and looked at the kneeling vampire. "Like what?" he whispered.

"If you don't think of something, I will make a suggestion." Tawaret replied, arms tightening around me until I couldn't breathe. I shook my head, making my ears flop, and struggled to no avail.

Everett's eyes widened, and then his face hardened, and he looked back to the vampire. He crawled over to the vampire, pushed him to the tile, and sank his teeth into his neck.

"Holy shit," someone in the crowd whispered. All eyes were on Everett and the struggling vampire pinned under him.

A few moments after, Goddess relaxed her grip enough that I could gasp and pant for air, although I was still trapped in her arms.

Everett kept drinking and drinking, even as the crowd murmured at how much Everett was taking. The vampire man's struggling stopped, and he moaned in pleasure. I put my ears back.

Tawaret just watched, her smile growing wider as Everett kept drinking.

"Stop!" I yelled, once, before Tawaret clamped her hand around my muzzle.

Eventually the man's groans faltered and soon after that, he went limp under Everett.

After far too long, Everett pulled back and sat up, licking his lips. The vampire's skin was dried out, and his body sunken. The vampire he'd been feeding on was dead, totally drained of blood. Not as drained as Tawaret had done to the women the other night, but the vampire was still clearly dead.

Oh god. Everett, what have you done?

Everett's cheeks were bright red and his eyes were glazed over. He tried to stand, but his legs buckled and he fell back to the tile with a giggle, holding himself up on one elbow.

The crowd was totally silent; not even the sound of breathing you'd get from a human crowd. You could have heard a mouse sneeze.

Tawaret set me down and walked over to Everett, her heels sounding like gunfire as she moved across the tile.

"A fitting punishment, High Priest." Tawaret crouched and put her hand on his head, looking like a proud parent.

Chapter Thirteen

Sowing Discord

The party lasted until after dawn. This house wasn't set up for the Sunrise Ceremony, but at dawn Goddess and I walked out the front door, coming back in with tanned skin.

Jack stayed as a jackal the entire evening, padding around at my side like a dog, at least until the sun came up and he disappeared into the guest room we'd been given for the day.

Once the clamor had died down around our little sun stroll, and Goddess and I nibbled on all the volunteers, I retreated upstairs. I reeled a bit on the steps; too much vampire blood again.

Inside our room, I found Jack pacing. He jumped when the door clicked closed and whirled to face me, crossing his arms across his chest. He wore a pair of borrowed pajamas.

"Now that we're finally alone..." I said, flicking the lock on the door and grinning at Jack. I tossed my shirt and Jack's clothing on the floor, having already taken it off to do the walk around the house, and moved towards Jack with a wink and a grin.

"Everett, no." Jack shook his head and stepped back out of my reach.

"No?" I stopped, more like stumbled to a stop, and blinked at Jack. I was having trouble thinking, my brain like mush from all the vampire blood. Oh, that must have been it. I detoured and threw back the covers on the bed. "Tonight then, after I've sobered up," I told him.

"It's not that." Jack sounded frustrated, so I turned to look at him again. "Everett, what happened tonight?" He stared at me, arms hugging his sides.

"A party..." I said, not following why he was so upset. I sat on the edge of the bed.

"No, the vampire. The one that slashed me." He fingered his back like it still ached, although he'd already healed.

"Oh, that." I cringed and bit my lip, looking away.

"What happened, Everett? Why didn't you stop drinking?" Jack came over to me and knelt in front of me, leaning to get into my vision again.

"Goddess said to keep going." I twisted my hands in my lap. "You heard her."

Jack took my hands in his. So warm. I wanted him to hug me, but I also wanted to run away.

"Everett, she didn't say anything."

"What? Of course, she..." I scrunched up my face as I realized what had happened. "Oh."

Jack cocked his head.

"She can speak directly into my head. I wasn't looking at her so I didn't realize that's what was happening. I thought she was speaking out loud."

Jack's expression brightened, and he smiled up at me. "So, she ordered you to kill him. But silently, so the others didn't hear."

I bit my lip. Had she given me an order? The night was a bit of a blur, and she'd been screaming in my head to kill him, but had it been an order? My head hung as I realized I'd never felt the compulsion.

Jack threw my hands away and snarled, jumping to his feet. "You did kill him then. It was your choice." He pointed an accusing finger at me.

"I don't know." I shrunk back.

"So then make her order you," Jack shot back. "Dammit, Ev, we just talked about this!" He raised his voice for the first few words but then caught himself and lowered it again.

The thought of being a passenger in my body again made me feel sick, and I shook my head, tears springing to my eyes. "You don't understand what it's like, Jack."

"But killing someone, Ev." Jack shook his head and turned his back on me. He slightly hunched over, as it curling in on himself. "I don't... I'm not sure I know who you are anymore."

Tears were rolling down my cheeks now. "Is this a breakup conversation?"

"I—" Jack threw up his hands. "I don't know, Ev. But I need some space, okay?"

"Are you going back to Portland?" I asked through my tears.

He shook his head. "No, not yet. She needs to be stopped, and the PCA is dragging their feet. I'm staying at least until you're free."

"Okay." I sniffed. That was logical, even if it didn't make me feel any better. I felt like a car had run me over, flattened me, and all my guts spilled out everywhere. I felt empty.

He walked over and grabbed his pile of clothes that I'd dropped by the door. He folded them up and then paused. "Where's my phone?"

"Here." I pulled it out of my pocket and held it out to him.

Jack came over and took it from me, then frowned. "This is the one you got for me."

"Yeah?" I asked. "Do you have another one?" I squinted at him, wiping tears from my eyes.

"... nothing." Jack shook his head. "I'm going to sleep downstairs on the couch."

"Are you sure that's safe?" I rubbed my cheeks. The tears had dried up for now.

"I think you made the consequences for touching me clear enough, so yes." He sounded bitter.

Grief punched me in the stomach again, driving the breath from me. Goddess had told me the vampire deserved to die. I'd *known* if I didn't kill him, that she would force me, even if she hadn't said so. At the time, I had wanted, well, I guess, it felt like I was taking back power by keeping control, but now I doubted my decision. I curled over and rolled onto my side, putting my back to Jack, expecting to hear the door open and close but there was only silence.

"I thought you were leaving."

"I realized we should maybe keep up the ruse." The bed moved as Jack sat down behind me.

"Is it a ruse?" I asked quietly. I felt numb, like I was floating ten feet behind my body and this all was happening to someone else.

Jack sighed. "That came out wrong."

"Look, if you need some space, go down and watch TV. *If* you happen to fall asleep on the couch, no one will question it," I said.

The depression filled back in as Jack stood up. "Thanks," Jack said softly. I heard his steps thudding across the carpet, odd because he usually walked silently, like a jackal, and a moment later the door opened and shut. I was alone.

I'D SEEN THE TELEVISION during the party—a giant thing hung on the wall in the living area. Remains from the party lay scattered around. Including literal remains. Or sleeping vampires, but I wasn't about to go about checking one way or the other.

I averted my gaze from a body slumped over the other arm of the couch and searched for the remote, revising my decision to sleep down here. I'd watch TV for a few hours and go back once I thought Everett would be asleep.

I was halfway through a daytime soap when a voice startled me.

"Jack, just the person I wanted to see," Tawaret purred.

I jumped and grabbed the remote to mute the television. I hadn't heard her come in. "Me?"

"Yes." She came over and sat on the other side of the couch near the corpse/possible vampire.

I shifted to the side to see her better and put an arm on the back of the couch. "What about?"

Tawaret reached into her blouse and pulled out a flip phone. The one that the PCA had given me. Shit. "Some interesting messages on here, Jack."

I just looked at her and considered if I could get to the back door behind me before she murdered me. Definitely not. Not that I would be safe from her, even outside. And I already knew I didn't have a chance against her even at night at my strongest in my half form. Finally, I said, "I already told you, I'm loyal to Everett, not you. I'm trying to do what's best for him."

"I expected better of you, Jack. What's best for Everett," Tawaret crushed the phone into powder between her hands, "is best for me."

I stared at her, trying not to wince as she dusted away the phone parts. "So, you say," I said.

"I do. Now, maybe the three of us need to talk this out?"

I shrugged.

"Go get him." Tawaret demanded. "Bring him down here, now."

"He's probably asleep," I said, looking meaningfully at the open blinds and the wide strip of afternoon sunlight coming in behind me.

"Wake him." Tawaret crossed her arms and settled back onto the couch.

Shaking my head, I got up and went to the bedroom. I had a feeling that if I didn't go, she'd do it herself and then punish me in some fashion.

Everett hadn't moved since I'd left him. I gently shook his shoulder, then harder when he still didn't open his eyes. Dang it, he wouldn't wake up. Not knowing how to wake him, I hefted him into my arms like a sleeping child and carried him downstairs and into the living room.

Tawaret lifted her eyebrows as I came in.

"Sorry, I couldn't wake him up." I went to lay him on the couch, but she pointed at the floor by her feet.

"Young vampires can sometimes be difficult to wake during the day," she said as I laid him down and arranged his arms and legs. I stepped back as she straddled his chest and leaned over his head. She glanced over at me. "Let me show you a foolproof method for waking them."

"Alright." I crossed my arms and sat on the couch, curious about what this method was. It would have been useful to know earlier, and might be again.

Tawaret put her hands on either side of Everett's head and looked up at me with a smirk.

"Wait—" I started to say.

Tawaret twisted Everett's head sharply to the side. His neck snapped with a crack and his eyes popped open, his mouth twisting into a scream that Tawaret smothered with a hand over his mouth.

I roared and jumped to my feet, lunging at her. She vanished and re-appeared on the other side of the couch. My dive took me over Everett. I rolled to my feet.

"What did you do!" I snarled at her.

"Nothing," Goddess said, putting a hand on one outthrust hip. "I was merely waking him up. No need to over-react, guardian jackal." Her tone was even, and her lip twitched like she was hiding a smile but there was real anger in her eyes. Shit. She'd baited me and I'd fallen for it.

Next to me, I heard a pop and then a gasp. I whirled. Everett sat up, clutching at his throat. The sight was enough to shock me out of my rage.

Everett's eyes widened, and he shrank back from me. "J-jack?" he stammered, kicking back from me. He was trembling. I wanted to comfort him, and reached for him but he flinched. Clearly, he was confused. Letting out a snort of frustration, I sat back in a crouch and counted back from ten to calm down.

"A little misunderstanding," Tawaret said with a slight laugh, appearing behind Everett and sitting on the couch. She put a hand on Everett's head to ruffle his hair.

The move made me snarl and Goddess's smile widened and she tilted her head at me, like she was daring me to take her on. Definitely baiting me, but why?

Still massaging his neck, Everett gave me a wary look and backed up to the couch. He pulled himself up and sat next to Tawaret. I swallowed another snarl when she took his hand. My jackal pushed at my skin, wanting to tear her to shreds but held back by the sun.

I suspected any kind of physical pain would have woken him, but she'd chosen to break his neck to set me off in front of him. Sowing discord.

Now I saw her game. But why try to turn him against me? I thought she liked that he had a guardian jackal? Had she heard us arguing earlier? Maybe she thought she had a chance to get me for herself?

I took a deep breath and focused on slowing my heart rate. Play along for now. Tawaret might think jackals are sacred, but that didn't mean I was safe, not by a longshot. "Yes, a misunderstanding. I didn't mean to scare you."

Chapter Fourteen

Supernatural Mediator

When Xander texted me about meeting up, at first it relieved me. It was an excuse to get out of the house at least. I'd been a bit of a hermit, hanging out with Oakley and Nate in the basement most nights until it was time for Sunrise Ceremony.

But then I realized I'd need to invite Jack as well, since Jack had wanted to meet Avery to get to the shifters and Xander had his number.

Xander wanted to meet at a local diner off the strip. He said the prices were better, plus it would be less busy.

As an added snag, Goddess made me take Oakley along as well, giving Jack a significant look. A memory shoved to the forefront of my mind, of pain and then Jack's face looking down at me. I'd gotten better at separating thoughts sent by Goddess from my own, and recognized it as her doing.

The three of us took a cab over from the mansion. As we got out in the parking lot, Oakley wrinkled his nose. "A diner?"

"You can wait outside," I told him, pointing to a bench that sat in front of the large picture window. "You'll be able to watch us from there."

I could see Xander seated at one of the larger booths visible from the window. Someone else was with him, but their head was down, looking at the menu. I pointed the booth we'd be at out to Oakley. He shrugged and took a seat on the bench.

Jack and I went inside, bypassing the host stand. Only when we got close did I recognize Avery.

"What's he doing here?" Avery and I said at the same time.

"Xander, move. Let me out," Avery snarled, shoving at Xander sitting on the outside.

"No, you two need to talk this out," Xander said, crossing his arms.

I stared back at Avery, barely able to keep my fangs up. But Jack needed to talk to Avery. I swallowed.

"Everett, sit down. He's right. We need to talk." Jack gently prodded me until I slid into the booth then he sat down next to me, trapping me directly across from Avery.

Avery stared daggers at me. "I have nothing to talk about with *him.*"

"Let's start with why you banned him from the meeting?" Xander threw up his hands. "Because it clearly upset him, a lot."

"I can't." Avery ground his teeth. "But he," he nodded at me, "knows why I did it." Avery's glance turned to Jack. "And who's this?"

"This is my boyfriend," I said, putting my hand on Jack's leg possessively. Only after it popped out did it occur to me that statement might not be true anymore. I took my hand back and scooted over against the booth wall.

"Jack." Jack held out his hand. He didn't contradict me, at least.

"Xander," Xander said, shaking it. When Avery didn't move, he added, "And this is Avery."

"He's the one," I whispered to Jack, doing my best to discretely point at Avery. I think I failed, though, as Avery's glare deepened.

"Everett told me what happened," Jack said to Avery in a mild tone.

The server came over to take our orders, a full pot of coffee in his hand. I turned over my cup for a fill. Jack got an appetizer and an extra plate to 'share' with me. Avery gave him a dirty look, but didn't say anything.

"Nothing you say will make me change my mind," Avery said as the server left. "So, I'm not sure why you set up this meeting."

"I didn't." I rolled my eyes, enjoying the warmth seeping into my palms from my coffee cup. "I only expected Xander, and," I held up my hands to stop the reply I could see Avery starting, "and I was going to tell him to drop it."

Avery twisted on the bench seat to look at Xander, who had the grace to look guilty. "I thought if you two just talked it out..." Xander's voice faded and he cleared his throat. "But honestly, tell me what about Everett is so objectionable."

"He's not trans," Avery huffed. "He's a chaser, trolling the meeting for fresh meat."

"I am trans," I objected, twisting my coffee cup. "I just wanted some support, like everyone else at the meeting." I had a quick flash of anger breakthrough the ever-present emotional numbness that had settled over me the last few days, but it faded just as quickly.

Avery snorted. "Yeah right. *Your* kind can't be trans. Never have been."

Xander started. "Damn, Avery, that's racist."

Jack shook his head. "Xander's right."

Personally, I wondered if *Avery* was right. I'd asked Stacy about contact info for any other trans vampires, just out of curiosity, but she'd never gotten back to me. Maybe because there weren't any? No, that was impossible. Still... might be rare, though.

I shrugged. "Just because there never have been, a fact I highly doubt by the way, doesn't mean it's impossible." I glowered back at Avery and took a sip of coffee.

Xander threw up his hands. "His boyfriend's right here. He can confirm, right?" Jack nodded. "See? So, Everett's welcome at the meetings."

"No, out of the question," Avery snarled, trying to get to his feet again, but stopped by the table, and I could see his wolf trying to come out. Wolf was a guess, but a good one. His eyes flashed golden. He sat back down, closed his eyes, and took a deep breath before opening them again. "His boyfriend is not a reliable source. He'll say anything Everett wants."

Xander's mouth dropped open, and he glanced back and forth between us. "What the hell? Am I missing something?"

Jack gestured with his own coffee mug at Xander. "We might as well tell him, Avery, so we can speak frankly. What do you think, Ev?"

"Yeah." I nodded.

Avery frowned. "I'm not sure that's a good idea."

"Look, if we need to, I can always call one of my roommates to make him forget," I said, half joking. I actually wouldn't do that. Still, Jack whacked my side gently with the back of his hand.

"Is that your idea of a joke?" Avery's lips pulled back from his teeth and I swear they were becoming pointed.

I shrank down in my seat. "Sorry, yes. You're right. That was in poor taste."

"Make me forget? What's that supposed to mean?" Xander frowned at me.

We were all silent and traded looks. Even Avery looked uncertain. After a moment, he clenched his fists. "Fine, tell him."

I didn't really want to, honestly, but no one else looked to be volunteering to go first. "Xander, I'm a vampire."

Xander burst out laughing. We were all silent until he laughed himself out. Finally, he wiped his eyes, still chuckling, and said, "No, really, that was hilarious, but what's the real secret?"

The server dropped off our food then. "Anything else?" he asked sweetly. We all shook our heads, and he retreated.

"So, what's your real secret?" Xander repeated when the server was gone.

"No, really," I said, glancing around. No one was looking at us. I dropped my fangs and showed them to Xander. His eyes widened and he let out a little squeak of surprise. I pulled them back up.

"Was that little display really necessary?" Avery sneered, cutting into his chicken-fried steak.

I shrugged, not really caring. I hadn't wanted to have a big back and forth with either of them. Only Jack's desire to talk to Avery had led to me agreeing to come. I was starting to think Avery and Lin had both been right; vampires and shifters shouldn't be mixing. It only led to heartache.

"How did you know?" Xander asked, glancing at Avery next to him.

"I just did." Avery took a bite of food.

Jack finished cutting his hamburger in half and put half on the plate in front of me. I gave him a little smile as he dug into his own food, despite all the smells making me queasy.

"Holy shit!" Xander was staring at me, his food sitting untouched. "That is so cool, dude. Duuuuddddeeee..." he drew the word out, leaning toward me. "Can you bite me?"

"NO!" Avery and I said in unison. Avery glanced at me, clearly startled by my refusal.

I cradled my coffee cup, shaking my head. "No, that's why Avery doesn't want me attending the meeting. Being bitten is..." I stared down into the black liquid. "Not good."

"Aww, c'mon, you can't tell me you're a vampire and then refuse to bite me." Xander pouted. He was really very cute.

"Vampire bites are addictive," Avery said, gesturing at me with his fork and knife. He glared at me. "Worse than crack I've heard. Don't dance around it."

I sighed and looked away from him at Jack. "That's true."

"Oh!" Xander's gaze followed mine. "That's why you said we can't trust Jack?"

"Exactly." Avery punctuated this with a bite of steak.

"They aren't addictive to everyone," Jack said. While the others had talked, he'd already polished off all the fries and the half burger on his plate. He traded the now empty plate for the one in front of me and dug into the second half of the burger.

"Now do you understand why I banned him?" Avery asked Xander.

"Not really." Xander shook his head. "He's nice enough and isn't the group here to help trans masc folk?"

"He's not—" Avery began and Xander cut him off.

"What, are we going to do genital checks on all new members now?" Xander poked a finger at Avery. "Because otherwise you're discriminating. Next you'll be saying members need to look trans enough."

"Xander," I said, shifting uncomfortably. "It's fine. Really."

"No, Everett." Xander didn't even bother to look at me, but held up a hand. "It's the principle of the thing. Right, Avery? So, what are your new rules for who can attend?"

"It's..." Avery groaned and covered his face, slumping back. "Oh my god, fine, he can come, but we'll have to have some ground rules." Avery dropped his hands and pierced me with a hard look. "If anyone gets bit, you can no longer attend."

"That seems unfair." I frowned. "I can't control every vampire in the city."

Avery crossed his arms. "Those are my terms."

Jack elbowed me, and I grimaced. "Fine."

"Good, now that's settled," Jack said. "Avery, when's the next run? I'd like to attend."

Avery almost choked on his bite of hamburger. "You what? You're a—" He cut off and glanced at Xander.

"Yeah, I am." Jack took another bite of his burger.

"No way." Avery went white. "But he's a..." He swallowed hard. "I thought you were dating him because you were an addict."

"No, I'm dating him because I like him." Jack rolled his eyes. "Anyway, I tried to ask Brun about the run, but they didn't like that I was dating Everett.

"You know Brun?" Avery blinked.

"Yeah. Everett's master is courting them," Jack said.

"Do *not* call her that," I growled, gripping my coffee cup so hard it exploded in my hands, sending pottery shards all over the table. I'd finished most of the coffee so it didn't go everywhere. "Oh, god, I'm sorry."

"It's fine, Everett." Jack tossed his napkins on the mess.

Xander was looking confused again, and his food was still untouched. ""Now what are you all talking about? Another secret?" He looked thoughtful, and then his eyes widened. Xander whipped his head back and forth between Jack and Avery. "Run? Wait, are you two were-wolves? Is that how you recognized what Everett was?"

Avery groaned and put his head in his hands. "Damn it."

"I take it that's a yes. That's amazing." Xander grinned, practically bouncing in his seat. "Can *you* bite me?"

"It doesn't work that way," Jack said. "Now, c'mon, eat before it gets cold."

Xander slumped down, his smile fading and picked up his fork.

"Brun's asexual," Avery said, looping back around to what had started this topic. "They don't court."

Jack shrugged. "That's why I said court and not date."

Avery shook his head. "No way."

I pushed at Jack. His plate was mostly empty. "Let's go."

"Not yet, Ev." Jack put his hand on my arm and turned his attention back to Avery. "Well, now, that it's out there, Avery, I still want to attend the next shifter run."

Avery narrowed his eyes at Jack. "Yeah, right. You hang out with vampires."

"So? I'm still a shifter. It's been weeks since I stretched my legs."

"No."

Xander smacked Avery's chest with the back of his hand. "C'mon, be nice. Jack just wants to meet the other locals."

"Did you move here?" Avery asked, glancing between us.

"Looks like." Jack sighed heavily and rubbed my shoulder.

I grimaced and nodded.

"So, what's the harm?" Xander poked Avery.

Avery snarled. "Fine. I'll take you out for a run, but just you, me, and Everett first. Then I'll tell you when the next shifter run is."

"Agreed." Jack nodded. "Just tell me when."

"Two days from now? I have the day off."

"Works for me." Jack reached across the table and shook Avery's hand. I worried about why he wanted me there, but Jack didn't seem concerned so I pushed my fears down.

FOR THE NEXT FEW days Jack and I continued sharing the room, but there was a tense silence between us. Jack told me the truth of what happened with Goddess, but I couldn't get over waking up in so much pain and then finding him standing over me. I felt betrayed; he'd said he'd protect me. I knew it was unfair to him, that he was doing the best he could, just like I was, but I still resented him.

As stories of her surviving a beheading circulated through the Las Vegas vampire community, Goddess' popularity surged again. To make more room, she solicited donations and built – with some quick last-minute construction – a proper chapel with more space. Human guards started patrolling the perimeters. Goddess said she wasn't in danger, but that I was still mortal. The *"still"* worried me.

My bite, well, killing, of that vampire during the party had made many reluctant to let us bite them. But enough still begged for the bite that Goddess and I started having to split them between us. Even then, I woke up hungover almost every night.

Tonight, another crowd packed the house. Even with the extra space, we had to have vampires RSVP ahead of time so that we didn't run out of room. Those that volunteered to be bitten had reserved spots. For that reason alone, many who wanted to attend again started signing up to be bitten.

After Goddess and I had fed this morning, we lay on the couch together while the vampires filed down into the basement to sleep for the day.

"Goddess, how did you end up sleeping for so long?" I asked. I'd been pushing the question around in my mind and the vampire blood this morning loosened my tongue.

Goddess languidly waved her hand through the air. "The sleep itself was planned. You'll see. When we get old, we can get tired of life so we'll sleep for a few years. Our amulets keep us alive and we came back refreshed."

"All right. So, what happened?"

"Honestly, I do not know." She sighed. "I've been searching the memories of all the vampires I've fed on. The last thing I remember of the last time my followers fed me through the amulet was that vampires were hunting down members of our church, killing them. My followers who had my amulet had found a hiding place and thought they were safe. But then I never got fed again."

"They were killing members of the church?" I blinked up, watching the play of light on the ceiling. "Why?"

She shrugged, bumping her shoulder into mine. "Who knows."

"Tell me about how the church used to be. In your time."

"Oh, it was marvelous!" Goddess sat up, leaning over me and taking my hands. Her eyes shone as she reminisced. "Golden temples to the Sun God Ra. Thousands of worshipers. Any partner you wanted. Armies of jackal warriors to protect us. Glorious."

"Golden temples?"

"The gold represents the shining light of the sun."

I tried to picture thousands of vampires lining up to be bitten. "I don't think the two of us could bite thousands."

"Of course not. We'd need to make more High Priests." Goddess put her hand on my stomach.

I wanted to sit up in alarm, but Goddess held me down. "More?"

"You're a little young to be making progeny." Goddess drummed her fingers on my stomach. "But we're already at the limit of what the two of us can do. And you're a strong vampire. Strong enough to make your own once you have an amulet."

I widened my eyes. "I'm really not interested in making another vampire, Goddess."

Goddess sat back up, getting off me. "The church cannot get bigger without more priests. I'm still too weak to make more. It has to be you."

"Does it need to get bigger?"

"Of course, it does!" Goddess jumped off the couch, twirling her robes. "We are higher life. We are destined to rule. Through the church we control. We rule."

"But why? I mean," I spread my hands up and out. "Isn't this enough? We have everything we need right here."

Goddess crossed her arms and pouted. "Everett, I'm used to much more luxury than this. You got me thinking. We need to prepare for emergencies. Without an amulet of your own, you are vulnerable. We got lucky the other week that they were after me only."

"Vulnerable." I snorted. "I'm a vampire." I swatted her hand away and stood up. "Now I'm going to go up and go to bed."

Goddess grabbed my hand. "No, no, no. Vampires are difficult to kill and don't age, but are not immortal. Not like me. And like you'll be once we get your amulet made."

"What's the difference? Isn't hard to kill and don't age what immortal mean?"

"No, it doesn't. Silver can still kill you. So can beheading." I flinched as she kept talking, her grip tightening on my hand. "Any number of things."

"I see."

"So, you see the need for an amulet."

I stared at her. "The *amulet brought you back to life*? How."

Goddess giggled. "Because my amulet is safe. Whole."

Shit. No wonder she freaked out when the mages had it. She must have mistaken my widening eyes for desire, because she squeezed my hand. "Don't worry. I'll start preparations to make yours. Then after that, you'll make your first progeny."

Make someone else into a vampire? The thought made me shudder, but I nodded along with her.

Chapter Fifteen

DESERT RUN

We met Avery just after dark, taking a cab over to the restaurant where we'd arranged to meet. Avery didn't want Tawaret to see him, and I didn't blame him.

I was surprised to see Xander in the passenger seat of Avery's car. Avery got out of the car and came around the hood.

"What's he doing there?" we both said at the same time. I pointed at Xander, Avery at Miles who stood at Everett's side.

We both glared at each other in silence for a moment. "You first," Avery finally said.

"Goddess insisted that Everett has to have a guard with him," I said, ushering Everett and Miles towards the back seat. I didn't like it either, but that had been part of her price.

"Stop." Avery stepped between us and the car door. "I need to prepare first."

"Fine," I said, crossing my arms.

Everett pressed close to my side, getting on tiptoes to whisper into my ear, "Are you sure this is a good idea?"

"Yes. You need a few hours away from your maker."

A smile played across Everett's lips, at least until Avery finished rooting around in the trunk and pulled out a blanket that he spread over the backseat.

"There, now the vampires can get in."

Everett's expression blanked out, the smile fading to nothingness. The same expression had been on his face a lot over the last week. It worried me.

We got in and Everett hunched over hugging himself, staring at his lap. I tried to take his hand, and he pulled away.

"So, Avery, why is Xander here?" I asked instead to distract myself as Avery pulled away from the restaurant.

"Stuck to me like a burr," Avery muttered. "Told him it'd be boring but he insisted."

"Look, I found out vampires and werewolves are real. You think I'm going to pass up a chance to see a werewolf change?" Xander twisted around to look at us in the back seat.

I gave him a half smile. "Who said I was a wolf?"

Xander squealed, half hanging off the headrest. "Oh, my, gosh! Tell me!" He fell back into the front seat. "No, wait, don't. I want to be surprised."

Avery snorted and looked at us in the rearview mirror. "I bet he's a cat. That smile. So mysterious."

I shook my head and glanced at Everett. He was still curled in on himself, staring at the floor of the car, not even glancing at the scenery outside.

Miles didn't say anything, just scowled. He must not have wanted this assignment either.

We headed away from the lights of Vegas. Since we'd started at the edge of town already, by now it was all scrub-brush and cactuses, the only lights came from the other passing cars heading into the city.

"How far out are we going?" I asked, checking my cell phone. I only had a single bar already.

"A couple more exits. There's a scenic bypass with a parking lot at the trail head, and nothing else," Avery said, glancing at me in the rearview. "Still time to back out if you were lying."

Maybe this was a bad idea. Avery was still being very antagonistic. Yet, I wanted to get Everett away from Tawaret for a while. I hoped it would improve his mood. I figured between the two of us, we could more than handle Avery.

After almost an hour of driving, Avery pulled off an exit that let out onto a small access road. We drove another ten minutes, until the highway was only barely visible in the distance as flashes of light when another car passed. He turned into a small parking lot, empty except for our car. We all piled out into the lot.

Other than the parking lot and the distant highway, there were no signs of civilization. The stars wheeled overhead. I'd never seen so many. I shivered in my thin shirt. The temperature had dropped rapidly during our drive over here, but once I changed, my fur coat would keep me warm.

With the car headlights off, the only sources of light were the stars and quarter moon shining overhead. It was so dark that in my human form I could barely make out Avery and Xander standing a few feet away. Even Everett standing next to me was a white blur of a round face in the inky black.

Miles crossed his arms and impatiently looked at his watch. I knew he'd fed before we left.

"It's beautiful," I said, staring up at the sky. So many stars. "I didn't know the desert could be."

Avery barked out a laugh. "Where you guys from that you've never seen the desert before?"

"Pacific Northwest," I said, keeping it vague. "And before than Northeastern US, around Maryland."

Xander shivered and cupped his hands in front of his mouth to blow on them. Everett opened the car back up, pulled out the blanket we'd been sitting on, and wrapped it around Xander's shoulders. He left the back door open, and the car's interior light lit up a strip of asphalt.

"Thanks," Xander said, closing the blanket around himself with another shiver.

"Let's do this then," Avery said, stripping off his shirt. He tossed it in the open back door, then continued undressing.

"Alright." I got out my wallet and phone and handed them to Everett. I didn't trust Avery enough that I was willing to leave them with Xander while we were gone. Everett put them in his pockets. That done, I stripped too and tossed my clothing in with Avery's. I kept my eyes averted from Avery, trying to be polite, but still couldn't help but see the scars on his chest.

Avery looked at me and raised an eyebrow. He shuddered and fell over onto all fours, fur sprouting all over him. He snarled, bones twisting, and a moment later, a massive white wolf stood where he'd been. An arctic wolf. I'd never seen one before. He was probably the largest wolf I'd ever seen. I revised my assessment of if Everett and I could take him to a maybe.

Xander let out a little squeal of excitement, bouncing on the balls of his feet. Everett tensed and swallowed hard, looking away from Xander and folding his arms.

Avery sat down and licked his chops, staring at me. "Well? I'm waiting."

I shook myself out and let out a deep breath, then let the change sweep over me. Pain hit me, making me fall over onto all fours as my limbs began changing, twisting. Gasping, I let it take me all the way to my jackal form. Now, standing on all fours felt natural. I shook myself again, from my ears to the tips of my tail, then gave Avery a toothy grin.

He snorted and shook his head. The tips of my ears barely came up to Avery's nose.

With my jackal eyes, the night came alive around me. I could hear the rustle of a mouse foraging in the underbrush, smell the lingering traces of a rabbit that had passed nearby, almost drown out by Everett's sharp vampire scent.

"Ahhh!" Xander was jumping up and down now, yelling in excitement. "You're not a wolf, what are you!"

"Humph, a coyote trickster. I should have known." Avery woofed. His voice didn't sound as human as mine did in changed form. Maybe that was intentional. "And you reek of vampire."

"Jackal," I growled, ignoring the insult. "Why does everyone think I'm a coyote?"

Everett came over and dropped to his knees next to me, wrapping his arms around me and pulling me into a tight hug. "So furry." He gave me a little smile.

I wagged my tail and licked his face.

"Did you want to run still?" I asked, prancing. Now that I'd changed, I was bursting with energy. My legs wanted to move.

Everett grinned. "Bet you can't catch me." There was a whoosh of displaced air and he was gone, racing off across the desert rocks. I let out a yip and chased after him. After his initial burst of speed, he slowed down, but was still moving at a faster pace than any human could manage.

Avery's white wolf pulled up next to me, moving at a loping run. I sprinted at full speed, yet he trotted along easily beside me. Of course, he was twice my size now.

Miles ran along after us, falling farther behind as we went, unable to keep up.

Everett let out a whoop of laughter and looked behind over at us. "That the best you can do?" he taunted. His eyes sparkled with joy, and I was glad we'd come. This is the first time he'd looked happy since we'd come to Vegas.

I put my ears flat on my head and pushed myself harder, my legs thundering on the rocky landscape, Avery matching my pace, but Everett slowly pulled away from the two of us.

Finally, he slowed down and stopped, turning to watch us. I slowed down to a trot, my sides heaving and my tongue practically licking the ground with each pant.

Miles caught up to us a minute later, looking very pale. His fangs were down and he was obviously thirsty. He gave me and Avery a thoughtful look but then scowled and wrinkled his nose. I'd have to keep him away from Xander when we got back to the car.

Avery let out a sneeze as we got close to Everett, then wrinkled his nose and stopped, still a good ten feet away, and sat back on his haunches. "Bleck, that smell. Don't know how you stand it."

"You get used to it," I said, continuing past him to Everett.

Everett grinned at me and put his hands on his hips. "Such a slow-poke," he teased. "You could keep up with me before."

Still panting, I lay down on the cool sand and rolled over onto my back, enjoying the chill. "You didn't run so fast before."

"What are you talking about?" Everett shook his head. "I didn't go any faster than last time." He referred to our last run through the woods outside Portland.

"You certainly did," I said around my pants, perking my ears up at him. "A lot faster. Even Miles couldn't keep up."

"Weird." Everett knelt down and reached for my chest, but then paused. "Can I pet you?"

I wiggled my butt and wagged my tail, sending a scattering of sand up. "Please, yes."

Everett smiled again and rubbed the fur of my chest. The sensation sent shivers of delight through me. I groaned and threw my head back, pulling my front legs up out of the way.

"God, this is sad to watch you debase yourself like this for a vampire," Avery growled. Everett's hand stopped moving. I opened my eyes and lifted my head to glare at Avery.

"Then go back to the car," I growled, shaking off Everett's hand and twisting up to my feet. "We'll be along in a few minutes."

"Fine." Avery huffed and stalked back away into the darkness, his white coat glowing in the moonlight.

Miles took a few steps after him, but then glanced back at us and stopped. At least he stayed a bit away. Far enough I could pretend we were alone.

"Do you know the way back?" Everett whispered to me as he left. "I... wasn't paying attention."

I glanced up at him crouched over me and gave him a doggy-grin. "Yes, our scent trail will be easy to follow. But you need to be more careful." I bumped his knee with my snout.

"Yeah." Everett fell to his butt in the dirt with a sigh and a scowl, resting his arms on his knees. "Story of my life."

I went over and sat at his feet so I could look him in the eye. "I want to apologize."

Now that we'd stopped running, the desert chill was getting to me. That and the long run in the dry air had left me dehydrated. I'd have to chug some water when we got back.

"For what?" Everett glanced away from me, looking out at the desert.

"For blaming you." I put my paws on his knees and licked his nose. Everett giggled and pushed me away. I sat on his lap, trying to ignore the burning in my nose from his vampire scent. "I should have listened better when you told me about your dreams and your sleepwalking. I want you to trust me. Talk to me about anything on your mind. I'll do my best not to minimize anything you tell me anymore, alright?"

"No, it's my fault." Everett's fangs came down for a moment, and his face hardened. He swallowed and pulled them back up. "You warned me. I thought I was taking back control, but I realized you were right again. She was herding me, and I went right where she wanted."

"She's a lot older than you, Everett. She knows what she's doing." I sighed. "Even I'm not immune. I only realized because I think she got impatient." I leaned into his chest.

Everett rubbed his neck. "I know you wouldn't do that. Even so, when I see your face sometimes, I can't help but remember that sensation. But why does she want to get between us?"

My ears flattened against my head. "Really? Think, Ev."

Everett scratched me under the chin. "But I thought she had her own jackal."

"They aren't really interested in her. I think maybe she can sense that they're just trying to spy on her, like me." I lifted my chin so Everett could get to that nice spot right at the base of my neck. My foot kicked involuntarily. "But honestly?"

"Yeah?" Everett giggled.

"I think she doesn't like you having someone else you can rely on." I leaned into Everett's hand. "Even a jackal that she considers sacred."

"Oh, that makes sense." Everett pulled me to his chest and flopped back into the dirt. I lay on his chest, looking up at his chin while he stared up at the stars wheeling overhead. His smell burned my nose; I'd lied to Avery about getting used to it, but I was finding it comforting. I relaxed into him, wagging my tail.

"So, what do I do?" he asked sadly, arms like bars across me, pinning me down.

"I know you don't like my plan, but do you have a better idea?" I struggled a bit, but Everett was so strong, I don't think he even noticed my fight.

"No, I don't." He sighed. "But we need to do it soon. She wants me to make another vampire for her, to expand the church. She said she's not strong enough yet to do it herself."

"Did she say when?" I sensed there was something else he wasn't saying.

"No, but I think she wants to do it soon." Everett snuggled me up under his chin and ruffled my fur.

"Was there something else?"

Everett stayed silent, looking at the stars. "It's not important," he said eventually.

I licked his chin and kicked my feet. "If you're sure."

"Yeah." Everett finally let me go and I rolled off him and to my feet.

"I'll talk to Avery about it when we get back to the car then." I pranced around his head, high stepping. "Speaking of car, it's getting pretty late."

Everett sat up and took out his phone. "Yeah, it's almost three AM."

"I'm dying of thirst." I licked my dry lips. Next time I'd have to bring water with me. Maybe I could use one of those dog backpacks...

We took a much more sedate pace back to the car. Partially because I had to sniff out our trail back, partially because Miles was too thirsty to run, and partially because I was exhausted. Everett had really run us way out into the desert.

Except when we got there, the parking lot was empty. Avery's car was gone.

"Shit." I looked up at Everett. "Can you call Tawaret to send someone to pick us up? I can give directions."

Everett pulled out his phone and mine, then shook his head. "No signal."

Miles took out his phone too, and shook his head. His red eyes looked at me hungrily.

I looked at the highway far in the distance. My paw pads were bleeding from the sharp rocks and my eyes were gritty with exhaustion after the run and the walk back here. My tongue felt like sandpaper.

"I'm too tired to walk to the highway," I admitted. "You'll have to go on your own and try to hitch a ride back to Vegas."

"I'm not leaving you. I'll carry you," Everett said.

I shook my head. "What, hitch a ride carrying a jackal? No one will mistake me for a dog. You'll have to go alone."

"I won't leave you. Change back..." Everett looked around, then cursed. "He took your clothes."

"Yeah." I sighed and flopped onto the cold blacktop. "They were in the car. What time is it?"

Everett pulled out his phone and checked it. "Four thirty AM."

"There's not enough time for you to get back before the sun comes up." I bit back a growl. "It took us at least an hour to drive out here, plus the walk to the highway..."

"We have to try. There's no place for us to get out of the sun out here," Miles said.

"That rat bastard," Everett muttered. "He did this on purpose. But he's hurting you too, a fellow shapeshifter."

"I bet you he'll be back a few hours after sunrise to pick me up." I did growl now, my hackles rising.

"At which point, if I weren't who I am, I'd be dead from the sun." Everett sighed and looked around. "But by the time he comes back, I might still be dead. I don't know how long I can last. It hurts... a lot." He rubbed his arms. "Why do you think the ceremony calls for us to take offerings right after? The blood helps us heal."

"And I will be dead," Miles growled.

"Miles, you can get to the highway in time to hitch a ride back. Go, save yourself," Everett said.

"If I did that to survive, Goddess would kill me herself." Miles crossed his arms and glared at him.

"We'll find you both some shade," I said, pushing back to my feet and glancing around at the featureless, flat landscape. "We'll find something," I said, mostly to reassure myself.

Goddess pounded my head with demands. I'd never heard her so angry.

"It was a miscalculation," I repeated in my head. *"We thought we could get a cab back, but the phones don't have signal."*

She snarled inarticulately, then, *"I'll come pick you up myself."*

"NO!" I yelled that out loud. Jack and Miles turned to look at me. *"No,"* repeated in my head. *"We'll be okay until dark. I don't want you to risk yourself."*

"Everett, you're too young to last outside all day."

She didn't even ask about Miles. I don't think she cared and a feeling of vague indifference that she sent me confirmed that.

"What about you, Goddess?"

I followed Jack and Miles over to a likely rock. We were still looking for shade for me. There was an opening underneath it, but it was too small. Jack dug at it with his paws.

Miles held his hands out in front of himself and flexed. The ends of his fingers turned into Talons, then he crouched down next to Jack and helped, throwing up huge plumes of dirt.

"You said yourself you're still weak. I don't want you to risk yourself for too long in the sun just for me. Jack found a hole for us to use. We'll be fine."

"Everett, you better be! If you die..." A picture came with it, of Goddess a mummy again.

"You'll just make another vampire. No big deal."

"If I lose you, I lose everything." Goddess fumed in my head, ignoring my words.

I winced. She was such a drama queen. Out loud to Jack I said, "Will this work?"

Jack stopped digging and looked up at me. "Was that Goddess? I didn't know you could talk to her mind-to-mind."

"Yeah, freaks me out, so she doesn't do it often. She's really mad. But saying she'll become a mummy again is just her being melodramatic." I rolled my eyes.

"Huh, that doesn't seem like her."

"She wanted to drive out here herself, but I think I talked her out of it." I sat back out of the way. I was thirsty, but I wasn't about to ask Jack to donate. He was panting hard and his paw pads were raw and bleeding. I'd survive until tomorrow evening. Miles... was another matter. His fangs had been down since the desert.

"Shit, if she came out and found Avery... You didn't tell her, did you?" Jack and Miles kept digging.

"Hell no." At least, I hoped she hadn't been able to pluck that from my memories. All I got from her were words and maybe vague images like the mummy thing, but I didn't know what she got from me.

"Good. This might be our only shot at connecting with the shifters. If she found out..." Jack paused his digging and looked back at me.

"I know." I swallowed. "But Miles could still tell her." We both looked at Miles.

Miles sighed and stopped digging. He hung his head and didn't look me in the eyes. "This hole isn't big enough for both of us."

Jack's ears pinned back to his head. "He's right, it's going to be tight just with you, and I'll have to put my body over you to keep you from getting burned."

They both went back to digging. Jack's paws throwing plumes of dirt out behind him.

The sky was becoming decidedly pink. "What about Miles?"

"It'll be an honor to sacrifice myself for the Goddess," Miles said. He sounded like he meant it.

I covered my face. "I shouldn't have come. I'm sorry."

"We couldn't have known," Jack said.

I'd had reservations, but I'd stayed silent. Now I felt guilty. "It's still my fault."

The sounds of digging stopped and something warm and furry pressed against my side. "I hope we've reconciled, at least. I still want to be your boyfriend, if you'll still have me."

I wiped tears from my eyes and lowered my hands. "I do too."

My skin started tingling like it did at the start of the Sunrise Ceremony.

"Time's up, this will have to do." Miles grabbed my arm.

"You should get in the hole. I can survive a little sun." I twisted from Miles' grip.

"A little being the operative word," Jack growled. "You almost burned to death when you were out for a long time when the house burned, remember?" He fixed me with a glare.

"There's no chance for me, but at least you can survive."

"Do you want... me... to bite you?" The videos I'd seen of sun deaths had looked painful. It was the least I could offer.

"Yes, please, High Priest. I'd like to go out with a final blessing." Miles dropped to his knees, pulling me down with him.

I let my fangs drop and zeroed in on his neck.

"No, bite his wrist," Jack said ears folded back. "When he goes up, you don't want to be close to him."

My hands shook as I took Miles' wrist and leaned over him.

"Hurry, please," Miles pleaded, looking over his shoulder.

I sunk my fangs in and drank deeply. I'd drained vampires dry before, maybe I could do that in time and spare him the sun. As I drank, it occurred to me that we were doing a bastard version of the sunrise ceremony.

Miles made sounds of pleasure as I sucked. My skin began to tingle and then Miles' cries of passion turned to pain, and then screams.

My face started feeling very warm, and the blood started tasting burned. Then Jack grabbed my hair and yanked me backwards off of Miles, kicking Miles in chest at the same time.

Miles' screams turned higher pitched as his skin blackened. He was burning a lot slower than the last vampire I'd seen burning at the sunrise ceremony. Then I remembered Goddess and me feeding on the burning vampire to save him. Maybe this had been a bad idea, extending his agony. I reached for him as Jack pulled me backwards.

"There's nothing you can do for him now," Jack said, pushing me into the hole and laying on top of me to keep me inside.

I managed to shove him off a few times, but he kept wrestling me back down. My skin darkened and then blackened from the sunlight.

I stopped resisting only when Miles' screams stopped. I covered my face and cried.

Chapter Sixteen

SUNBURNED

THE SUN HAD COME up hours ago, forcing me back to human. Thank God for my darker skin, or I'd already be sunburned.

Miles hadn't been so lucky. I could avert my eyes from the greasy burned patch on the ground where he'd died, but I couldn't do anything about the smell. A greasy cloying thing that clogged my nostrils and made my eyes water.

My paws, well, hands, had healed when I'd changed back, but I was starting to hallucinate from thirst. And even I would sunburn, eventually. Everett had given me his shirt to cover my more sensitive bits from the sun, but there was only so much it could do.

Everett moaned in pain underneath me.

Avery had better come soon.

I couldn't see the parking lot from here, but eventually I heard the roar of an engine coming down the road, then the sudden silence when the car turned off. A car door, then another, slammed.

"Jack?" Avery called. "Where you at?"

"Over here!" I yelled back after a couple of tries.

"C'mere, I've got your clothes."

"Bring them to me!" I glanced over my back at the rock. "And a blanket."

"Jack, are you serious? We both saw you last night."

"You heard me!" I snarled.

"Fine, fine." Avery said. "Keep talking so we can find you."

"You're a bastard, Avery. Now bring my shit now." I really should have been more diplomatic, since I still wanted Avery to connect me to the shifters, but he'd just tried to kill my boyfriend, he had killed Miles, and I was too tired and thirsty to be tactful.

Avery and Xander came into view. Avery carried my clothes and Xander a blanket.

"What is that?" Avery made a face and pointed at the burned spot. I made the mistake of glancing that way. His skull and a few blackened bones were all that was left. His clothes had burned with his skin.

"What's left of Miles." I met his eyes. He glanced away.

"Sorry about Everett and that other guy," Xander said in a low voice. "I didn't know what Avery had planned." He dropped the blanket at my feet and dashed back towards the car.

I shielded my eyes from the sun with one hand and squinted at Avery as I pulled the blanket over my lap. "Bring any water? I'm dying of thirst."

"In the car." Avery stomped over and dumped my clothes a few feet from me. This close, I could see the dark circles under his eyes and smell the coffee on his breath. "Now get dressed."

"Can I get some privacy?"

"What are you sitting on?"

"Everett." I met his gaze.

"You were guarding him?" Avery snorted and shook his head. "Whatever. Hurry, I'm tired." He turned and stomped back to the car.

I covered the hole with the blanket before standing. After I was dressed, I said, "Ev? Crawl out. Sorry for any stray light. I'll do my best to keep you covered as I carry you back to the car."

"Just do it." Everett called back. The blanket shifted as he wiggled out of the hole. It took some maneuvering, but I got him up in my arms still covered.

"How you doing?" I whispered as I hefted him up.

"Do I have to answer that?" He moaned.

"Just do your best to keep still and silent," I reminded him. "If Avery realizes you're still alive, he might try to finish the job."

"Avery's a coward," Everett said. "He's too chicken to attack me directly."

"I don't want to take that chance. I squeezed my arms around him.

Everett wiggled. "Fine."

Avery and Xander leaned on the car waiting for me.

"What the hell is that?" Avery yelled.

"It's Everett." I met his eyes. "Obviously I'm not leaving his remains to rot in the desert." If I'd been thinking I would have gathered up Miles' as well, but I didn't want to prolong Everett's suffering to go back for them.

Xander burst into tears and turned away, covering his face. I felt bad for deceiving him. I'd have to text him later and let him know Everett was fine.

"Why isn't he a burned spot on the rocks like that other guy?" Avery asked.

Shit, that was a good point. I'd have to think fast. "I shielded him from of the worst of it. Don't worry, I'll buy you a new blanket," I said, hoping he'd buy it.

"Ugh. Fine, but put that thing in the trunk."

I narrowed my eyes at him, gripping Everett tighter.

Avery pressed his key fob, and the trunk creaked open. I walked up to the open trunk and stopped, my muscles locking up. Putting him there away from the sunlight would have been the smart thing, but my instincts were screaming at me not to let Everett out of my sight. I couldn't help but remember what had happened last time I'd made Everett ride in the trunk. If I held him, he could discretely feed on me if he needed to, rather than risk him going feral.

Avery stared at me impatiently, then checked the time on his phone. "Hurry this up. I'm already going to be late to work as it is."

I couldn't do it. "No," I said, shaking my head. "I'll hold him."

I walked around to the passenger door, shifting Everett's weight so I could open the handle. Avery snarled and slammed the trunk, then got in the driver's seat while I slid into the back, balancing Everett in my lap. I awkwardly pulled the door closed just before Avery pulled away.

"What the hell is wrong with you, Jack?" Avery growled, glaring at me in the rearview.

"What's wrong with me?" I yelled back, my voice hoarse with thirst. "You tried to—" I stopped, hugging Everett to my chest, reminding myself that they thought he was dead. "You left us in the desert, outside cell phone range. That's murder."

Avery scoffed. "Can't murder something that's already dead."

"They seemed pretty alive to me, Avery," Xander said in a low voice, sniffling.

"How many people do you think they killed to extend their un-natural lives, Jack?" Avery sneered, glancing at me in the mirror.

Everett shifted in my arms. I tensed up, pinning his arms down. "What, in the whole four months he was a vampire?" I didn't know how old Miles was. I didn't know anything about him, now that I thought about it.

Avery frowned and Xander twisted around in his seat to look at me over the headrest, his eyes wide.

"What, that's it?" Avery asked.

"Wait, wait. Now I know why he looked familiar." Xander sank back down in his seat and fiddled with his phone. "Portland, four months ago," he said, thrusting the phone screen towards the back seat. He'd pulled up the news report about the city-wide manhunt for Everett, wanted for the death of his roommate Lindsay.

I nodded. "Yeah, that's him. Where'd you see that, anyway? I thought it only showed on local news."

"Yeah, I remember that," Avery added, glancing over at the phone Xander held out. "It showed up on some trans news sites. The trans community was outraged about them using the wrong pronouns and dead naming him on television. Then more when they found out he was buried under his dead name."

"I went to the funeral," I said, hugging Everett when he tried to move again. "I tried to talk to his parents about it, but they had me thrown out instead."

"You never told me that," the blanket wrap in my lap whispered.

"Shh," I hissed.

"What was that?" Xander asked, but Avery cut him off.

"Why the fuck did he not bring this up when I accused him of not being trans?" Avery bitched.

"We both wanted to forget the whole thing," I said with a sigh. The memory of finding his roommate dead, her throat slit, was burned into my mind. "I was the one who found his roommate."

"Geez, I'm sorry," Xander said in a low voice. "Was this... was that when he was turned?"

"Yeah, that same night they killed her. They tried to kill him too, almost succeeded." I shook my head again. "Let's talk about something else, huh?"

"I guess I thought he'd been a vampire longer," Avery muttered. "He feels... felt older." He frowned and glanced at me again in the rearview, his eyes narrowing.

"That's probably because of his maker," I said.

"So, he agreed to be turned to stay alive?" Avery said, louder this time.

In his blanket cocoon, Everett wiggled again, and I hugged him tighter. "No, it—" Everett said.

I smothered his face with my hand to cut him off.

"Did the blanket just move?" Xander asked. He'd twisted around against his seatbelt to look at me over the headrest again.

"No—"

"Thirsty," Everett rasped, wiggling against my grip. Shit.

"What the hell!" Avery jerked the wheel in surprise and we skidded across the lanes.

"Watch the road!" I yelled back, struggling to hold the thirsty vampire who was now thrashing and gnashing his teeth.

Avery struggled with the car, slowing down and getting it under control. Luckily the highway was almost empty.

"Everett, stop," I pleaded with him. "You're going to get burned if the blanket comes off."

"Hurts," Everett rasped, but stopped moving.

Shit.

"He's still alive?" Xander smiled down at me over the headrest.

"Yes, but the sun's getting to him a bit, as you can see."

"Should have put him in the trunk like I requested," Avery snarled.

He was probably right, but... "The last thing he needs right now is to be alone," I growled back.

"How the hell is he still alive?" Avery asked. "That blanket isn't enough to keep the sun out."

"It's not," Everett muttered. "Still hurts."

"Less sun on the floor, all right?" I said.

"Okay," Everett said.

I gently pushed him off my lap and he slid down my legs to sit on the floor, unwrapping the blanket and pulling it over himself like a shroud, then rested his head against my leg.

"Better," he said with a sigh.

"How is he still alive?" Avery repeated in a deep growl.

"Because his maker is old," I said, glancing down at Everett's blanket-covered form again, although I was pretty sure that wasn't the reason sun didn't hurt him. "He'll be fine once I get him back home and get him fed."

"You mean feed him your blood," Avery muttered, his hands white-knuckled on the steering wheel.

"No, I don't. He doesn't drink my blood." I licked my lips, feeling my tongue rasp against them. "Do you have any water?"

Xander tossed me a bottle, and I twisted the top off and drank the whole thing in one long gulp.

"Yeah, right," Avery scoffed. "And I've never heard of a vampire so old that even their progeny are resistant to the sun. How old is he, anyway?"

"She, and oh, I don't know." I lowered my hand to where I thought Everett's shoulder was. "How old would you say?"

"At least four thousand years old, maybe older," Everett said, his voice raspy and muffled by the blanket.

"Shit." Avery's voice turned low and gravely.

"Yeah. We've been trying to figure out how to get Everett away from her," I said, stroking Everett's blanketed shoulder. "But she's something else."

"What, this isn't what he signed up for?" Avery let out a little laugh.

"I didn't sign up for anything," Everett said. "I was an accident."

"How is that possible?" Avery asked.

Everett pushed against my leg. "Thirsty."

"A little longer, Everett," I said.

"I'm glad you're okay, Everett," Xander said. "If you need something sooner, you can bite me."

"No, you can't," Avery reminded both Everett and Xander.

"What's stopping you from getting away?" Xander asked. There was disappointment in his voice, but he sounded interested.

"Tawaret, she's stopping Everett from leaving. We're basically prisoners," I said.

"So, your bodyguard the night of the trans meeting wasn't actually a bodyguard?" Xander asked. "The cute blonde one, Oakley, who invited me to a threesome?"

"Don't take him up on that!" Everett yelled from the blanket. "Trust me."

"Wait, he was serious?" Xander groaned. "Dang it, he's so hot. I thought it was a joke."

"Yeah, not a bodyguard so much as a guard." I confirmed.

"You were looking to hook up with the shifters to what, find a way to kill her?" Avery said.

"If we have to," Everett said.

This was a good a segue way as any. "That's why I wanted to meet the shifters. To—"

"To get us to do your dirty work for you?" Avery snorted. "Much as I relish the thought of killing a vampire, I will not do it to protect *another* vampire."

"Okay, think of it as protecting your city then," I growled. "Besides, I honestly don't think we *can* kill her."

"She's gathering an army, Avery," Everett lifted the blanket to look up at him. "Our bloodline, we can control other vampires. We already have hundreds at our call, and she's talking about having me make a progeny so we can expand."

"Shit, really?" Avery pounded on the steering wheel with one hand.

"Yes. He's not exaggerating."

"The PCA—" Avery began.

"They know. They've tried to take her out a few times and failed. If it takes much longer, it'll be too late for Everett."

"He's a vampire," Avery growled.

"C'mon, Avery," Xander said, reaching across the gap between the front seats to put a hand on Avery's arm. "He's a fellow trans-guy. We should help him."

"Xander, you don't understand." Avery shook his head. "Even if I wanted to help him, no way could I get the rest of the pack to agree. Vampires and shifters don't like each other."

"We work together at the PCA. My boss is a vampire," I said. "That's how I met Ev. It's not impossible."

"Lucky," Xander muttered.

"Come to the next hunt with me, then," Avery snorted. "You'll see."

At least it was an invite, even if it was a reluctant one.

As soon as we came into cell phone range, both the phones in my pocket, mine and Jack's, started vibrating furiously with missed calls and messages. Mine were from Goddess, although a few were from Nate and Oakley. I ignored them and put the phone back in my pocket. Goddess already knew where we were.

I tightened my grip on Jack's leg. I was so thirsty and having my mouth this close to his warmth wasn't helping, but his scent was helping ground me. If I wasn't clinging this close to him, the smell of Xander just on the other side of the seat would've been too much for me.

"We're almost there," Jack assured me, probably mistaking the source of my agitation as thirst.

I felt Goddess trying to control me, but I fought her off as I had been all morning. Although this time it was harder than it had been. Her power over me grew stronger as we got closer to her.

I'd been lucky she hadn't popped in during the discussion with Avery. If she found out what he'd tried to do... Well, I don't know what she would do to him, but it wouldn't be pretty.

In my head Goddess said, "You're almost here, I can feel it. I'll meet you on the front steps." Abruptly, her presence in my head vanished.

"Avery, drop us on the street. We'll walk to the house from there," I rasped out from bone-dry lips. The effort tore up my throat. So thirsty. My fangs came down and pressed against my lower lip.

I couldn't see anyone from under the blanket, but I could hear the disapproval in Jack's tone. "Everett, no. End of discussion."

"Goddess," was all I got out. I swallowed and licked my lips, trying to say more. "Knows. Meet. Steps."

"Street it is," Avery said.

"What, no!" Jack growled. I felt him lean towards the front seats and a shadow fell over my blanket. "She won't know who you are. We'll tell her we hitchhiked."

"Street fine," I lisped against my fangs.

"Everett, if your fangs are out, we can't walk that far." Jack set his hand on my head. "You're already burned."

"He's already had this much sun," Avery said with a laugh. "What's a bit more?"

The voice of reason, Jack's tone was calm and even. "He's already close to feral. What if he catches sight of a neighbor and loses it? How long do you think before someone pulls out a cell phone camera and vampires are on the six o'clock news?"

Avery groaned.

"We won't tell her who you are," Jack said. "We'll say that we hitchhiked. It was what I would have done if I didn't know you were coming back."

"You were so certain that I was coming back for you?" Avery sounded surprised.

"I was." Jack laughed. "Or maybe I didn't relish the idea of hitch-hiking naked."

The rest of the ride was silent. I let out a sigh of relief as the car rolled to a stop in the shadows at the front of the house. Even under the blanket's meager protection, the sun stabbed my skin. It was like being constantly stung by wasps.

I knew it would be worse if I hadn't drunk from Miles. Guilt and gratitude warred in my chest over his death.

I grinned and threw off the blanket and crawled up into Jack's lap, back against the door. He smiled at me and gently took one of my hands in his, turning it over and kissing my palm.

"Ouch," Xander commented, and I twisted around. He winced and touched his cheek. "Your skin is black. That's not a sunburn. Does it hurt?"

I nodded.

"Even with that blanket, any normal vampire would be a burned-out husk already, like that other one," Avery growled, gripping the steering wheel tighter. "Now where's this master of yours?"

I pointed. She'd appeared at the top of the steps in the deep shade of the porch overhang, smiling widely, as Avery had rolled to a stop.

She'd done up her makeup with big swooping black lines around her eyes, and wore a tight white sleeveless dress with a neckline that plunged nearly to her naval.

"Holy shit," Avery whispered, craning his neck to stare up at her. His eyes were enormous and locked on her. "She's really hot."

Goddess ran to the bottom of the steps and pulled open the door I was leaning on. I fell backwards into her arms.

"Everett, so glad you're all right," she purred, setting me on my feet. I swayed and clung to her. Miles, it seemed, was not even a blip on her radar.

To my surprise, Avery turned off the car and got out. Goddess turned to him with a dazzling smile as he came around the car. "Thank you so much for rescuing my two *stupid* boys from the desert." Her grip on my arm tightened, but her smile widened. "Whatever I can do to repay you, just let me know."

Xander watched it all with wide eyes from the passenger seat, but didn't open his door. Smart guy.

"Of course, yes, no problem," Avery stammered as Jack got out of the car. Jack slammed the car door harder than he needed to, and Avery jerked, tearing his eyes away from Goddess. Immediately he whirled, putting his back to her.

Goddess took a step towards him, dragging me with her. "Why don't you two come inside?" She sidestepped still closer, sidling around Avery. "I'd like to repay you properly."

"No need," Avery choked out and shuffled back around the front of the car. He got back in the driver's seat, studiously avoiding looking at Goddess, and drove off.

As soon as he was out of sight, Goddess' smile slid away. She dragged me up the steps and into the house, totally ignoring Jack.

"How could you be so stupid?" she hissed into my ear. I winced.

"It was an honest mistake," Jack said, shutting the front door behind him and cutting off the painful sunlight. He walked over and took my free hand in his and giving it a light squeeze. I almost swooned at how warm his hand was; my fangs ached. Jack kept talking, oblivious. "We've both been feeling cooped up, and then during our run we got a little... distracted."

"And what if you hadn't snagged that driver to stop for you?" Goddess snapped at him. "You got lucky. Once Everett is a couple hundred years old or we make his amulet, he'll be alright all day in the sun. But as young as he is, he's still vulnerable."

"We did get lucky a passing driver helped us," Jack agreed. "Even if it was too late for Miles."

"But if something had happened to Everett. If he'd died, you would have never been found," Goddess growled back, her fingernails dug into my skin.

Like she cared. She'd just make another vampire apprentice.

"Not true, Everett," Goddess said, answering my thoughts. I jumped and glanced guiltily at her. I hadn't even felt her slip into my head, although now that I was aware, I could feel her in the back of my mind.

"I'd need the amulet for that, and if I'd lost you..." Her eyebrows drew down sharply and her lips thinned out as she pressed them together. "If I lost you, all would be lost."

I exchanged a confused glance with Jack. He shrugged, clearly as baffled as I was.

Chapter Seventeen

Ill-Timed Interuption

Everett had been sleeping in a little nest on the floor, a pile of blankets and pillows. I hated seeing him like that, even though I knew that when sleeping he was dead to the world, literally. Still, before I left for the day, I scooped him up and returned him to the bed, tucking him in.

He looked so peaceful laying there that I couldn't resist kissing his forehead. His skin was icy to the touch, and he was white as a ghost. Feeding on nothing but vampires could not be good for him. I wondered if it wasn't contributing to his more recent cruel streak, like his willingness to kill that vampire.

Everett had said he needed to concentrate to access the memories in the blood. But on the subconscious level, they were still there. Could they be affecting him in ways he wasn't ready to acknowledge? Feeding on humans or me was one thing, but vampires... even the kindest of them had a dark side.

Nothing I could do about it now except stay close and keep reminding him of his humanity. The human bodyguard Tawaret had put on our door gave me a dirty look, but didn't stop me from leaving.

I texted Avery when the taxi dropped me off at the strip. He met me at the bar inside the Bellagio, already sitting at a table with Brun. They glowered at me as I sat down.

"Hey Jack." Avery fist-bumped me with a grin. I wondered when we'd become best buds, but I humored him. After all, I needed his help.

"I didn't know that you invited them," I said, jerking my head in Brun's direction.

"They agreed to come after I told them what I saw at the house," Avery said. "Brun, this is—"

"We've already met," Brun said, narrowing their eyes at me.

"What, do all jackals know each other?" Avery joked.

I shook my head.

"No, Tawaret is obsessed with jackal shifters. Brun here," I bobbed my head at him, "is why she dragged us to Vegas. Though now that we're here I think she's intending to stay."

"I still can't believe there's a vampire that can walk around in the sun," Brun muttered.

"You should take Tawaret up on her invitation to visit the house," I said. "They do it every morning at the Sunrise Ceremony."

"Haven't built up the courage yet. She keeps texting me about it." Brun scrunched up their face and rolled their shoulders forward. "How do you stand it, being helpless around all those vampires after dawn when you can't shift?"

"It's not a walk in the park. I'm not going to say I haven't been scared out of my mind a few times," I said, remembering the first night at the house. "I just keep in mind that I'm doing it for Everett. What are you fighting for?"

Brun scowled and looked away.

Avery took a swig from his beer, then said, "Jack's looking for shifters willing to help go after this goddess before she can get more powerful."

"*More* powerful?" Brun snorted.

"You laugh, but she's told Everett that she's still weak." The server dropped off my beer and I thanked them, then took a swig.

Normally I didn't drink this early in the afternoon. It was only 3 pm, but I needed to settle my nerves.

"Shit." Brun slammed the rest of their drink.

"Exactly. But the PCA—" I started to say, but Avery cut me off with a muttered, bitter comment.

"Is useless, like always."

"What do you mean?" I asked.

Avery shook his head and got up, retreating to the bar without saying anything else.

"How do you know Avery?" I glanced at Brun.

"Met them at a trans event. Recognized him as a shifter." Brun kinda shrugged. "He told me your boyfriend is trans too?"

I nodded, not liking the fact that Avery was outing Everett to people like that.

"Why didn't you tell me?" Brun shot me a look over the rim of their mug.

"That's not my information to be sharing," I said with a frown. "I wish Avery hadn't said anything either. Besides, isn't your issue with him being a vampire? I'm not sure how being trans changes anything."

"I don't know, we trans people need to stick together. And I didn't know there were any trans vampires. Guess I never thought about it."

I hoped I'd been able to change Brun's mind. At least it seemed like they were reconsidering their blind hatred of vampires, or at least Everett.

After leaving Avery and Brun I stopped by the PCA office. They told me Stacy was sleeping and no one else was around. I left a message, but didn't expect to hear back. I hadn't been texting them anymore, too worried that Tawaret might be monitoring my phone.

I made a few more stops while I was out, doing some grocery shopping, and picking up an apology present for Everett.

When I returned, I found Tawaret lounging on our bed, wearing nothing but the silk robe from the dawn ceremony and stroking a sleeping Everett's hair. As I came in, she rested her hand on Everett's head. "Been a busy boy, Jack?"

"What do you mean?" I set my bags on the dresser and moved to the end of the bed. "Some of us need to eat food, Tawaret."

Her eyes flashed. "Do not call me that. I have not given you permission."

I crossed my arms and leveled my gaze at her.

"If it's food you need, I'll stock whatever you want. My servants will take care of it." Tawaret swirled a finger through Everett's hair.

I still didn't respond.

She pointed to the side of the bed and the pillows and blankets piled on the floor by the bed. "I see you're sleeping on the floor."

I raised my eyebrows but didn't correct her about who had been sleeping there.

She seemed surprised by my lack of response.

"Hmm, well," Goddess twisted a lock of Everett's hair around a finger. "You left your boy unprotected. What will he say if I wake him, tell him you abandoned him, hmm?" She gave me a razor-edged smile.

I kicked off my shoes with a shrug. "He knows I left. Go ahead, wake him up and ask him." A bluff, but one I didn't think she'd call me on.

She frowned and I knew I was right. "Why leave him unprotected just for a meal you could get here?"

I gave her a hard look. "You saying he's in danger with you nearby to protect him?"

She snarled, eyes turning red and her fang dropping. The asymmetry of her fangs made the symmetry of her face and the beauty of her fine features stand out even more. "Never!"

"Then I'm not sure what the problem is if I pop out for a jog, shopping, and to get a bite to eat. Now if you'll excuse us, I'm exhausted." I pointedly looked at the door.

She got up and stalked past me without another word. I wanted to lock the door behind her, but the doors of the bedrooms didn't have locks. I suddenly wondered how many times she might have come in during the day while I was sleeping.

I didn't understand why she was still trying to drive a wedge between Everett and me; it had to be clear by now that I would not serve her. If anything, I would just leave.

I turned this over in my head as I stripped down and hid Everett's present under the bed. I started to climb into bed, but stopped when I touched Everett's cold body, got back out and looked at the pile of blankets. Frowning, I shrugged, and crawled into bed next to Everett. Maybe I should have waited until after I apologized again to cuddle, but I didn't want to wait.

As I spooned up to him from behind, the coolness of his skin made me shiver, but my body heat would warm him up soon enough. I'd missed cuddling him and his smell.

I'd thought Everett totally out of it, but as I settled my arm down across him, he stirred enough to put his hand over mine and gave a little contented sigh before lapsing back to his death-like state. That sigh made a bolt of understanding go through me: she wanted Everett to be more dependent on her. With me gone, he wouldn't have any other support. If she got me for herself, that was a bonus.

Everett had told me how he'd begged for her to leave me behind. Clearly, she'd miscalculated when she'd kidnapped me. Either she'd thought that by threatening me she could keep Everett in line, or she'd wanted me as her own jackal guardian. Or perhaps both.

She might respect the jackals, but she wanted to control him more.

I'D FALLEN ASLEEP IN my nest on the floor where I'd been sleeping since Jack had asked for a break. However, this morning I woke up in the bed next to Jack. Jack twitched in his sleep and rolled over as I crawled out of bed, but a moment later his breathing returned to normal.

My ringing phone pulled me out of the shower. I dove to answer it before it woke the still sleeping Jack.

"Hello?" I whispered, ducking back into our private bathroom.

"Why are you whispering?" Avery asked from the other end of the line with a bemused tone.

I sat on the toilet, keeping my voice low. "Jacks still sleeping," I said. "Why are you calling me, anyway?"

There was silence for a long moment, and then Avery sighed. "To apologize. After meeting, what was her name, Tawa..." he paused for a moment. I had no I idea what he was trying to call her. When I didn't say anything, he continued. "She's scary. Almost got me with her vampire mojo and I was aware and on guard."

I groaned and rubbed my face. She didn't have any mojo, or vampire mind powers; but I didn't want to argue with him about that. Avery probably wouldn't take kindly to being told he was just really attracted to her, nothing supernatural about it. "Apology not accepted. What do you want me to say, Avery?"

"You said you became a vampire by accident? How's that work? I thought all new vampires lately apply and know what's up."

"Not with her. She's more into signs and omens and things. I was leaving work one minute; next I wake up a vampire. Now is that all?" I didn't want to get into the whole complication with the amulet.

Avery laughed. "God, I can't stop thinking about her. She's so beautiful. Is she ace, really?"

"Ace?" It took me a moment to realize he meant asexual. "Oh, no, I don't think so. She found out I was trans when she came on to me and stuck her hands down my pants and found nothing, cause I had lost my packer in the fire."

"Fire? Damn, you've had a busy few months, huh?"

"You have no idea." I got up and started pacing. "So did you call 'cause you're looking for a date with a four-thousand-year-old vampire, Avery?"

"As tempted as I am, no. I really did call to apologize."

"Thanks," I said, and hung up before he could say more. I was glad he'd come around, but I wasn't in the mood to deal with him. Goddess was furious with me, and I still didn't understand why. So, what if I'd died in the desert? At least I wouldn't have to make any more vampires into slaves.

Oakley and Nate had totally abandoned their friends. One evening I'd heard a vampire pleading with them to come back, that he missed them. They'd walked right past him without even acknowledging his words.

Although, I would have hated to cause Jack's death, too, at least we would both be free. When I came out of the bathroom, wiping the last of the tears from my eyes from my crying session, I found Jack sitting on the edge of the bed yawning.

I raised an eyebrow as I put my pajamas away. "Still tired?"

"I went out today. I had an errand to run." He leaned down and pecked me on the cheek as he passed on his way to the bathroom.

I touched my cheek and smiled. Maybe Jack really was changing his mind about us staying together.

"Where'd you go?"

"You're the one who warned me you can't keep a secret right now, Ev." Conspiracy. Exciting. I hoped he was coming up with a plan to deal with Goddess, more than the long-shot with the shifters. Clearly the PCA didn't know what to do; since the beheading, there had been no more attempts on her life.

I waited to hear more, but Jack shut the bathroom door in my face. Pouting, I went to sit on the bed to wait.

Jack grinned at me when he came back out and saw me there. He crawled onto the bed and rested his head in my lap looking up at me. I ran my hand down his cheek to stroke his short beard.

He groaned and cupped his hand over mine, pulling it to his lips and kissing my palm. I shivered, looking down into his dark brown eyes.

"Your skin is so cold, Ev." He grinned, his eyes dancing with mischief. "I know a way we can warm you up."

Now I grinned down at him and smoothed back his black hair with my other hand. "Does that mean our break is over?"

"I... honestly don't know." Jack sighed and reached up to touch my face, then rolled off my lap and knelt in front of me. "I want to apologize. When she snapped your neck and tried to blame it on me, I realized how much psychological manipulation T— I mean Goddess must be putting you through when I'm not there." He sighed and kissed the back of my hand while looking up into my eyes. "Why didn't you tell me?"

I frowned. "It's hard to put into words, and it's not just one little thing. And I thought maybe I was imagining it. Really, it hasn't been a big deal what she's been doing."

"Everett..." Jack sighed and half stood to gently kiss me on the lips. He pulled back after a moment and looked up at me. "We both made mistakes. But how about I make it up to you?"

"What did you have in mind?" I said, giggling.

"Well." He dropped my hand and sat up to slide off the edge of the bed. Jack knelt down and fished under the bed, then stood up holding a plain pink bag. "I won a bit in the slots yesterday when I went out."

He upended the bag onto the bed. Two boxes with pictures of dildos on the front and a tangle of leather fell out.

I picked up the closer one, turned it over, and read the box. Double sided vibrating strap on.

Jack laughed and picked up the leather harness with both thumbs. "I wondered if you were serious about topping me."

I blushed bright red, unable to hide my smile, and glanced up at him under my lock of hair. "I'd love to."

"I got two types. When we've had sex before, you wanted me to use your front..." He stammered, flushing bright red. Jack had been great dealing with my vagina when we'd had sex, but as a gay guy he freaked out talking about it. I didn't like mentioning it either, so he humored my front and back hole language.

I glanced at the second box. Standard vibrating dildo with a base to use with the harness. "I want to try this one," I said, popping open the box I already held.

"That one works with the harness, too," Jack said. "It—"

The door to our bedroom opened suddenly and Kurt popped his head in. "Goddess wants to see you in her room, Everett."

"Goddamn it!" Jack yelled, whirling and hiding the harness behind his back. "Can't you knock?"

Kurt shrugged, grinning, eyes roving over the bed and the half-unpacked dildo I held. "Not my problem."

He pushed the door the rest of the way open and crossed his arms. He was so wide and tall he filled the doorway like a looming black shadow.

I set down the box and slid off the bed. As I passed Jack I whispered, "We can pick this up later tonight." He frowned and gave me a tight nod.

A vampire I didn't know the name of was in the hall dusting. As I passed him, he put a hand across his chest and bowed to me. I nodded back to him, blushing, and turned sharply to head down the hall. The bowing had begun recently and I wasn't sure how to stop it.

When I got to Goddess' room, I figured turnabout was fair play. I went in without knocking, but stopped dead before I'd taken one step into the room. Goddess sat in a pink armchair, totally nude, one leg thrown over an arm, her hand rubbing herself as she watched Nate and Oakley on the bed. Nate was buried deep in Oakley's ass, rhythmically pumping. I blushed and averted my gaze.

A warm hand hit my shoulder, and I jumped, snarling, before I realized it was Jack.

"Sorry Goddess, I couldn't stop him from coming," Kurt said from behind the two of us.

"It's fine, Kurt. Now go." Goddess waved her free hand languidly at him.

Jack moved up next to me, wrapping his arm around my shoulder.

"Care to join us?" Goddess asked.

"No," I said flatly, reassured by Jack's warmth at my back. "That had better not be the only reason you summoned us."

I normally wouldn't have snarked at her; she scared me too much, but I was already a little wound up and sexually frustrated myself.

"Us?" Goddess laughed. "I only summoned you, High Priest."

"After yesterday I'm not leaving his side." Jack squeezed my shoulder. Except he apparently had after I'd fallen asleep. He wouldn't have left to buy something as frivolous as sex toys—I was guessing those had been an impulse purchase—so what had been so pressing as to take him out of the suite?

I stayed silent, waiting. The only sound was the slap of skin as Nate pounded Oakley.

"I had hoped you'd join them." Goddess sighed and gave a little pout. "I wanted to introduce you to some of the benefits of your position as my High Priest, since Jack broke up with you. It's better that way anyway, you shouldn't date your jackal, it only leads to heartbreak."

"We're not broken up." Jack slid his hand down my arm and pulled me to his side. "We were just taking a break. But we're back together now."

I flashed a smile up at Jack and put my arm around his back.

Goddess scowled. "Is that so? Well, that wasn't the only reason I called you in. Brun will be coming over at midnight to show me a movie."

Jack sucked in a breath. I glanced up at him, curious, but he didn't say anything.

"Brun's the other jackal, right?" I asked.

Jack nodded.

"Correct," Goddess said, frown deepening. "I will introduce you to them, and you will say nothing in their presence. Understood?"

"Yes. Is that all?"

"From now on, you are not to leave the suite without a vampire bodyguard. Obviously, Jack needs some lessons in how to protect his charge." Her eyes slid to the guys on the bed and her hand, that had slowed while we talked, sped back up. "That will be all."

Chapter Eighteen

BRUN FOR DINNER

Jack wrapped his arms around me when we got back to the bedroom and began kissing my neck.

"I'm sorry, Jack." I gently pushed him away and hunched my shoulders, sitting on the edge of the bed. "I don't know that I'm in the mood now."

"That's alright." Jack sat next to me and rubbed my back. "We can just talk."

"Am I your boyfriend?" I asked, snuggling up to his side. I reached behind me, grabbed one of the dildos and shook it at him. "Or are you just as horny as I am?"

Jack let out a little laugh and kissed my forehead. "Maybe a little of both. I have missed being close to you, in more than one sense of the word."

There was a knock at the door, and then Kurt opened it without waiting for us to answer. Really, again? I was glad we hadn't already undressed. I stuffed the dildo between Jack and me to hide it.

"There is a vampire downstairs asking for you." Kurt crossed his arms and stood there staring at me.

I groaned. "Tell them to wait for the ceremony like everyone else."

"Not you." Kurt's eyes flicked to Jack.

"Me?" Jack stood up and headed downstairs with Kurt, me on his heels.

The house was strangely empty; normally vampires waiting to attend the ceremony roamed the house. Not at random, but waiting to serve the Goddess, doing tasks for her and cleaning, remodeling the mansion to be more like the temple she envisioned. But today there was almost no one around. She must have cleared the house for Brun's visit. As we went down the stairs, I heard chanting out front. I stopped halfway down the stairs and peered out the window on the landing.

Thirty or so vampires were gathered on the lawn. A few of them held signs. *Goddess [heart]'s you* and another with my name on it, although Jack pulled me on before I could see more.

Downstairs, a familiar red-haired vampire stood in the front entryway clutching a suitcase. Her normally pristine clothing was rumpled, her long hair was tangled, she was paler even than normal, and her hands shook on the suitcase.

"Stacy?" Jack stopped.

She whirled towards us, her eyes wide. "Everett. Oh, thank God." She dropped her suitcase and ran towards us.

Kurt shoved me behind him, putting his body between me and Stacy. She clawed at Kurt's face and shook off Jack's attempts to grab her. "Everett, please, Everett!" she cried.

"Everett, go upstairs while I take care of this," Kurt growled, holding Stacy back with one arm and pushing me away with the other.

"No, she just needs me to bite her," I pleaded.

"Only at the Sunrise Ceremony," Kurt snapped back.

Kurt had no imagination. All he could do was follow orders, just as Goddess had said.

I leaned over and bit down on Kurt's arm, right through his shirt. He bellowed and went down on his knees almost immediately. Seconds later, he was prostrated in front of me, moaning with pleasure. Stacy crawled over him and flattened herself down on her face next to him, then slid one shaking arm across the tiles towards me.

I withdrew my fangs from Kurt's arm and sat up, licking my lips. Jack crouched next to Stacy, touching her back, trying to get her attention without success.

Oakley watched from the shadow of a doorway, his eyes shining with want. I hated this. I felt like I was separate from the other vampires, separate from Jack and his shifter friends. I was starting to see why Goddess considered herself as above them all.

"Everett, please," Stacy pleaded again, pushing her arm closer. Sighing, I took it and gave her what she wanted.

"God, thank you, Everett," Stacy groaned after she'd recovered enough to talk.

Jack helped her stand and led her into the sitting room.

"Are you moving in?" I asked from the doorway. "You know, with the suitcase and all."

"Of course not," Jack said. "She's got to get back to Portland to work."

"About that..." Stacy wrung her hands together. "I quit."

"What?" Jack and I gasped at the same time.

"You love that job," Jack said.

"Jobs come and go. I can't work in Portland if Everett is here. You saw me." She glanced down at herself and then touched her hair. "Is there somewhere I can freshen up?"

"Who is this?" Goddess said, appearing at my back.

"This is my boss from Portland," Jack said, crossing his arms and standing up to get between them. "She just came to check on us."

"How are you liking Vegas so far?" Goddess ducked around me and Jack, and sat on the couch next to Stacy.

"Well, I just got here." Stacy offered Goddess a small smile. "Came here straight from the airport. But now that I'm recovered, I guess I should go find a hotel room."

"Recovered?" Goddess asked. She glanced at me. I bit my lip and looked at the floor. I didn't want to give her to Goddess. Stacy was mine! I bit down my snarl as Goddess smiled knowingly at me. "You're welcome to stay here. We have plenty of rooms." She was talking to Stacy, but looking at me.

"I wouldn't want to impose..."

"No, never. There's just one thing I want from you in return." Goddess smiled sweetly and took Stacy's hand.

"Of course." Stacy smiled at her and squeezed Goddess' hand. Her smile widened and her eyelids drooped as Goddess lifted Stacy's arm to her mouth and bit down.

I OPENED THE DOOR to Brun's knocking. Tawaret had thought Brun would be more comfortable with me greeting them than one of the vampires. She was probably correct.

"What's with the fan club?" Brun shot a thumb at the vampires on the lawn.

I shrugged as I shut the door behind him. "No idea. It's new. But, well," I said with a shudder, remembering Stacy earlier tonight, "I think they're vampires that Everett and Tawaret bit. They've had to limit attendance at the Sunrise Ceremony."

"What is that anyway?" Brun asked, glancing around the hall.

"You'll see at dawn!" Tawaret said, skipping in from the living room. Today she wore a bright white sun-dress decorated with little red flowers.

Everett came in behind her, hands folded in front of himself and looking at the floor. He'd changed into a suit and tie. Behind him were the rest of Goddess's servant vampires: Oakley, Nate, and Kurt along with three others that I vaguely recognized. And Stacy as well. It was terrible to see my strong, confident boss reduced to the strung-out addict begging for a fix that she'd been this morning.

"Tawaret, how nice to see you again." Brun offered her a smile and took her hand to kiss the back of it.

Tawaret giggled and batted her eyelashes at him. "The pleasure's all mine." She stepped back and took Everett's arm. "This is my apprentice, Everett."

"My boyfriend," I said, stepping over to Everett's other side.

Brun snorted and raised an eyebrow. I met their gaze, daring them to say something. They stepped forward; a hand outstretched. "Nice to meet you."

Everett shook it hesitantly, glancing over at Tawaret as he did so. She pursed her lips, hand on her hip.

When Everett tried to take his hand back, Brun held on and met Everett's eyes. "It's polite to respond to a greeting, Everett."

"You may greet him, Everett, then you and Jack will go," Tawaret said, inflecting the words with the slip of power that I'd learned to recognize when she gave him orders.

"Nice to meet you too, Brun," Everett recited in a monotone. Tawaret had ordered him not to say a word to Brun while they were here, so I guessed she'd made an exception. As soon as he let go, Everett grabbed my arm and pulled me away.

"Everett and the others won't be joining us for the movie, but they'll be back for the ceremony." Tawaret shooed Everett and I, and introduced them to the line of vampires.

"What about Jack?" Brun asked, cutting her off. "And I was hoping to get to know your apprentice as well. What's he got to do that's so important?"

"Oh, well, nothing much honestly." Tawaret pouted. "I just wanted to spend time with you alone."

She gestured at Everett, who had pulled me all the way over to the base of the stairs, and he stopped.

"I really want to learn about all of you." Brun crossed their arms and glared around at everyone.

Shit, Brun, could you be more obvious about it? I tried to signal but Brun wasn't looking at me.

"Brun, they'll be plenty of time for that later," I said. "I bet you'll be by the house practically every night."

Brun took a step back towards the door, their eyes widening. "Maybe." Damn, they were a terrible liar.

"I thought it might be less intimidating if it were just you and me for the evening." Tawaret lowered her hands, frowning. "Would it be better if we go out? I haven't yet visited a modern theater."

"No, no." Brun shook their head. "It's..." they swallowed and started over. "It's too late for the last showing."

Tawaret pouted. "What's wrong then? You seem awfully nervous."

Brun smiled broadly and threw back their shoulders. "Nervous? What makes you say that?"

They were so bad at this. I thought Everett telegraphed his emotions, though he had been getting better lately, but Brun practically lit a neon sign at every thought. I'd told them earlier that I could handle spying on the house, so I'd been extra surprised when Tawaret had announced they were coming over. Perhaps Brun had taken my words earlier as a challenge.

"Then let's go." Goddess swept over, took his arm, and tugged him into the house. "Wait until you see the theater..."

Chapter Nineteen

PARANOIA

I REALLY ENJOYED WAKING up with Jack's arms around me. Warm. Safe. I snuggled up to his chest and hugged his arm. Jack had been so tired he'd wanted a nap after we'd been dismissed.

"Good evening to you too," Jack mumbled into my back.

I smiled as he kissed the top of my head. "You owe me a night of passion."

Jack growled and nipped the back of my neck. "Do you know what I want to do?"

"What's that?" I giggled at the feel of his teeth.

"I know you enjoy the front, but I really want to take you from behind." He nuzzled my neck again.

I squirmed and gasped at the fluttering kisses. Wetness slicked my underwear already. My fangs wanted to come down at my arousal, but I was getting better at controlling them and could keep them up. "I don't know..."

Jack chuckled. "Are you nervous?"

"Yeah," I admitted. "I've heard it can hurt."

"Ev, you're a vampire." Jack licked my neck. "But, if we go slow and take our time, it shouldn't hurt at all."

My toes curled as he moved his kisses around my neck to my ear. "Alright."

"Just let me do one thing." Jack kicked off the covers and climbed over me. He pushed the desk over in front of the door before getting back into bed with me.

I giggled. "Tired of Kurt waltzing in?"

"Among others." He tugged at my shirt. "Now, off."

I raised my arms so he could pull my shirt off over my head. He pushed me back onto the bed and kissed me on the mouth, tongue probing at my lips. He ran his hands down my chest, gently tweaking my nipples. When his hands got to my pants, he tugged at the waistband of my pajama bottoms and he growled, breaking off the kiss.

"Here, let me," I said.

Jack backed off me. We both stripped, and Jack grabbed a bottle of lube from his bag and I got one of the vibrating dildos from the shopping bag.

"Now on your hands and knees on the edge."

Butterflies fluttered in my stomach, but I did as he said.

"It might be a little cold at first," Jack warned. A moment later, his finger swished around my butt. Honestly, his finger felt like it was on fire and the lube cooled it down to a bearable level. "How's that?" Jack asked, gently pushing his finger inside me. I hardly felt it.

"Fine. It didn't feel cold at all." I clenched up as he put a second finger in with the first. No more than he'd done before, but I was still nervous. Both fingers stretched me a little.

"Relax, Ev," Jack crooned, using his other hand to rub my ass.

"I'm trying," I said, craning my head to look at Jack.

Jack grinned at me, gently twitching his fingers. A few moments later he added a third finger. I gasped, but really it wasn't any worse that the two. The sensation was odd, but also enjoyable.

"Ready for more?" he asked after a few minutes.

"Yes."

The fingers pulled out, and then I felt the tip of his penis press against me. It slid in easily and throbbed inside me.

"That's not too bad," I said.

"I've only got the head in so far," Jack said, gently squeezing my ass with both hands.

"You can go farther," I encouraged him, trying to focus on relaxation.

Jack pushed farther in, groaning with pleasure as he filled me. "That feels good," Jack moaned. He rocked back and forth slowly, going a little farther each time. "Let me know if it hurts and I'll slow down."

I closed my eyes, shuddering and clutching at the sheets as he filled me more and more. It was different that having him in my front, not as pleasurable, but still nice. "Harder," I growled, enjoying the way he slid in and out.

Jack grabbed my hips and started thrusting harder until I could feel his balls slapping at me. While I loved the sensation, my front ached to be filled like this, wet dripping out onto the sheets beneath me. Many people had bottom dysphoria, but my vagina had never really bothered me, and in fact, I enjoyed using it for sex even if I would have preferred to have been born with a penis.

The bed bounced, and the vibrating dildo rolled against my hand. I grabbed it and blindly pawed at it until the vibrations started. I reached down and pressed it near my pulsing clit, grown oversized by the T I had before being changed. I groaned and my fangs popped out, unable to control them any longer with the pleasure as I used it as a vibrator.

Jack was still thrusting, balls slapping me. He wasn't pulling far out anymore, moving only slightly as he rocked against me. Combined with the vibrator, the motion put me over the top and an orgasm ripped through me, clenching my stomach and curling my toes. My anus spasmed around Jack's cock, and he cried out, coming right after me.

Jack stiffened, cock fully filling me, stretching me. His seed was almost too hot as it spurted into my body, but it quickly cooled to manageable levels. Jack groaned and collapsed on top of me, a pleasurable warm weight pinning me to the bed, although with my vampire strength I could have moved him anytime I wanted. I turned off the vibrator and wiggled it out from under my body.

"You were right. I don't know why I was so nervous, that was amazing." I sighed.

Jack kissed the back of my head. "To tell the truth, I was super nervous my first time too."

"If you're quite done," Goddess' voice echoed in my head, "It is time to prepare for the sunrise ceremony."

I flushed bright red.

"What's wrong?" Jack asked, rolling off me and propping himself up on one arm to look at me.

"Goddess just summoned me for Sunrise Ceremony." I sat up with a scowl. "I wanted to do round two."

Jack laughed. "I need time to recover, anyway. We can pick up after the ceremony."

I got up and got dressed in my robe and boxers. "You coming?"

Jack stood and pulled on jeans and a shirt. "Yeah, since Brun will be there." Normally he hid in the room, but I'd seen him watching from the second-story balcony that looked out over the backyard where the Goddess and I went outside.

Vampires already packed the room, kneeling in ordered concentric rows that radiated out at an angle from the back door. By having them kneel on pillows, we could fit more bodies in than if we had chairs. At least that's what Goddess told me, although honestly, I think Goddess really just enjoyed having everyone kneeling before her.

Palpable excitement and anticipation came from the assembled vampires. What little quiet chatter there was went silent when I arrived.

Brun and Goddess weren't there yet. All eyes turned to watch Jack and me as we came in. I directed Jack to stand in a spot where the sunlight would hit when I opened the blinds.

A few minutes later, clocks throughout the mansion chimed and bonged; Kurt had reprogramed them all to go off at sunrise as a final call for any stragglers.

As the last chimes finished, Goddess appeared in the doorway. Her outfit had gotten more elaborate as time went on; today over her white robe, she wore a leopard skin shawl, a thick gold necklace, and a tall white crown adorned with colorful feathers.

Brun wasn't with her. I glanced around, wondering if perhaps I had missed them in the crowd—not likely given their height and broad chest—but there was no sign of them. Kurt and Nate were also conspicuous in their absence.

The ceremony went as it always did. Starting with the chanted prayer, then Goddess and I coming back in from the outside none the worse for wear but a little tan on our pale skin that would fade back to our normal tone within a few minutes of feeding, and ending with us giving blessings to the followers that requested one. We split the room nearly in half, although Goddess could still tolerate more than I could.

After the followers shuffled down to the basement to sleep for the day, Jack asked Goddess what I'd been wondering.

"Where's Brun?"

Goddess pouted and flipped her dark hair. "They wanted to leave early. I'm very disappointed that they don't seem to be bonding with me as I'd like."

"Give it time," Jack said, coming up and draping my robe over my back. I pulled it on and belted it shut, still hating that Goddess insisted I leave the robe off for the last half of the ceremony.

Goddess gave Jack appraising looks up and down that had me swallowing a jealous growl. "I see you and my High Priest have made up."

"Yes," I said, taking Jack's arm and dragging him back towards our bedroom. "In fact, we have some unfinished business upstairs. Good day, Goddess."

She watched us go in silence, lips pursed. I couldn't read her expression, but I still didn't like the way she was looking at Jack.

MY ALARM BUZZED LOUDLY in my ear. I groped over and grabbed my phone, stabbing blearily at the screen until it turned off. Only when I sat up did I realize Everett wasn't in the bed beside me.

Rubbing sleep from my eyes, I threw my feet off the edge of the bed and looked. Everett sat at the desk holding his phone. Tears streaked down his face, still despite him scrubbing at it with one sleeve. That woke me up more effectively than a cup of coffee.

"What's wrong?" I slid off the bed to kneel next to him. I put my hands on his arms, pulling them down from his face. His phone screen had gone dark, so I couldn't see what he'd been reading.

Everett clutched at my hand. "I couldn't sleep; it's not like when I was human. Now when I feed it's like a shot of adrenaline, and all the blood at the ceremony..."

"You don't have to explain." I stroked my thumbs across the backs of his hands. I couldn't blame him for being bored while I was sleeping. Sex twice in one day had knocked me out more effectively than a sleeping pill. "What did you read that upset you so much?"

He took a shaky breath, and I smiled at the human gesture. Tawaret never made those kinds of movements. I wondered briefly how long before Everett stopped making them too, but squashed the thought. "I just was looking at pictures of bottom surgery."

Everett tried to gesture, but I kept his hands pinned in mine. He let out another sob. "I don't know that I even wanted it, but now I don't even have the option anymore!" His voice rose in pitch at the end and he wrestled his hands from mine with a burst of strength to cover his mouth.

I sighed and hugged him from the side, lying my head on his shoulder. "Don't give up hope. The mages did top surgery on you."

His shoulders hunched. "Lots of surgeons do mastectomies, Jack, so there was a mage surgeon who could do it. Bottom surgeries are much more specialized. Not to mention..."

I cocked my head, discretely glancing at the time on the nightstand clock. I shouldn't have cut it so close with my alarm, but I hadn't counted on Everett being awake. "We'll figure something out after we take care of Goddess."

But I could already feel him shaking his head against my shoulder. "No, Jack. They were taking something away. And even then..." He winced. "They had to use silver."

"Taking away?" I paused, thinking about what I knew about vampire healing. Healing, oh, I got it now. "You'd heal. But you didn't heal the top surgery because they were taking away."

"Yeah..." He sniffed and wiped at his face again.

I kissed his cheek. I didn't have an answer for him.

"Why'd you have an alarm set? Are you going somewhere?"

"Yeah, I need to go run a few errands."

"Okay." Everett yawned.

I picked up my shirt from the floor and sniffed it, wrinkling my nose at the stale sweat smell, but then glanced at the clock. I had to leave now, or I'd be late. No time to change. I leaned over Everett and pecked his cheek again. Or at least I meant to. He turned his head so I got him on the lips. I lingered a few moments, savoring his cool lips on mine, before straightening. "Get some sleep. I'll be back shortly."

"Can I come with?" Everett asked suddenly. "I don't want you to leave without me."

"You need to get some sleep."

"So do you," he countered with a smirk.

"That's what coffee's for."

"Which I can totally drink." Everett stood and put his hands on his hips, sticking his tongue out at me.

"Everett, you know Taw, I mean, Goddess," I corrected, since Everett still couldn't hear me say her name, "is as prone to day-walking as you. If she finds me gone, she won't care, but if she realizes you're missing she'll be pissed."

I crossed my arms. If I ran, I could still make it in time. As long as Everett stopped arguing. He deflated like a balloon, hunching over on himself. I felt bad pulling that trump card on him, but I'd make it up to him later.

I walked past him and pulled back the covers. Ev climbed in and I tucked him in. "I'll make it up to you." I said, kissing his forehead.

Probably a good thing I hadn't changed clothes, because after the cab dropped me off, I had to sprint almost the entire way across the pedestrian walkway to the casino. Even then, my contact, Annabelle, from the PCA had gotten up to walk away by the time I arrived.

She frowned when she saw me, but sat back down at the nearest machine. I sat down next to her, wiping sweat from my forehead. Running in one-hundred-degree heat was not my idea of a good time. Whose bright idea was it to build a city in this hellhole, anyway? And why couldn't we meet at the PCA? Annabelle had insisted on meeting this way again, which had me baffled, but I complied.

"What is going on?" she hissed at me under her breath, eyes fixed on the machine in front of her.

"Sorry, Everett was awake when I got up to leave. Took me a minute to get out without arousing suspicion." My hands shook as I got my wallet out, and then three tries to get my card in the machine.

"You said you had something important to talk to us about?"

"Yeah," I said, finally getting the card in the slot. The game started up with fanfare. "Everett told me Tawaret is having him make a progeny," I said under the music of the game.

"Do you know when?"

"No. I don't think they have a date planned yet. But you need to take her down, now."

Annabelle was silent for a moment, considering. "You saw what happened. I *cut off her head personally, Jack!*" she finally hissed.

I clenched my fists and banged on the game buttons. "She can't heal from everything, Ana—"

She cut me off. "We've been discussing it."

"*Discussing it?* You need to act now! You wait much longer and she'll be too powerful. She's already got a vampire fan club camped out on the front lawn of the mansion!"

"We know. But we also need to make sure the next attempt is the final one. We can't rush this. We're waiting to hear from the office in Egypt that has the records from the last time this cult gained power. They're still trying to translate the documents they found."

I sighed. "Fine. Just please emphasize the need for haste."

"Jack, have you ever tried to rush an old vampire?" She turned fully from her game to look at me with a frown. "But I'll do my best."

"Thank you."

I waited fifteen minutes after she'd left, mostly to finish getting my breath back, before standing and leaving the casino.

Maybe I was just being paranoid, but as I turned onto the street and started down the sidewalk, I caught sight of a bright orange floral patterned Hawaiian shirt. That shirt was distinctive and ugly, and I'd seen the same man in the same shirt when I'd been running into the casino.

I started using the reflections I passed to keep watch behind me. The orange shirt wearing man followed me as I turned down a side street.

Perhaps not so paranoid. Tawaret was having me followed now. Damn. I hope they didn't overhear me with Annabelle. Had they also seen my meeting with Brun and Avery? I got a terrible feeling about Brun's no-show at the sunrise ceremony.

I took a detour into a souvenir shop, buying some postcards and other knick-knacks to send to friends back in Portland; I'd told everyone I was on vacation here with Everett. Couldn't hurt to play into that a bit, give credence to the lie.

My phone rang as I left. Avery's name popped up on the screen.

"Jack, hey, glad I caught you awake."

"I'm not a vampire, Avery." I ducked into an empty doorway out of the flow of traffic on the sidewalk.

"You live in a house full of them, so same difference."

"Why are you calling?" I asked, watching the sidewalk through the reflections in the windows of the store across the street. No sign of the orange shirt guy. Had I lost him? Or had I just been being paranoid?

"Oh! I was going to invite you to the run. It's tonight."

"That's not the full moon," I said, catching myself as I remembered the brightness of the stars overhead in the desert the other night. "Sorry, the timing just surprised me. The forests in Portland are too dark for a lot of animals without the full moon. And why give me so little notice?"

"I'll pick you up at eight at your house." He paused. "No vampires though."

I chuckled. "I figured. All right, see you this evening."

Chapter Twenty
The Las Vegas Pack

When I woke up that evening a bit before dark, Jack had already showered and was getting dressed.

"Sorry to run out on you again. I'm going out," he said, pulling me in for a kiss.

I leaned against him, pouting. "Can't I come with?"

"No, I'm going on a run with the shifters. At least this first time I need to go alone." Jack checked the time on his phone. "Avery's picking me up in a few minutes."

Much as I still wanted to come to spend time with him and get away from the creepy bowing and too-formal behavior of the vampires, I understood. After all, last time I'd gone to a run a crazed mountain lion shifter had attacked me.

"I guess." I huffed. "But maybe you and I can go on a run of our own later this week."

"Count on it." Jack leaned down and gave me one more kiss, deeper this time.

"Bye," I said, pulling away with more than a little regret. Jack dashed out the door, waving one last goodbye as he went.

I puttered around the room for a bit until Oakley poked his head in and told me that Goddess wanted me.

"Goddess?" I knocked gently on her door, hoping maybe she wouldn't respond and I could go back to being miserable on my own, which was actually preferable to enduring more of her training.

"Enter," Kurt boomed in his London accent.

So much for that. I paused and took a deep breath, then went inside.

Goddess languished along one end of a plush couch, fully dressed this time, thank God. When she saw me, she sat up and put her feet on the floor, then patted the seat next to her. "Everett, come, sit with me."

Dragging my feet, I walked across the room and sat.

"Kurt, go attend to those other duties I gave you."

"Yes, Goddess." Kurt put a hand to his chest, inclined his head to her, and then left the room.

"Now, Everett, have you given any thought to who you might like to make your apprentice?"

I blinked at her, mouth dropping open. "I thought that was a more distant hypothetical?"

"For now. After all, we still haven't made your amulet. But we'll be doing that in a few days. Then after that, you'll turn your first vampire."

"We will?" Shit.

Goddess nodded, her eyes shining. "I've had our followers gathering supplies. I can't have you unprotected any longer."

"Okay." I shifted uncomfortably.

"Once that's done, we can make your progeny at the next full moon," Goddess said.

"What if I don't have anyone in mind by then?" I asked, my mind racing. You'd think I'd pay attention to when the full moons were, being I was dating a shifter.

"I'll use the signs to choose a likely candidate off the street."

I stared at her, hoping she was joking, but knowing she likely wasn't; she wasn't given to humor. "Oh." I didn't want to be responsible for some random person dying. I needed to let Jack know that we needed to move up the timeline of the plan he'd hinted at. "If that's all?" I stood, but Goddess pulled me back down.

"It is not all," she said. "I need to teach you the spells to make your amulet. I can help with parts of it, but certain ones need to be cast by the amulet's owner."

Great. But before we could get started, Goddess' door swung back open and Kurt poked his head in.

"Goddess, Jack is not in the house," he said.

"Is that right?" Goddess turned to me. "Everett, where is your jackal?" She didn't make the question an order, but I knew that if I hesitated or disassembled that it might become one.

"He's on a run with the Vegas shifter pack." I hoped she wouldn't press because I didn't want to tell her about Avery. Luckily, that answer seemed to satisfy her.

"I will wait for him to return then, Goddess."

"Excellent, Kurt. You are dismissed."

Kurt bowed his head, doing the hand gesture to the heart. As the door closed, I asked, "What do you need from Jack?"

"Nothing urgent," Goddess said, leaning over to her side table to grab a lined notebook. My suspicion level shot up. "Now, I have the spells written here phonetically—"

"Goddess, before we start, I need to use the bathroom." I wrung my hands and shifted.

She frowned. "Fine. You may use mine."

I dashed inside, locking the door behind me and sitting on the toilet. I didn't have much time; vampires only needed to pee out excess liquid from the blood we consumed, so we never needed long in the bathroom. I pulled out my phone and shot off a quick text to Jack.

"Making vampire on full moon. Kurt is looking for you and I'm worried."

I wiped my phone message history to conceal that I'd sent them, then I flushed the toilet and turned on the sink like I was washing my hands, hoping that was enough to keep Goddess from asking about what I'd been doing in here.

Unfortunately, my luck did not hold. As soon as I stepped out, Goddess held out her hand to me. "Phone."

It wasn't an order, but I silently gave it to her.

She unlocked it with my passcode that I had never given her and started scrolling through my messages. After a moment, she looked up at me. "Who did you text?"

I hunched my shoulders. "Jack, just to let him know Kurt was looking for him."

"Hmmm..." Goddess made a little humming noise and tucked my phone away into her own pocket. "You know, Everett, I wasn't going to tell you this until I gathered more evidence, but..." she trailed off and got out her own phone. "I've been having Jack watched when he goes out." She looked at me expectantly.

I glared at her and crossed my arms, not wanting to give her the satisfaction. "So?"

She sighed and showed me a picture on her phone of Jack at a table at a restaurant with Avery and Brun. In the photo, Jack leaned across the table towards Avery and both of them were smiling widely at each other while Brun scowled in the background. I shrugged at the photo, although a stab of jealousy caught me off guard at the way Jack and Avery were looking at each other, and I struggled to keep it from my face.

"He's cheating on you, darling," Goddess said, her eyes brimming with sympathy. "I have more photos than just this. Think. Where is he tonight?"

With Avery, of course. She must have figured out Avery was a shifter. I looked away from her, a tear sliding down my cheek. I was sure she was lying. She had to be. A second tear followed the first and I tried to discreetly wipe it away with the back of my hand.

Goddess leaned towards me, and I expected her to embrace or touch me like she was always trying to do, and tensed up, but she just handed me a tissue.

"This is why we don't date the jackals. True, they're drawn to vampires, but they love their own kind more," she said as I dabbed at my eyes. One benefit of being a vampire was that I no longer got the runny noses I used to get when I cried.

"I'm okay now," I said, tossing the tissue in the nearby garbage. "Let's get to training. I'll talk to Jack tonight when he gets back, but I don't want to think about it anymore."

"Brun isn't coming?" Avery asked when I hopped into the passenger seat of his car.

I gave him a sideways look as I clicked on my seatbelt. "Brun left the other night."

Avery frowned and leaned over me to look up at the towering mansion filled to the brim with vampires. Twilight deepened the shadows in the corners of the house and the fake windows, giving the house a sinister air in the fading light. "They were supposed to call me when they got home. I assumed they'd stayed." Avery sat back, shaking his head, and put the car into gear. "I'll have to chew them out when we get to the run."

"I'm surprised it starts so late," I said, mostly to change the subject. I didn't know why they hadn't called Avery, except for maybe their meeting with Tawaret had been more unsettling than they'd prepared for and it embarrassed them. "Back in Portland, we always met up a couple hours before dark to have a cookout and socialize."

He shot me a grin and snorted out a half laugh. "Yeah, but there it probably wasn't hot enough to fry an egg on the ground."

"That is true," I admitted. "Is that why the run doesn't officially start until later?" I knew from our last trip out here that it took nearly an hour to drive out there and it was already almost dark.

"Yeah, give it a chance to cool to semi-reasonable levels. Even then, it's still murderously hot until at least midnight." He reached over and cranked up the AC until I was shivering in my thin t-shirt.

"I bet." I sympathized and my fur was meant for warmer climes. As thick and bushy as Avery's coat was, he could probably have slept in a snowbank and been fine. As an arctic wolf, Vegas temperatures must have been murder. "How'd you end up in this hellhole, anyway?" I gestured at the flashing scenery, and only after did I realize my question might have offended.

Luckily, Avery just shrugged a large shoulder. "Followed a boyfriend out here, and then stayed because cost of living was so cheap. For instance, how much you think the vampire's mansion would have would cost in Portland?"

"A million? Or more? More than I could ever make in my lifetime. I could barely afford my tiny one-bedroom, and it was only a couple hundred thousand."

"Well, what you paid for that one-bedroom could probably get you a decent way to something like that out here," Avery said.

"I guess."

Conversation trailed off after that until we pulled into the crowded parking lot. A couple hundred people milled around in the dirt nearby.

"I don't see Brun," I commented as we got out of the car. They kinda stood out from the crowd in their human form, but none of the milling silhouettes looked like them.

Even with the sun down, it was still hotter than hell. My thin shirt soaked with sweat after just a few steps.

"Maybe they've already changed." Avery started for the largest knot of people to ask after Brun. But no one had seen them and everyone was still human.

Avery impatiently checked his watch as more cars trickled in, but Brun didn't emerge from any of them.

Eventually, someone blew a whistle and the scattered conversations died down. There was a quick lecture for the newcomers about if you were separated from the pack to be sure to return to the cars before dawn. A naked, unprepared human with no supplies wouldn't last a full day out in the summer heat, a fact that I knew well.

"Alright, if there's nothing else, let's get this run started!" the leader called through her bullhorn.

"Actually," I yelled over the sudden flurry of people shucking off clothing. "I have a quick request to make!"

"Who the heck are you?" a heckler called from the crowd. In the dark my human eyes couldn't make out who had spoken.

"This is Jack. He's new in town. I'll vouch for him." Avery slapped me on the back hard enough to rock me forward a step.

"Alright Jack, but make it quick." The leader moved aside and handed me the bullhorn she'd been using.

"Hi, I'm Jack." I waved, but almost no one waved back. "I'll just get to it then. I have a request to make. I need some help to get my boyfriend away from the vampires—"

"No way!" The leader practically tackled me as she tried to wrest the bullhorn back from me.

"What's the big deal?" I snarled, wrestling her for it. She was taller than me but I had more muscles.

"We stay out of the vampire's way. We don't antagonize them," she growled, finally getting hold of the handle and pulling it out of my hands. Then she turned to Avery, hands on her hips. "Did you know what he was going to say?"

"Yes, I did." Avery stared right back at her. "This new vamp in town is bad news, and it really is in our best interests to run her out."

Everyone scoffed and the flurry of clothes shedding started again. Less than a minute later, the air was filled with growls, howls, barks, and wuffs.

Avery growled, his voice going lower and lower as he started changing. His clothes ripped apart as he blew up into his giant wolf state.

A tiger stalked near me, growling. "You smell like vampire."

Avery threw back his head and howled. All the wolves in the crowd joined him.

Sighing, I pulled off my shirt, dropped my pants, and let the change wash over me.

The big white wolf lowered his head and sneezed, violently, then took a step away from me. "She's right. You totally reek of vampires, Jack."

"I live with them. Not much I can do about it." I gave a shake, setting my fur right. He was right, though. The smell burned at my nose, and I couldn't get away from it like all the shifters backing away from me.

"I'll try to work on them during the run." Avery shuffled back two steps, his lips curling. "I have a feeling everyone is going to stay away from you."

The run was great, although Avery was right. After we got going, no one got within ten feet of me, or downwind of me. However, I saw Avery chatting with different people every time I turned around. A few shot sympathetic glances my way as they talked with him.

My muscles pleasantly ached by the time we got back to the car. Dust coated my fur, almost covering the burning vampire scent. Almost.

The temperature had dropped during our run, and now my breath plumed in the air with each pant. I changed, then quickly retrieved my clothing and dressed, shivering in the cold. My phone said it was almost three in the morning. Avery went into his car to get a pair of sweatpants out of the trunk.

"That looked like it might have gone well, at least with a few people," I said when Avery got into the car. He was still shirtless and shivering in the cool night air. The scars from his top surgery stood out red against his paler skin.

"A few, yeah, once I explained about seeing both of them prancing around in the sunlight." Avery started the car and flipped the temperature dial all the way around. "More might come around in the next few weeks. I told them to drive by the mansion to see the followers already gathering around her."

"Good call."

"And, Brun hasn't talked to anyone since they went over to see Tawaret the other night. You sure they left the house?" Avery glanced my way as he drove.

"No," I admitted. "Everett and I were a little distracted."

"Damn it," Avery pounded the steering wheel. "Take a look for them when you get back?"

"I will," I promised.

When we got back closer to Vegas, my phone started buzzing with text messages.

"That's weird." I frowned down at Everett's message.

"What is?"

I shook my head and shot a quick text back to Everett asking for more details. "Looks like Tawaret pushed up the ceremony to make a new vampire. We'll need to get him out of there before the full moon, which is in..." quick google search later, "a week and a half."

Avery winced. "Gonna be tight to get enough shifters to be security for you."

"Yeah," I agreed, also wondering why Kurt wanted me. The other vampires mostly ignored me, pretending I didn't exist unless they had explicit instructions to talk to me. Tawaret must have given him instructions to talk to me, but why?

"Is there something else?" Avery asked.

"He also said Kurt was looking for me. And now Everett isn't responding to my texts asking for more information."

Avery was silent for a moment. "Combined with Brun being missing, it's not a good sign. You should come stay at my place."

I grimaced. "I have to go back, Avery. Everett's still there."

"How about this? I'll stay in the car, you run in, get him, and bring him out."

"What about Brun?" I asked, tensing up. It wasn't a bad plan: it was still night so I could change to protect myself if I needed. But I was tired from the long run, and Everett could be anywhere in the house.

"I'll get together a group to go in with me during the day to look for them. But it will help if you could tell us where they might be."

"Nowhere upstairs. I would have heard something, at the very least. But there's a big basement with a theater and a gym. The vamps sleep down there during the day, so I avoid it mostly. If they are keeping them at the house, that's where it'd be."

"Shit."

"Sorry."

CHAPTER TWENTY-ONE

EVERETT'S AMULET

GODDESS SASHAYED PAST ME. "Now, let's get started on that amulet."

"Now?" My stomach twisted. I'd hoped to escape with Jack before making it, but he hadn't even returned from his run yet. "Shouldn't I rest first? We've been up all-night practicing."

"It's the perfect time for exactly that reason. You've got the words down, so let's not give you time to forget them."

"I can barely summon magical energy yet," I protested.

"It's enough for the spell. Now, kneel, put your hands behind your back, and drop your fangs," she ordered. "You will not move from there until I give you the order."

The spell compelled me to obey, although I protested as I got into position. "Fangs down? Why?"

"Would you like the left or right pulled?" Goddess asked me, taking a pair of pliers from her desk.

My hands shook against my back and my mouth went dry. "Pulled?"

Goddess frowned and lightly tapped first one fang and then the other. "That's not an answer. Left or right. It's your choice."

"Why?" My whole body shook now from the fear and my tooth rattled against the pliers she still held against my mouth.

"The fang creates a connection back to you, tying your soul to the amulet." Goddess placed the tool in her lap and leaned down, taking my chin in her hands and kissing my forehead. "I'm sure you've noticed my own missing fang," she whispered. "All the Dawn's children go through this."

I shook my head. "I want to wait until Jack has returned."

"No. You won't see him again until he's fully trained."

"What does that mean?" I struggled, or tried to, but Goddess' words held me immobile.

"He's a loyal Jackal. He just needs some encouragement." She gave a cruel smile. "I'm already training Brun. He'll come back to you much more pliant."

My eyes widened, but her order compelled me to stay kneeling. "No, no, no, no!"

"In the meantime, if you get lonely, I'm sure Nate or Oakley would be happy to keep you company." She patted my shoulder. "Best not to date your jackals in the future, hmm?"

I closed my eyes, fighting back tears. "No! No!"

"Speaking of Jack," Goddess said as my phone buzzed in her pocket. "I should give him a little encouragement to return quickly to your room." She sent a message on my phone and then stood, tousling my hair with an affectionate smile. "Be silent," she ordered, cutting off my continued screams.

The door to Goddess' room creaked open and Oakley stepped inside. "Everything is prepared."

"Good." She smiled and patted Oakley's cheek on the way out the door. "You can hide here. Everett will not interrupt. I'm going to go check on Brun."

Oakley turned off the lights and crouched down near the door, which he left cracked open after Goddess left.

I was trapped silent, immobile, and helpless as the trap closed around Jack. Sometime later, I heard a quick creak from the steps, only because I was straining my ears for any sound.

Oakley threw open the door and vanished into the hall. I heard yelling, followed by a loud crack and the shattering of glass. A howl. Sounds of a fight.

"Jack," I whispered, intent on the continued sounds of fighting. A moment later, silence. A tear rolled down my cheek. Even Jack couldn't win a fight against so many vampires. I shuddered to think what Goddess' idea of training entailed.

Goddess confirmed it when she returned a short while later, smiling down at me with predatory glee. "Now that Jack's out of the way, let's get back to the amulet making."

Goddess picked up the pliers from the desk. "You may talk again. Choose a fang." She tapped my fangs again. Strangely, while she made the first part an order, the second part was not.

"No."

Goddess sighed. "I see you're going to make this difficult."

A knock on the door interrupted her. "Enter," she called.

Kurt cracked the door. "Goddess, Jack is—"

"Stop." Goddess threw up one hand. "You are not to mention his name in Everett's presence until he's been broken. I'll join you in the hall. Everett, silence until I return."

She left me there, still kneeling. I growled and fought to move, but the magic that bound me to her demands wouldn't let me do more that turn my head. She'd shut the door behind her, and I couldn't hear what they were saying.

From where I was, I couldn't see the clock either. She came back in an unknown amount of time later and she didn't look happy.

She took her time arranging her robes and picking back up the pliers. "Now, which fang?"

"Neither." I glared at her. I had a feeling I knew why she wasn't making the demand a magical compulsion. The spell must require my voluntary donation; something that she couldn't force me to do.

"It seems your jackal isn't the only one that needs training." Goddess scowled and stood. "We'll see what your answer is in a few hours. You will be *silent*," she ordered.

She leaned over and grabbed my arms, twisting them behind me and up my back. My joints strained, and I would have screamed except for her order for silence.

"Don't move a muscle, Everett." Then she let go.

Staying like this was torture, but I couldn't move.

"I'm going to go lead the Sunrise Ceremony." Goddess blew me a kiss. "When I return, we'll try again." She flicked the lights out as she left, leaving me in darkness.

I was already thirsty. Lately I'd only eaten during the ceremony. If she was doing it without me... I tried to lick my lips, but I couldn't even do that much. Her order kept me locked in place, frozen like a statue.

The minutes ticked by. My body kept trying to heal, but my position was just too extreme. Each jolt of healing eased up on the agony a bit, but then it came back as bad as ever when I didn't relieve the pressure. I was ready to cry with relief when Goddess came back in. I didn't even know how long I'd been there. Time had lost all meaning. There was just the constant agony.

The tangy scent of vampire blood wafted off of her. My vision zeroed in on a red spot near the neck of her robe. My fangs ached to bite, my mouth and tongue felt like sandpaper. I wanted that blood so badly. I tried to whimper.

Goddess took her time walking back to the chair, sitting, then carefully arranging each fold of cloth from her robe before she waved a hand lazily at me. "You may lower your arms."

Oh, thank God. I let my hands drop and the agony immediately went away. I would have sagged, but I couldn't move the rest of me, only my arms.

Goddess picked up the pliers. "Which fang?"

I'd had a lot of time to think in between the screaming agony. Without Jack, I had no allies here. Any vampire worshipers would be as loyal to, or more loyal, Goddess than to me. Not to mention the fact that I was helpless before her, with or without the amulet.

Still, I remembered Jack's words. I wouldn't give up. He'd want me to fight. A tear rolled down my face as I thought about where he must be right now. Chained up somewhere, helpless. I couldn't help him like this. But if I went along with her, made the amulet and a progeny, I'd be even more closely tied to her. Trapped on both ends. Enslaving my former friends.

"Answer, now. Or do you need a few more hours to think about it?" Goddess tapped my fangs again.

What should I do? I shook my head, shaking, crying harder now. "I want to see Jack. I need to know he's okay."

"No," Goddess snapped, her eyes blazing red and her fang dropping. "You will not say his name again without my permission, Everett."

I still tried to call out his name, but my tongue refused to move.

"I can see you need a bit more time to think."

Goddess set down the pliers and came over to me. She forced me facedown onto the floor, grinding my face into the carpet. She pulled my arms so sharply that I felt them pop painfully at my shoulders and elbows. I screamed.

"Silence! You will maintain this position," she ordered, cutting my scream off with a gurgle. "I'm going to bed. We'll see how you feel tonight, hmm?" She flicked off the light, and I heard the rustle of bedsheets. Then silence.

DESPITE HOW TENSE I was as I went up the steps to the house, I couldn't hold back a yawn. The run and the shifts had exhausted me. I wasn't sure this plan was going to work, but I had to try.

Avery waited out in the street with the car running. I'd have liked him to have been closer, but cars of worshiping vampires packed the driveway.

I'd eventually gotten a text back right before we got home, "I want to ravage you. I'll be waiting in bed. Naked. Hurry back."

I could tell right away that Everett had not sent it. My stomach had dropped and twisted, although I hadn't wanted to worry Avery so I hadn't said anything.

The door opened easily; the vampires always left it unlocked. They weren't worried about being robbed, after all. As I went inside a peculiar smell tickled my nose, making me sneeze. Something about it was familiar...

A murmur of conversation came from the living room. Two vampires stood in the front hall conversing quietly when I came in. They cut off their conversation to stare at me. One smiled and lowered his fangs but his partner put a hand on his arm, leaned close and whispered into his ear. His fangs went back up and he scowled, but let me pass them to the stairs.

The new smell grew stronger as I headed upstairs. Where had I smelled this before? It didn't hit home until I saw the wreath hung on the door to our room. Purple flowers. Wolfsbane.

Why?

I stopped still in the middle of the hall and took stock of my surroundings. This was worse than I'd anticipated. Shifting from foot to foot, I contemplated the door to our room, then glanced up and down the hall. No sign of any vampires. The door to Tawaret's suite was cracked open. I didn't see anything but darkness beyond that, but I'd never seen the door left open before. The other close by doorway, set a few feet down from our door, was also cracked slightly open, and I felt eyes on me, though I couldn't spot any watchers.

Everything about this screamed trap.

Given the wolfsbane, the feeling of being watched from the two doors, and the text that designed to lure me to the bedroom... I turned and bolted back down the stairs.

The door to Tawaret's room banged open and Oakley streaked out, lunging at me with his fangs bared. Moments after I heard another bang and the pounding of feet on carpet.

Even expecting the move, I barely evaded his grab. Oakley slammed into the wall on the landing. I careened down the stairs two at a time. Kurt leapt over him, laughing as he chased me down the stairs.

I jumped the last few stairs and landed hard on the tile. I needed to get outside. Rage and fear fueled my steps, speeding me along as I sprinted for the front door.

My body ached to change, but the wolfsbane perfume lingered in my nose, stopping the change. Inside my jackal half growled in frustration and my skin itched with fur trying to sprout and failing.

"Jack, stop!" Kurt yelled after me.

I hit the front door with a bang. As I tried to open it, Kurt slammed into me from behind. The force of his impact tore the door free of its frame and sent us both tumbling outside. We landed on the porch in a shower of wood and glass as the cheap door shattered beneath us.

I rolled over, trying to get back the breath that Kurt had knocked out of me. On hands and knees, Kurt grabbed at my clothing. I rolled again, tearing my shirt, and landed in the decorative bushes.

Gasping, I crawled out of the bushes, right into Kurt's legs. He grabbed me by the hair and forced me down to the grass, grinding my face into the dirt. I sneezed, sending dirt flying, and continued without success to change to my jackal. Another set of hands grabbed my arms, forcing them behind me, and I heard the snap of a ziptie. Shit.

Then a loud snarl shook the ground, followed by a howl that sent me back to struggling against the hands on me.

A flash of white hit the two vampires on me, bowling both of them off of me. I pushed up, spitting grass.

A snarling giant white werewolf, half man/half wolf on two legs fought with Kurt and Oakley. He had Kurt's leg in his mouth, holding him off the ground so that the vampire couldn't get any good leverage in his wild punches. With his claws, he kept Oakley at bay, slashing and driving him back anytime he tried to get close.

I could hear a commotion in the house and knew it wouldn't be long before we were swarming with vampires. As soon as my feet were under me, I sprinted down the driveway to where Avery's car still idled in the middle of the street, trusting Avery in his warrior form could handle the two vampires.

Avery howled behind me, and I glanced over my shoulder to see that he'd dropped Kurt and run after me, five vampires on his heels. More poured out of the house behind us and joined in the chase.

I jumped and slid over the hood to get to the driver's side door.

Avery was taller than me, but I didn't stop to adjust the seat, throwing it into drive before I was only halfway in the car. Avery didn't even try to open the passenger door. He leaped, landing on top of the car, and dug his claws into the roof.

We careened off down the street, almost out of control, as I struggled to see over the dash while flooring the gas. Vampires chased us for blocks, even as I blasted through red lights and stop signs. I don't know how I managed to not get hit, as I blew through the residential streets trying to shake them off our tail.

"Jack, stop, you've lost them!" Avery growled from the roof as I blasted down yet another side street. At this point, I was totally lost.

Heart pounding, I slowed and then stopped the car. There was a thump, and the springs on the car eased up. A moment later Avery, totally nude, opened up the passenger door and crawled inside.

"Well, that was exciting," he panted, wiping sweat from his eyes. Understatement of the year.

I WAS SO TIRED, but the constant wracking pain as I continually pulled my own arms out of the socket trying to stay in the position she'd contorted me into kept me awake and in constant agony.

When the lights eventually flicked on and Goddess said, "Everett, you may move and talk again as normal," I sagged into a gibbering heap, unable to even form words.

Goddess picked me up and set me on the couch as I struggled to come to my senses.

"Thirsty?" she asked.

"Yes." The word stuck in my throat and I could barely get it out. My fangs pressed into my lip, aching with need.

Goddess gave me a cruel smile. My thoughts were so hazy and muddled I barely could remember why she'd been torturing me. At least until Goddess picked up the pliers again and turned towards me.

"Which side, Everett?" she asked again.

"Left," I whispered. I felt emotionally wrung out and defeated. I'd had vague plans the night before to rescue Jack and escape, but now I was just glad to not be in pain anymore. I couldn't go back to that; I'd let her take my fang if it meant the pain would not come back.

"Good." Goddess grabbed it with the pliers. "Now, concentrate on calling magic to you and recite the first three pages of spell."

We'd practiced both skills separately, but not together. Plus, we definitely hadn't practiced with one of my fangs held by pliers and with me so thirsty I could barely talk. After the first recitation, she shook her head.

"No. You mispronounced the third word. Again."

After the fourth time, I could feel the magic catch when I finished the spell. It pulsed through me, doing... something. Goddess had been vague about what the spell did.

Goddess twisted and yanked the pliers, pulling my fang out in one sharp motion. One spurt of blood came with it, and I blacked out. When I opened my eyes again, I lay on my back on the floor, my hands folded awkwardly underneath me.

Something clinked, and somehow, I felt my tooth hitting the inside of something stone. It was like it was still part of me.

"You feel that?"

"Yes." I poked at the space where my fang had been. I could feel it there, but it wasn't. "How?"

Goddess sat at her desk. "That's what the first part of the spell does. We need to establish a connection between you and the amulet. Sympathetic magic."

Goddess picked up the pestle. "I recommend you stay lying down. This next part might hurt a bit. And no screaming." That last bit was an order. She gave me a significant look.

I flopped down on my back on the bed just as she began grinding my tooth between the mortar and pestle. I arched my back, gasping and tearing at the sheets at the pain. It was like she was grinding up a tooth that was still in my mouth. Each smash and scrape was pure agony. It made my earlier pain with my arms feel like it had been nothing. I should never have agreed to this.

By the time she finished, I was sobbing uncontrollably, fat tears rolling down my cheeks. The worst part was that I could still feel the dust. Now that each grain was so small, every time they slid across each other it was like something scraped the inside of my mouth.

"All done," Goddess sang. "Now, come help me with the next part."

Shaking and wiping tears away, I slid off the bed. Goddess pulled a Bunsen burner from underneath her desk and a container of gold chunks from a drawer, which she fed piece by piece into a shallow bowl on the burner.

"When the gold is melted, we'll mix the tooth dust in with it," she said conversationally, as if she hadn't just been torturing me for the last day.

I wanted to ask if it would hurt, but had a feeling I wouldn't want to know the answer to that question.

At least she pulled the bowl off the burner first, but still it felt like she'd poured molten gold in my mouth when she dumped it in. I clutched my mouth, swallowing back another scream.

As she stirred, she said, "Recite the next spell as I pour it into the mold. Your notes are there if you need a refresher."

After it had cooled, she had me say the last part of the spell while she helped me carve my name into the front of the amulet.

My amulet didn't compare to Goddess' one; the gold on the edges had a seam where the mold had held it, and my name going from the top of the disc to the bottom wasn't perfectly straight and the letters were shaky.

As I held it in my hands, my vision twinned. I could see the amulet there in my palms, but I also was looking up at myself from below. When Goddess took it from me, where her hands touched the gold of the amulet, it also felt like they touched my skin.

The sense of wonder even pulled me out of my despair, at least a little, although I still felt like I was going to throw up every time I thought of Jack.

"This is so strange," I said. "But I thought you said you couldn't feel the amulet, only me?"

I don't know how I could ever lose track of it; I could no more lose my right arm. Also, if she felt me as completely as I felt this amulet, there was no escape from her.

"Mmm, yes," Goddess handed the amulet back to me. "Once your apprentice uses the power in it to rise, you trade."

"Trade?" I frowned, clutching my amulet to chest. My feelings about it were far more intense than the ownership I'd felt over Goddess's amulet; I didn't think I could give it over to anyone.

"You'll see." She patted my hand in a surprisingly motherly gesture.

Chapter Twenty-Two

Be Careful What You Wish For

"Shit, what are we going to do?" I paced Avery's living room, running my hands through my hair in frustration.

"They've taken Brun hostage," Avery said around a mouthful of food. "We at least need to report that to the PCA. And who knows, maybe that will force them to get off their butts and act."

"I already did report it." I held up my phone. "No response."

"Then let's head over there. They can't ignore us if we're in their faces." Avery growled, grabbing his keys.

"What. The. Fuck." Avery growled as we walked inside.

I kind of agreed with the sentiment. An enormous portrait of Tawaret dressed as a Pharaoh took up the entire wall across from the entrance. They'd hung an 8x10 of Everett next to it.

A familiar red-headed woman walked out of the back room.

"Stacy?" I said.

She glanced at me and did a double-take. "Jack!"

Oh, shit. "Stacy. Last I saw you, you were at the Goddess' house." I took a step back, ready to run. "I thought you quit the PCA."

"Goddess asked me to come in and take my job back." Stacy clasped her hands together. "I'd do anything for her and Everett."

"I suppose you have something to do with that, then?" I tilted my head at the framed pictures of Tawaret and Everett.

"Of course. I brought Goddess in and introduced her to all the vampires here!"

"Stacy, you're helping them?" I probably didn't have a job to go back to when this was all over.

"Of course. I'd do anything for my Goddess." Stacy's eyes turned red and her fangs dropped. "And she wants you, Jack. Grab them!"

I grabbed Avery's arm and dragged him back towards the door, but two more vampires were already there blocking the entrance, fangs down and red eyes fixed on us.

"Why aren't they asleep?" Avery hissed, glancing around us with wide eyes. "It's almost noon!"

"It's Goddess' bite," I said, pulling out a silver bracelet. I cracked one across the face, using the bracelet like brass knuckles. She fell back with a hiss, black lines of silver poisoning running up her skin where the bracelet had hit.

Avery shoulder-checked the second vampire, and we ducked out the door, running for our lives.

"That might have been something important to mention before we came in here," Avery growled, huffing.

"I didn't think it mattered." I vaulted over a startled gambler, who dropped her cup of coins. "The Portland office is only staffed by mages and shifters during the day."

"Usually ours is too."

Vampires dashed after us, led by Stacy. We burst out a side door into the sunlight, huffing and panting. A snarling vampire couldn't stop fast enough and burst into flames when he got too close to the glass door as it was still swinging shut. I didn't have it in me to be upset at his death.

God, so hot. I shielded my eyes and yawned. I'd been up for over 36 hours so far.

"What do you think happened to the day staff?" Avery mused.

"Probably the same thing that happened to Brun." I rubbed my eyes.

"Why do they want you so badly?" Avery asked, cracking his neck. He was taller and larger than that vampire he'd body checked, but vampires were tough, especially more so than shifters during the day. He had to be feeling it.

"She's from ancient Egypt. She thinks jackals are the protectors of the dead." I mean, maybe she wasn't wrong. I still wasn't sure why I'd been so intent on helping Everett when I first found him, or why I was so attracted to him. But honestly, it didn't really matter to me. I cared about him, and he was in trouble.

"*That's* why she wants Brun?"

"Yeah."

"We have to rescue him."

"And Everett."

Avery paused. "Sure, I guess."

"What do you have against vampires, Avery?" I snapped when we got back to his car.

"You haven't been in Vegas long. You don't understand." Avery slammed his door. "It's different here."

Sweat rolled down my face. Hopefully, I wouldn't be here much longer. I turned up the AC and angled the vent to hit my face. "So, tell me."

He snorted. "You don't care."

"I do." I needed to learn what I was up against here.

"Vampires outnumber shifters here at least ten to one, Jack." Avery paused, as if just realizing something. "Wait, you're dating a vampire. Why are you carrying around silver?"

I shrugged. "I trust Everett, yes, but not all those creepy vampires that he lives with."

"Silver brass knuckles...silver knuckles?" He cocked his head. "Not a bad way to fight off vampires."

"Or, you know, silver bullets," I pointed out. "Getting into melee range with a vampire is generally a bad idea. This is more of a last resort weapon."

"Maybe if we were prepared. Do you know anyone who can make silver bullets?"

"Like vampire hunters?" I said, thinking of the hunters from Portland. "Shockingly, no. Do you?"

"Vampire hunters don't last long in Vegas."

I examined the silver bracelet. "Well, I guess a plus with the silver knuckles is that we could use them in our animal forms. Can't handle a gun with paws," I said.

I hadn't considered that before, but anything to give us an advantage.

"True."

"Wait, where are we going?" I sat up as Avery left the strip.

"My house. I'm exhausted."

"No! They're at the PCA! Find a hotel or something."

"What?"

"They have your address, Avery," I snapped. Avery glanced at me blankly. "Everett knows your name, and with access to the PCA's record, they'll know where you live. By dark your house will be swarming with vampires."

"Shit. Thanks." Avery rubbed his head.

THREE NIGHTS SINCE I'D seen Jack. Two since we'd made my amulet. Goddess had kept my phone, saying I needed to focus on picking someone to change.

All that happened was I was bored out of my mind. It didn't help that I was still distracted by my feelings of the amulet. And I wondered why I could feel it, but not Goddess' amulet.

Who could I change? I remembered Xander begging me to change him. I didn't like the idea of turning anyone into a vampire, but if I had to pick someone, I might as well pick someone who was enthusiastic about the idea. Still, I had not a little trepidation as I knocked on her door to tell her my proposal.

"Everett, come in," Goddess sang from inside.

Ugh. I hated that she always knew where I was. I sighed and went inside.

"What do you need?" She was sprawled out on her bed, naked, lounging between Kurt and Nate.

"First, can you tell me how J—" struggled to say his name and gave up; Goddess' orders still forbid me from saying it. "How he's doing? Can I go see him yet?"

"Not yet." Her face darkened. "If that's the only reason you are here, leave us. We're busy." She gave me a hungry look. "Unless you'd like to join us?"

"No, and no." I crossed my arms. "I have an idea for someone to turn, but I need my phone back so I can text him."

"Oh? Who?"

I took a deep breath. "Xander." I felt bad doing this to him, but if I didn't choose someone, Goddess would choose for me. I could end up with someone transphobic, or worse. And at least I knew he was excited about the supernatural. Heck, he'd probably volunteer.

"Good choice." Of course, she'd been going through my phone while she had it. Goddess sat up and picked up my phone from the nightstand. "I'll text him for you."

I met Xander downstairs an hour later, waiting on the porch to make sure a visiting vampire didn't eat him. He was grinning from ear to ear as he got out of the cab. His hair had been dyed bright blue since I'd seen him last, but otherwise he looked the same.

"Everett!" He waved at me and bounded up the steps two at a time and stopped in front of me, hands clasped in prayer. "Please, please, please tell me you weren't joking with your text. Will you really turn me?" I wasn't sure exactly what Goddess had told him, but apparently, he knew already. That would make things easier.

I glanced around at the vampire guards and took Xander's arm. "Let's talk more in my room."

"You doing alright?" he asked, squeezing my hand as we went upstairs. "I heard about Jack."

"J—" I tried to say his name, and failed again. Swallowed hard. "I'm fine." I burst into tears on the steps.

Xander stopped and hugged me. "Everett, it's okay. You'll be fine."

I pulled back and wiped my eyes.

Xander turned my hand over to look at my tears. "Dang, it's not blood." He pouted.

I had to laugh at that. "Why would it be blood? Honestly. We have to pass as human. You know?"

We continued up to my room, passing a vampire dusting the paintings in the hallway. She put her hand to her chest and half bowed to me as we passed. I barely noticed the genuflecting anymore, but Xander frowned and glanced back at her.

When we got to my room with the door shut behind us, he asked, "What's with all the bowing and stuff?"

I took a seat in a plush lounge chair and gestured for Xander to join me. "Goddess, the ancient vampire who made me, is the leader of this church. As her progeny, I'm her High Priest."

He laughed and flopped next to me. "Weird, but okay."

I fidgeted with my amulet that hung on a necklace under my clothing and looked away. "I was serious about the text. Are you interested in becoming a vamp—"

"Holy shit, Everett! Yes, yes, yes!" Xander jumped up off the couch and whooped. "I cannot believe this is happening. Oh, my, gosh, I need to put this on my twitter!"

"No, no. Xander," I jumped up and dashed across the space between us. Xander yelped when I plucked the phone from his hand. "Super naturals have to stay secret. You can't talk about this."

"Oh."

"I'll give you your phone back, but you have to promise not to post anything about this." I held his phone out of reach.

"Fine, I promise." Xander pouted and held out his hands.

I handed the phone back. "You'll need to fake your death if you're going to become one of us."

"Pff," Xander blew a piece of errant hair from his face. "No problem."

"There's something else." I sat down next to him. "Where are you at in your transition? Was there anything else you wanted? Other surgeries? Because you won't be able to get any more once you're changed."

He screwed up his face. "Nothing?"

I shook my head. "Look at me. Testosterone doesn't do anything anymore. I'd only been on it a few years, so I'm still really androgynous."

"I'd kinda been hoping to get bottom surgery, but..." he pushed up his upper lip and put two fingers down like fangs for a moment. "I'm not turning down the chance to be a vampire. I mean, I'd rather be a shifter, but—"

"You have to be born a shifter."

Xander's shoulders slumped. "Yeah, Avery told me. I guess vampire's good though." He perked back up and grinned at me.

I tried to grin back, but my smile faltered.

"I'd feel remiss if I didn't mention the last little," I pinched my fingers close together, "downside of being a vampire."

"What?" He snorted and held up a hand. "Wait, don't tell me. The legends about a vampire not being able to disobey their makers are true."

I winced and pulled out my amulet. "Not normally, no. But with our bloodline... yes."

Xander bit his lip, staring at my amulet. I had the side with my name up. "That's why you couldn't just leave Goddess, why Jack said he'd have to take you away?"

I nodded.

"That's a pretty big negative, Everett," Xander said, giving me a sideways look.

I shrugged. "Yeah, that's why I wanted to warn you."

"I'll have to think about it," Xander said, stripping off his jacket and tossing it to the end of my couch. He took off his shirt next, throwing it after the jacket. I stared at him, puzzled. His top surgery scars were just thin white lines, barely visible under the hair on his chest. He must have had it done a long time ago.

"What are you doing?"

"Bite me." He tapped his neck and threw back his head. "I want to see what all the fuss is about before I commit."

I slipped my amulet back into my shirt. Goddess had given me orders; I couldn't bite humans. "I'll have to get permission from Goddess first."

He stared at me, eyes widening. "Wait, who's Goddess?"

"My maker. You've seen her before, that morning when Avery tried to burn me."

"That's your maker?" Xander laughed. "I think Avery simultaneously was terrified of her and wanted to bone her."

"Yeah, she can be intense. You better meet her before you decide." I hauled him to his feet and out the door as he protested.

"Come in, Everett," Goddess called from inside before I could even lift my hand to knock. She'd changed into a dress and reclined on her sofa reading a book. Kurt and Nate were gone.

"Really, you're reading Dracula?" Xander giggled when he saw the cover, and I elbowed him to shut up.

"Goddess, this is Xander. The one I want to turn."

She lowered her book and looked him over, pursing her lips. He blushed. "He'll do." She went back to reading.

"One more thing," I said. Goddess lowered her book again, frowning. "Xander would like me to bite him."

"Good idea." Goddess said. "Go ahead and do it now."

I let my fang come down and turned to Xander.

"Holy shit, Everett." Xander backed up until he hit the door, his voice quaking. "That's creepy as fuck. And what happened to your other fang?"

I ignored his question and I dove for him. I latched onto his neck. Hot blood spurted into my mouth and I almost spit it out. So hot compared to the vampires, it felt like it burned my throat on the way down. Too hot. I could only manage a few swallows before withdrawing. I didn't even lick the last few drops that spurted from his puncture wound.

Babbling with fear and lust as the venom hit him, Xander went glassy-eyed and slid down the door to land on his back.

Chapter Twenty-Three

Metric Magic

Xander spent the night, too out of it from the venom to drive home. Especially after Goddess had bitten him again after I'd finished.

"I suppose I should give you a tour," I told him the next night when I woke up.

"Yeah, I guess." He glared at me. "Then I need to get home. I'm gonna lose my job if I miss another day."

I shrugged. "Not like you're gonna keep it as a vampire. Actually, you should just go home and pack, then come live here for the next few days until the ceremony."

"I tried to leave, but your flunkies wouldn't let me." Xander opened the door and pointed to the vampire standing guard outside.

"That's new," I admitted. "But it doesn't surprise me. You've agreed, and Goddess gets possessive."

"I tried to wake you, but it's like you were dead."

"Vampire, remember? Now let's go."

"I still haven't agreed." Xander crossed his arms.

"I don't think you have a choice anymore. Goddess likes you."

His eyes widened.

"Sorry." I laced an arm through his and started steering him through the house. "So, the good news is that being a vampire is actually pretty fun."

"Can we go to the kitchen first? I'm starving," Xander said, his stomach growling loudly.

I ignored him, marching him past the entrance to the kitchen. I was on a mission. "After we're done. Now, here's the chapel where we do the Sunrise Ceremony. You missed it last night."

"Imagine that," he laughed and touched his neck.

I dragged him to the basement door and opened it. "And down here we have a huge personal theater and a bowling—"

Pain stabbed at my head and I collapsed. *"Everett, stay out of the basement,"* Goddess screamed the order in my head.

"What's wrong?" Xander dropped down next me, grabbing at my arm.

"It's Goddess," I said, climbing to my feet. I had a feeling that's where they'd been keeping Jack. I'd been waiting for an excuse to go down there hoping that might keep me from being noticed. Guess it was too much to ask for.

"Sorry that she hurt you. I don't need to see the basement that badly." Xander's voice was low as I took him to the kitchen. "She's a little scary. Why doesn't she want you to use the theater?"

I sat at the kitchen table while Xander rooted through the fridge. "Because I'm not allowed to see J— him right now. But I miss him. I was trying to sneak down there."

I wiped away a tear.

"See who?" Xander said from the kitchen.

"I can't say his name." I sat up, crying hard now. "Goddess told me I'm not allowed."

"Jack?"

"Yes." I sniffled, and scrubbed at my face with my shirt sleeves.

"He's not in the basement." Xander scoffed. "I saw him yesterday."

"What?" My tears dried up almost instantly. I lowered my hands and stared at him across the kitchen island where he was making a sandwich with some of Jack's food.

"He's staying with Avery in some motel. Not sure where." Xander looked at me and shrugged. "I called Avery when I got your text. He didn't want me to come, but being bitten by a vampire was an amazing experience. Ten out of ten. I don't know why Avery was so bent out of shape about it. Who cares if it's addictive?"

I couldn't believe Goddess had lied to me. Relief followed by terror and then shame. "Jack's... alright."

"Yes, like I said. He's fine."

God, I wished I was better at pulling memories from the blood. Maybe if I'd known yesterday when I first drank from Xander, but I still wasn't very good at getting specific information from people. Goddess on the other hand...

My eyes flew open. Oh no! Goddess had bitten him too.

"Please tell me they're not still at the same motel!" I clutched at Xander's hands. If so, Goddess probably already had captured him, and really did have him in the basement.

Xander shook his head. "No, they've been moving hotels to stay away from the vampires. They said they were going to move again after I talked to them so that, quote, 'you won't betray us' end quote."

"Good." I sagged in relief. "But then how am I were supposed to let J—, him, know that I'm alright?"

"Goggle voice number. I text it and Jack gets an email. I messaged him today, while I was stuck here."

I twisted my hands together and gave him a shaky smile. "I'm sorry about dragging you into this. But thank you for letting me know he's not being tortured by...*her*," I finished with a whisper.

"I volunteered, Everett. I knew what I was getting into when I came over here. Do you know when you'll be changing me?"

"On the first night of the full moon. At midnight." I paused, hands shaking as I realized I was going to have to kill Xander. I liked him; even knowing he would rise as a vampire later... the thought sickened me.

Xander lit up, his eyes sparkling. "What? You sound like it's horrible. That's wonderful, Ev."

"Don't call me that. Only J— he can call me that nickname."

"Sure, sorry, Everett."

"It's fine. Will you tell... them... about when the change will happen?"

"Yes, it—"

"Wait, no, don't tell me. Anything I know, Goddess will know too." Crap. She bit him already though. She probably already knew he'd been sent in as a spy. So why had she let him keep his phone?

"Why do you call her that and not her name?" Xander pulled out his phone and started swiping away with one finger.

"It's another order, I think. I don't remember it, and when people tell me I just hear nothing."

Xander wrinkled his nose. "She can do that, just with her orders?"

I looked at him sideways. "I... can't promise I won't give you orders like that. I mean, I won't want to, but I don't know how it works. If she gives me an order, will I have to pass it along to you?" I shrugged helplessly.

"That part of being a vampire sucks."

"Yeah, it does."

"THAT WON'T BE SOON enough!" I yelled into the phone, pacing back and forth in the newest hotel room. "They'll change Xander before that."

I hadn't liked the plan of sending him into that house alone, but I hadn't been able to come up with anything better. No way we could snatch Everett and Brun while they were in that enormous house surrounded by hundreds of vampires. And it was too dangerous to have the house watched, but we needed to know when they left. This was the only way, much as I hated it.

On the phone, Dave tapped away at his keyboard, typing as we talked. "Look, they say they'll leave soon, but they're still researching her."

"They got Stacy, Dave." I ran my hand through my hair. Avery had gone to work, judging it safe enough. He was more than a match for any human agents the vampires might send after him during the day. At least we hoped. But I'd agreed, seeing that it wasn't him they were after.

"I know." Dave sighed heavily.

"Wait, back up. They've found Tawaret in the old records?"

"Yeah, it took a while because they had to find a translator. Tawaret is a Priestess of the Church of Ra. The vampires destroyed it during the time of Cleopatra."

"What's the hold up? What else do they need to know about her?"

"They think the texts might show how to destroy her. Obviously, the ancients knew how. They have translated enough to know that when their amulets are intact, they are immortal. Even cutting off their heads won't kill them."

"Yeah, that was something." I grimaced. "So, Everett was right about the amulet being the key. But the thing's just gold. Toss it in a fire."

Dave snorted. "We tried that when it was at the mage house. I was there. That thing has so many protection spells layered on it that nothing happened. And no one could figure out how to undo the enchantments on it. The spells the ancients use are different than the ones we use today. Think of it like... metric and imperial measuring systems. You might eventually be able to modify your metric ratchet to take off the bolt, but first you need to experiment to see what size you need. And if you aren't careful you might end up doing more damage trying to take it off. Stripping the bolt as it were. If we had the amulet, we might be able to eventually untangle the spells on it, but it'll be faster if we know where to start."

"The problem is that we don't know where the amulet is now. Wherever she hid it, even Everett can't feel it anymore."

"That's impossible. Isabella said it's soul-bound to Everett. The only way he wouldn't be able to feel his own soul..." Dave gave a helpless sound and I could feel the shrug through the phone. "It's impossible."

"His own soul..." I remembered how Tawaret had made it so Everett literally couldn't remember her name. "Could she order him to forget how to connect to the amulet?"

"I don't know." Dave hummed thoughtfully. "I'm not very familiar with control spells like the one attached to the amulet."

"Let me guess, super illegal." I walked over to a wall and bumped my head against it a few times.

"Ohhh yeah. I mean, not that it stops people, mind, so it pops up now and again. Been a few cases since I started."

"Well, tell me what you know." I knew Dave was older than he looked, but I'd never asked how old or what had happened.

"For starters, she can't order Everett to do anything he really, strongly objects to. It's more like coercion that's been magically strengthened."

"Okay." That tracked with what I'd seen. And she didn't use it often, instead using trickery, fear, and threats to get Everett to do what she wanted.

"But the amulet is part of Everett now. Like a finger, and don't think she couldn't block Everett from feeling himself."

"But then how did she hide it?" What had Everett said? That he only felt calm when he was holding it. And he was calm. So how could he be holding it, yet not holding it? It hit me. I knew where it was. "Everett has it! He's had it the entire time."

"Wouldn't you have seen it?" Dave sounded skeptical, and I didn't blame him. "You've been living with him."

"I would have if he was holding or wearing it." I felt like an idiot for not considering it before. "But he's a vampire, and heals instantly. Think about how smugglers hide drugs in drug mules."

"It doesn't matter if we don't know how to destroy it, Jack." Dave's voice droned in my ear, but I hardly heard him.

"But we'll kill two birds with one stone if we can get Everett away from her. Can't you at least send some shifters or mages to help?" As I said that I remembered my contact, Annabelle, and the elder vampire, Rowan, from the PCA. Pembroke too, if he hadn't flown home already. They might help me. The shifters are all pretty pissed at her kidnapping Brun. Quite a few volunteered, but they are all civilians. A couple were security guards, including the tiger shifter I'd met on run. Most just worked service jobs at the casinos. But the elder vampires might be able to recruit some powerful vampires to shore up their ranks.

Dave sighed heavily. "I'll see what I can do. You at least know a time or place when Everett will be out of the house?"

"Xander said full moon, at midnight. Just like Lady Ann's ceremony. But the problem is that we don't know where yet and I haven't heard anything else from Xander."

Dave gasped. "So, more bad news."

"What?" I growled. What else could go wrong now?

"The jackal that lives in Montana, the one you told me she asked about?"

"Yeah? What about her?"

"She was kidnapped last night."

"Fuck."

CHAPTER TWENTY-FOUR

THE SACRIFICE

THE FULL MOON WAS bright overhead. We took two cars over to the Mandalay Bay. Goddess wanted to do the ceremony there, on the roof overlooking the Luxor.

"In the shadows of the pyramid" was actually what she'd wanted. We had settled on the roof to keep humans from interrupting.

Goddess set up a circle similar to Lady Ann's from the park all those months ago back in Portland. Instead of tiki torches, we used votive candles barely an inch tall. The specially carved bowl and knife were replaced with a stainless-steel bowl and chef's knife borrowed from the kitchen. What we had was like a dollar store version of the spell. Goddess had overheard me telling that joke to Xander as we'd gathered things up to head over to the Luxor, and told me that it was the intent that was more important than the tools. I still thought it was tacky looking though.

Now that the moment of truth was here, Xander was wide-eyed, pale, and trembling next to me. I kept my eyes fixed on the door to the roof, expecting Jack to pop out at any moment, come to save Xander... and me. But as the moon drifted higher, my hopes fell.

Goddess had brought along a jackal with her, held on a short lead with a choke collar around its neck. I knew without even looking at the tag on the collar that it had to be Brun. Jack's animal form was mostly tan and gold all over, but this jackal had a dark black and gray stripe along their back.

I drifted away from the other vampires to the edge of the rooftop, staring out over the flashing lights of Vegas. A cool night breeze swept over me, bringing the smell of car exhaust. I clutched my amulet to my chest, trying not to feel hopeless and trapped, and failing. I was terrified of what was going to happen to Xander after I changed him.

Nate came up behind me and stood quietly by my side for several long moments.

"Everett, come here." Goddess words were not an order, but I had no reason not to obey. I drifted over to her. She tugged the choke chain tight as I approached.

"Sit," she said. Brun whimpered and sat. "Good jackal." Goddess stroked between their ears with her free hand.

"Yes, Goddess?"

"When it's time, do you know what to do?"

I shook my head.

Goddess tisked. "It's ever so simple." She pointed at Xander, the chain rattling. "Xander will kneel in front of the bowl, which will have your amulet in it. Holding his head over the bowl, you'll slit his throat with the knife, making sure to catch as much of his blood as possible in the bowl."

"What!" Xander yelled, clutching at his neck. "I thought you were going to make me a vampire."

"I am" I glanced at him. "That's how I died too."

"Nate, tie Xander up. It's almost time."

"Then what?" I prompted her as Oakley and Stacy held Xander down. He started screaming as Nate zip-tied his arms and legs together.

"After his blood is all drained, lean his body forward so that his forehead touches the amulet. Then you wait."

Hands bound behind his back and legs secured at the ankles and knees, Nate dropped Xander in front of the bowl in the center of the circle.

Goddess pressed the knife into my hands.

"Now?" I whispered, staring down at the knife.

Goddess glanced up at the moon, considering. "Not quite yet."

Nate and Oakley had their hands clamped on Xander's shoulders, keeping him in place. This is what Lady Ann had gotten wrong with her ceremony; the sacrifice was yourself. I'd been changed in the dumpster without any theatrics. Maybe they were just window dressing. If that were the case, I didn't know why Goddess had bothered waiting, except for tradition's sake. She liked tradition, as I'd seen with the sunrise ceremony.

Xander and I had bonded over the last few days; Xander too nervous to leave the room and me too depressed. I'd known this was coming, but even then, I hadn't prepared for the reality of standing in the cold and being expected to slice the throat of my best friend.

He'd rise again, a vampire, but also as my slave.

I hope Jack had gotten somewhere safe. Gone back to Portland, maybe.

"I need a moment." My hands shook as I set the knife down in the gravel next to a crying Xander.

He looked up at me, panic clear in his face. "Everett, I changed my mind."

"Almost time, Everett!" Goddess called. "You'll need your strength. Vampires, I want you each to let Everett give you a blessing before we begin."

"Yes, Goddess," they chorused, then made their way over to me. I took a long gulp from each one.

I swayed as I got to my feet. The others returned to setting up, lighting the candles, their eyes slightly glazed from my venom.

"Everett, when you are ready, place your amulet in the bowl," Goddess called to me. "It is time to get started."

Shit. "Yes, Goddess," I said back.

She hadn't given me an order, thank God. I wondered if this was like the amulet making process, where it had to be my choice. I frowned, thinking about it. No, probably not, and it didn't need to be the sacrifice's choice either, I knew that from experience. Even if she didn't order me to do it, she might just do it herself, and I didn't want to do that to Xander. No, I'd at least do him the honor of killing him myself.

Still, I turned my back on the proceedings to stare back out over the city, delaying as long as possible. I was still swaying a bit on my feet, this time from the effects of the vampire blood. The sensation was a bit like being drunk back when I'd been human, but more pleasant, and came with a buzz of energy that alcohol had never given me.

"Careful," Nate said, putting a hand on my shoulder and drawing me back a step. "You're too close to the edge. I'm not sure even you would survive that fall."

The horizon line stared back at me, tempting me. Except, with my own amulet now, going over the edge didn't matter. I definitely would survive. All jumping would do would delay things until the next full moon. Which... maybe that would be enough time for... for what? If Jack were smart, he'd be far away and getting farther.

A tear ran down my cheek. I was between a rock and a hard place. Nothing I could do would stop this.

I craned out over the edge to look down at all the little people scurrying about with no idea of the vampire drama going on right under their noses.

But another four weeks or more... maybe by then the PCA would be able to act. I owed them the delay. I owed it to Xander.

Not letting myself think too much about what I was doing, I threw out my arms and leaned forward, letting gravity take me.

"It's already dark, Jack," Avery protested as I hurried him down the sidewalk. "Even you aren't crazy enough to go after vampires at night."

"I'm not going after them, I'm just rescuing Everett." I pulled him along.

"Jack, this is madness. It's just the two of us." Avery tugged at my arm but I shook him off.

"Did you message everyone to get to the rendezvous point?"

"Yes, but—"

"That'll have to be good enough," I said, and meant it. "Now, are you with me or am I on my own?" In reality, I had no idea how I would to do this alone, but I'd been wracked with guilt since running away last week. And now Xander's life was on the line.

"I'm not abandoning my friend, either. Who do you take me for?" Avery threw up his hands and pushed away from me. The crowd parted around us. "But why did Xander wait so long to message us the location? There's no time to get anyone else. With just two of us, it's a suicide mission."

"Because this is a trap," I snapped back. "We knew this was a possibility going into it if she bit Xander, but I'm not giving up on either—"

Abrupt screaming cut me off. "Oh my god, someone jumped! Call an ambulance!"

Avery and I both whirled along with the rest of the crowd to see a form plummeting off the roof.

"No!" I screamed bolting towards the falling figure. I had a sick feeling I knew who it was; I hoped I was wrong.

I fought against the crowd, who was rushing away from where the body had hit. Shoving people aside with abandon and ignoring the cries of protest. I burst out into a cleared circle.

Everett lay in the center of the sidewalk on his back, spread-eagled with blood spreading in a pool out from his body. He wore his white ceremonial robe over a pair of jeans and tennis shoes. One Good Samaritan was trying to give him CPR already. Snarling I shoved her off.

"Shit, Everett," I said, dropping to my knees next to him. His eyes were open, but he didn't respond. I glanced up to the roof and shook my head. Made my job easier. I scooped him up in my arms, ignoring the cries of protest from the Good Samaritan and the other onlookers. No breath, but that was normal.

"He's not breathing! You need to wait for the ambulance," one of the bystanders called.

I ignored them, hoisting Everett up into my arms. Avery clapped his hand on my shoulder. "Let's go, my car."

"What about Xander?" I huffed, dashing after him. Everett was bleeding all over my shirt, but I didn't care.

People parted for us with wide eyes and I noticed more than a few had cell phones out recording.

Avery glanced at the moon. "They can't do it without Everett, right?"

"I don't think so." Everett was deathly still in my arms.

"So Xander should be safe for now."

I didn't respond, but I hoped so. Climbing into the back seat, spread blood everywhere, but Avery didn't seem to mind though. He just started the car and peeled away from the curb.

Everett's skin was stone cold under my hands. I touched his forehead and then held my wrist in front of his mouth. No reaction. Prying up one eyelid, his eye was rolled back in his head. Still no reaction. Everett's clothing was covered in blood and his body moved oddly in my arms, and I suspected he had multiple broken bones. I could feel them popping and healing under my hands, but he was so hurt that it was going slowly.

Better to do this now. He was already hurt, probably not aware anything around him. But where would she have put it?

"Do you have a knife?" I asked Avery.

"A knife?" Avery laughed. "No, why?"

I just shook my head and started poking at Everett's wounds and body with my fingers and hands. Mostly at his chest and stomach. That was the only place that had enough room.

There it was. Palpitating his stomach, I felt something hard there, deep down. I traced the outline with my finger. Maybe I should leave it where it was for now.

"Why do you need a knife?" Avery repeated.

"He's not healing and he's not biting me. I need to feed him."

"Goddamn kidding me," Avery mumbled, then louder he said. "Isn't it better to leave him unconscious? This way Tawaret can't control him. Besides, he might be, like, dead, dead. I'm not sure even a vampire could survive a fall like that."

Sighing, I pulled Everett closer. Avery was wrong. He had to be.

Something hard in Ev's pocket ground into my hip. I fished out a gold disc the size of a fist, a little rough around the edges, with Everett's name chiseled out in block letters on one side.

I hadn't known about this part, but it made sense that she'd forced him to make his own amulet. Dave had said that with the amulet, she was immortal. If Everett had one now, too, then... he had to be still alive. But then, why jump from the building? He had to know it wouldn't kill him.

"No, he's still alive." I heaved a deep sigh. "But you're right, better he stays unconscious."

I put Everett's amulet in my pocket and then pushed his hair back away from his face.

"What were you thinking, Ev?" I whispered.

Avery pulled into the parking lot out in the desert. It was about half full. Most had already changed, and animals flitted in and out of the small area illuminated by the headlights before Avery shut them off. I spotted a massive bear, a tiger, and some wolves before the light died. Annabelle, Rowan, and a handful of others stood a ways apart from the shifters.

"I'm going to go remind everyone about the vampires being our allies," Avery said, getting out of the car and then stooping to look inside.

"Find me something sharp first," I told him. "I need to take the amulet out before *she* gets here."

Avery growled but gave a sharp nod before getting out. He popped the trunk then came around and handed me a small multi-tool covered with grease stains.

I popped open the tiny little knife tool, then stopped and took a deep breath. "Everett, if you're awake, I'm sorry for what I'm about to do."

I stabbed the little knife into Everett's stomach and started sawing. He didn't so much as twitch.

Red flesh yawned, but no blood came out. Falling that far had done a number on him. Any other time he'd be healing too quickly for this to work.

Good, better that he not be awake for this. I stuck two fingers in the hole, and after a few tries fished out a very slimy ziplock bag.

The back door opening startled me out of my contemplation.

"What is that?" Avery wrinkled his nose, pointing to the bloody ziplock.

"This," I said, holding it up, "is the key to defeating Tawaret."

"Yes!" he pumped his fist. "So, we just need to destroy it to kill her?"

I shrugged. "I think so, but we can't do it right now. We don't know the spell—"

In my arms Everett shuddered. His eyes popped open. Blood red, they flicked up at me, barely seeming to register I was there. Everett turned his head and buried his teeth into my bicep. I yelped and grabbed his hair, trying to pull him away, but tugging at him ripped his teeth further into my arm.

"Holy shit!" Avery reached for Everett, trying to drag him off of me, but all that happened was the three of us tumbled out of the backseat onto the asphalt.

I landed on Everett, and Everett's head cracked against the blacktop. That seemed to bring him out of it. His teeth withdrew from my arm. He looked like Tawaret now, only one fang.

Avery kicked at Everett's head while pulling me to my feet.

"Avery, stop, he's fine."

Panting hard, Everett froze, but his single fang stayed down. His eyes flicked back and forth over me from where he still lay on his back.

"What happened to your fang?" I asked, clutching at my bleeding arm.

"Amulet." He closed his eyes. "I feel it again, Jack!"

"I know." I'd dropped it in the chaos and it lay a few feet from Everett. I didn't want to touch the thing directly, so I picked up the bag by the edges and stuck it in my pocket with Everett's amulet, heedless of the blood. My clothes were already ruined anyway.

"Where?" He hissed it out slowly, still not moving. One of his legs was bent at an odd angle and the cut I'd made on his stomach gapped open. His skin clung to his bones, he half looked like a mummy.

"Inside you." I pointed at his belly.

"Plan?" he hissed.

"I'm taking a group of the shifters to the vampire house to look for Brun," Avery said. "You'll stay here with Jack to draw out as many vampires as possible."

Everett's head rocked back and forth. "Brun... with... Goddess."

Avery swore. "You sure?"

Everett's eyes opened, fading back to their usual brown and his fang pulled back in. "Yes. On... leash..."

"Xander?" I asked, trying to keep my dread down.

"Fine. That's why jumped." He winced. "Hurts."

"Thanks." Avery crouched down and reached for Everett but then pulled his hand back.

Ev took a shuddering breath and closed his eyes. "Thirsty."

"Sorry, Ev. When Goddess gets here, it's safer if you're too weak to attack us." I crouched next to Everett and stroked his hair.

He whimpered. "Understand." He slid an arm a few inches towards me. "Amulet?"

"I'm going to keep them, just in case you..." I couldn't finish the sentence. I didn't want Tawaret to take him back, but I wasn't sure even this group could take her on for long. I glanced over at Avery. "Actually, if I took Everett now and started driving, she wouldn't be able to catch us before dawn."

"But if Brun and Xander are with her..." Avery shook his head. "We need her to come here, to give us a chance to rescue them."

"PCA?" Everett asked, his words slurring.

"You don't know?" Avery snarled. "Your Goddess took it over. They can't help us."

"But the good news is, the brains in Africa have been going through the archive. They found a spell that can destroy the amulet, make her vulnerable." I rested my hand on his forehead. He was colder than I'd ever felt before. I knew with the amulet he'd be fine, but I still worried.

"Cast..." He hissed in pain as he sucked in a breath for another word. "Now?"

"So, the bad news is that they're having trouble translating it." Dave had sent me an email with more details, but I didn't want to blow up this last stand with bad news that the documents might be too damaged for them to ever be able to finish. Everett and Avery deserved at least a little hope.

Avery glanced at his phone and stood. "She's not going to be far behind us. We need to start getting our defenses ready." He tossed his keys to me. "Jack, you stay human. Carry Everett out past the end of the parking lot. We'll distract Tawaret. Once we've got Brun and Xander, you take off, away from Vegas."

I nodded and scooped Everett up in my arms. Everett yelped. He turned his face to my chest, and I tensed, but he kept his mouth shut.

The shifters parted around us, growling and stalking in wide circles.

I went about ten feet off into the dirt before Avery's giant white wolf trotted up.

"This is good. Don't want to get too far away from the car." He sat down on his rump, cocking his head as he looked both of us over. His muzzle pulled back. "You both smell like blood."

"Shocking," I muttered, rolling my eyes as I crouched to gently set Everett in the dirt. He slumped against me, shaking. I think he would have been crying if he weren't so drained. I was impressed by his control to not bite me while I carried him.

Rowan and Annebelle joined me, and Avery and I laid out our plan. Annabelle had two other mages with her, and Rowan had three more vampires. They'd help the shifters.

Chapter Twenty-Five

Clash of the Supernaturals

AFTER I'D HIT THE ground, I'd lost all sense of my body. All I'd been able to feel was the amulet in my pocket. I felt trapped, unable to move or speak. It was horrible. If this is what Goddess had dealt with for thousands of years while she'd been sleeping, I was surprised she was as sane as she was.

I don't know what woke me up, but I kinda wished I hadn't. *Everything* hurt. I knew whose arms I was in, I recognized Jack's smell, but I couldn't resist a small bite. His blood tasted nasty, but it did help lessen some of the pain.

Being surrounded by animals when Jack pulled me out of the car was disconcerting. I hadn't known where we were going, but it made sense. Who better to protect against vampires? Still, I was nervous. Especially with all the pulled back ears and growling being directed my way.

Goddess raged in my head a moment, trying to move me, but I was just too drained and exhausted. Even she couldn't do more than make me twitch. Defeated, I felt her leave, but I knew she was on the way. She wouldn't give up that easily.

I wasn't sure about Jack and Avery's plan, but I hoped it worked. Xander and Brun deserved to be free of her.

Unable to do anything else, I closed my eyes and listened. Jack's heart pounded against my ear. He'd tried to project calm, but I could smell the fear in his sweat and the way his heart hammered. Our advantage was that Goddess couldn't feel the amulets, only me. If Jack could get away, he could take them to the PCA to destroy when they translated the spell.

"Jack?" I rasped, my throat dry.

"Shh, Everett, don't talk. Save your strength." Jack stroked my back. A nice gesture, except for the stabs of pain it sent through me.

"No, important." I took a moment to recover. "Leave me. Take amulets, go. Destroy." I wanted to say more, but even that much was almost more than I could do.

"I can't." I felt moisture hit my head. "I won't."

"Can't..." the words died in my throat. I swallowed and tried again. "Can't follow without me."

"Everett..." Jack's voice broke and he hugged me tighter to him. The hug was agony on my broken bones.

I think I passed out a moment. When I came to, I was lying on the dirt. I could feel Jack's heat nearby.

I wished I could be as confident and strong as Jack. I rolled my head to look up at him standing over me. Imagined it was me standing there, protecting Jack. The amulets in my pockets; taking them to be destroyed.

Suddenly I stood in a hotel room, pacing, talking on the phone. I recognized Dave's voice on the other end. Dave was telling him that they didn't have a translation ready. Then I was in front of the computer reading an email from Dave. Dead end. The scrolls and texts were too damaged. They were probably never going to be able to finish.

"Better hurry up with whatever you're planning," Avery said. His voice pulled me from Jack's memories. "Two cars just got off the highway headed this way."

"Thirsty," I managed to get out. I tried to push up, but was too weak. Jack had lied about them being able to destroy the amulet.

Avery glanced at me and snorted. "Vampires. And I think you lied about getting used to the smell."

"Maybe. But I find it almost comforting now."

The animals prowled up to form a line between me and the road. Why were some still human? But then another of Jack's memories told me they were vampires and mages who'd volunteered to help. I felt so helpless lying here.

If we couldn't destroy the amulet this was all going to be for nothing. She was already so powerful. Hundreds of vampires already at her beck and call. Even the vampires not with her were too scared to stand up to her; look how few Rowan was able to gather against her.

With the amulet, she was unkillable. The most they could do was incapacitate her. Put her in a coffin for another thousand years. And what about me then? And Xander if I made him one of us? Would I be too dangerous to be allowed free? Of course, because otherwise she could control me.

Fuck.

Goddess had made the amulet. Maybe she knew a way to destroy it? Even if she did, though, she'd never tell me.

But there were other ways. I knew that. Just like I'd seen what Jack had tried to keep from me.

Avery padded out into the road. A few of the largest animals joined him; the tiger, a massive brown bear, a lioness, and a timber wolf. Though the smaller brown wolf only came up to Avery's shoulder, the four of them were still pretty intimidating.

In my human form my eyes couldn't penetrate the darkness, but I knew the others stalked around us. Occasionally I saw a shimmer of eyes in the growing reflections of the headlights coming towards us.

The two cars screeched to a stop in the middle of the road about 10 feet from where Avery and the rest waited. I shifted to better hide Everett's body behind my shadow; not that it would matter with Tawaret, but the rest hopefully might take a moment longer to spot him.

Vampires hopped out of almost every door, red eyes flashing in the moonlight. They formed a line across from the shape shifters, mages, and rival vampires, hissing and barring their fangs at them.

Tawaret got out last, dragging Brun on a short chain out after her. Brun's jackal form was much larger than mine. A black stripe ran down their back that I didn't have. Tawaret had a thick choke chain wrapped around their neck, held so tight that Brun walked on tiptoe.

"Sit," Tawaret ordered, standing a bit behind the line of vampires, lit from behind by the car's still running headlights. Brun sat, curling their fluffy tail around their feet. I found myself rubbing my throat in sympathy.

Even from here I could hear the low growling that rumbled from Avery's throat. When he saw Brun, his ears went back and he snarled.

Much as I wanted to change and join them at the front line, I knew the plan. Also, if I did, I'd lose my pants and the amulets in the pockets. Even if we couldn't destroy them, keeping them away from Goddess at least limited her power.

A scrape behind me drew my attention and I glanced back to see Everett dragging himself across the rocks in Tawaret's direction, leaving a bloody streak in the dirt. I was almost impressed. I hadn't even thought he could move.

"Oh! I see that not only have you brought my apprentice, but you've found my errant jackal!"

"We won't let you take him," Avery snarled. I knew he meant me, but Tawaret took it the other way.

Tawaret pulled tighter on Brun's leash and gave Avery a predatory smile. "Take him?" She gestured towards me and Everett behind me. "As you can see, he's clearly coming to me of his own volition."

Hair sprouted along my arm and I had to count back from ten to calm down. "No," I growled.

"Give us back Brun and Xander," Avery snarled.

"Where is Xander?" I whispered. I didn't see him in any of the car windows. Had they left him behind?

Despite my whisper, Tawaret heard me. She glanced my way, her smile crinkling up her eyes. "Xander is here. Kurt? Fetch him. It's late enough now we'll need to do the ceremony here anyway." She sighed heavily, glancing around and tugging at Brun's leash. "I'd wanted to do this at the pyramid, but I suppose here will do."

We all tensed as Kurt flashed back to the car and opened the trunk. He dragged out a crying Xander, bound hand and foot with zipties.

"Xander!" Avery yelled, taking a step forward. Stacy and Oakley mirrored him, crouched and growling, blocking his way.

"Stacy, it's me," I pleaded. Her eyes were blank and she looked at me without recognition.

Everett had crawled his way to my feet. I casually put a foot on his back and pushed him down. He let out a hiss and went limp. Passed out again I hoped.

"Give me what's mine and I'll let you and the others stay and watch the ascension of my newest high priest and demi-god." Kurt dropped Xander at her feet and Tawaret nudged him with her foot.

"Never!" Avery snarled and charged. That broke the seal, and both sides charged at each other, fangs, claws, and teeth bared. The mages hung back, fire sprouting from their hands.

Four vampires darted past Avery and his three lieutenants, heading towards me and Everett. I tensed, but prowling shifters emerged from the darkness like vengeful shadows to tear into the vampires. I winced as three wolves tore into Nate with their teeth. A fourth pounced, swinging a silver bracelet held in her teeth into Nate's face. He screamed loud enough that I clapped my hands over my ears. Black lines snaked up from where the bracelet hit him and he collapsed clutching at face and screaming.

With Nate down the wolves retreated, dashing away to help a lynx and a cheetah that were nipping at Stacy. I almost felt bad for her, but I wouldn't stop the shifters from attacking her. She'd clearly chosen a side.

Two vampires rolled together in the car's headlights, Rowan wrestling with Oakley.

I crouched, trying to see past the chaos. I caught glimpses of Tawaret, still standing proud holding Brun's leash. She caught my gaze and winked, stroking Brun's head between his ears.

The fighting rolled closer to me, the vampires gaining ground on the shifters and their allies. The mages threw bursts of fire at the approaching vampires. A few went up in flames but most were able to dodge the spells.

Although we outnumbered the vampires at the moment, but more cars were pulling up and dumping out more of her vampires.

Shifter teeth and claws hurt the vampires, but after a few minutes their injuries healed, whereas the shifters had to change to heal and the intense fighting didn't leave time to change. Even if it did, changing was taxing all on its own. Not something you could do over and over again all night. But the vampires never tired. Even with the improvised silver weapons, Tawaret's vampires were slowly winning.

Many of the shifter's feral forms were too small to do much damage, and few of them were able to maintain the half form to fight. Even those that could tired after a few moments, reverting back to their feral shapes.

A mage went down screaming under a pile of vampires. The other two were fighting back-to-back, slinging fire as fast as they could chant the spell, but the vampires were closing in by dint of sheer numbers.

An injured wolf limped past me, running further into the desert, one paw held high. Then the cheetah, a large gash bleeding along her side.

Kurt fought with two wolves and a massive badger; he was covered with bite marks and cuts, and looked like he'd be going down soon. Nearby Oakley held off another wolf and a lynx from going after an injured Nate, who still clutched at his blackened face.

Shit. No one had even gotten close to Tawaret.

I spoke too soon. Avery roared as he and the bear trampled Kurt, heading right for her. Avery was in warrior half form, almost as large as the bear.

"Brun, attack!" Tawaret dropped his leash.

The jackal stood up on two legs, muscles growing on their chest, muzzle lengthening as they transformed into their warrior form. Then with a howl they leaped between the charging shifters and the Goddess.

Avery backpedaled, tail tucking between his legs. The bear gruffed and made a half-hearted swipe at Brun, but pulled back before connecting.

Tawaret twisted her fingers in Xander's hair and dragged him back towards the cars, away from the fighting.

Damn it.

Then I had more important things to worry about. Stacy slashed down at the last wolf between me and her then locked red eyes with me.

My hackles rose again, hair sprouting up my arms, and I couldn't hold back the change any longer. I managed to stop halfway, keeping up on two legs so I didn't lose my pants and kept use of my hands, even if they did have massive claws on them, I'd still be able to pick up Everett and run if need be. But I wanted to wait and see before running off if we might still come out on top and rescue Brun and Xander.

I roared, well, howled, jackals weren't really good at roaring, in Stacy's face as she swiped at me. The blow was deflected by the thick fur on my shoulder, but it did tear away most of my shirt. In retaliation I snapped my jaws at her, managing to catch her arm. The vampire blood burned in my mouth like hot sauce, but tasting of rotten meat.

Stacy's other hand snapped out in a backhand blow that caught the side of my head. I snapped my jaws open in surprise, stumbling a few steps to the side. My head rung. While I was distracted, she pulled out a pocket knife, flicked it open, and stabbed it into my leg. I yelped in pain and fell, my leg no longer willing to support my weight.

My former boss fought dirty, it seemed.

I grabbed the handle with one oversized paw, and tried to pull it out, but it was buried all the way up to the hilt. Even a small tug on it sent a wave of agony through me, so I left it where I was.

Stacy scooped up Everett under one arm like a football and dashed off between one blink and the next. The shifters let her pass, too busy with fighting to care about one fleeing vampire.

I limped after her, but the pain was too much. My body shifted the rest of the way into jackal form, shrinking and pulling in on itself and knitting up my wounds as I changed.

The knife popped free as the bone knit, falling to the dirt with a metallic clink. Even with my shifting, I still bled some. I shook off the rags of my bloody clothing and gave chase. I realized after a step that I'd forgotten the amulets, but Jack was more important.

Avery and the bear still fought with Brun. The black-backed jackal was still in warrior form, holding back the other two shifters who were reluctant to hurt them. Brun had no such hesitation. Avery's white fur was stained with red on one side and he'd reverted to wolf form, but he looked more pissed than hurt.

I limped by on four legs, and Brun glanced over at me. The bear took advantage and used his massive size to drive Brun to the pavement. Brun clawed and snapped at the bear but the bear didn't even react.

Stacy had laid Everett out at Tawaret's feet already. She gave me a bloody grin as I limped towards them, ears flat and tail tucked between my legs.

Tawaret spotted me and gave me a wide smile. "Jack! So glad to see you've come to your senses."

My hackles rose and I dropped into a fighting stance, snarling at her. "No, I'm here to get Everett back."

"Oh? And how's that going for you?" She pointed behind me and I risked a peek over my shoulder.

A few shifters were up and fighting, but they were being quickly overwhelmed by vampires. All three mages were down. Injured shifters, some already back in human form and some still in animal, were scattered around on the pavement and dirt. The bear had subdued a snapping Brun, but she and Avery were surrounded by four vampires. No sign of Rowan and his allies, but in the dark the vampires all looked like red eyes to me.

"Shit," I panted. The backup plan was shot too. My pants along with the amulets and the keys to Avery's car lay in the dirt on the other side of the parking lot. I'd been so angry about my boss, or former boss, taking Everett that I'd lost myself.

"Stacy, go start setting up for the ceremony. Kurt, you and the others start tying up the shifters. I don't want any more interruptions—"

She was cut off by a burst of light and a pair of overlapping screams, followed by a wave of magic washing over us that made all my fur stand on end like I'd just been zapped by static electricity. I whirled.

Oakley screamed with his head thrown back. Red light poured from his mouth and eyes. As abruptly as it started, the light cut off, and Oakley collapsed in a heap.

I froze, unable to process what had happened. Nate let out a howl of grief, dropping the tiger he'd been carrying to dash towards Oakley.

"Nate, no!" Tawaret gasped, but she was too late.

He dropped to his knees next to Oakley and let out another howl, then pulled Oakley's body to his chest. Oakley's body looked shrunken in and the skin dried and leathery. And the smell coming to me on the wind... I wrinkled my nose and gagged, wishing I were human right now. My jackal nose was too sensitive.

Nate yelped, pulling at Oakley's hand. Something gold there glittered in the light of the full moon. He picked it up, moving his hand as if to throw it, when the magic swirled in the air again. Nate screamed, shinning briefly with light before collapsing on top of Oakley.

Tawaret hissed out something in a language I didn't know, but was fairly certain was a curse.

A gasp from behind me made my ears prick up. I turned to see Everett sitting up, his eyes wide. His skin was rosy and healthy looking, and all his wounds were gone. Totally healed.

Chapter Twenty-Six

SHATTERED

I GASPED, LIFE FLOWING through my body. My eyes snapped open and I sat up, momentarily confused about what was happening. All the pain was gone, and I was no longer in the dirt, but on asphalt.

"Everett?" Jack said in a whine. He stepped towards me, tail wagging and touched the end of his snout to my forehead.

"I'm fine..." I trailed off, spotting Xander lying next to me, still bound in zipties and crying. "What happened?" I reached for him and he cringed away from my hand.

"You let your amulet out of your hands." Goddess dropped my amulet in front of me. It clattered against the asphalt, sending reverberations through my mouth where my missing fang had been.

I could still taste the blood in my mouth. I nodded and picked it up, feeling numb. My heart ached. "Who did it kill?" I whispered.

"Nate and Oakley. But no matter, we have more than enough followers now. Besides, this worked out. You had to have eaten someone regardless before changing Xander. Otherwise, you would have been too weak." Goddess tossed her hair over her shoulder with a sniff.

I buried my hand in the rough of Jack's neck fur and swallowed hard, noting as I did so that his fur was matted all over with blood. More blood covered the asphalt around me. Practically saturated the air. The wild tang of shapeshifter blood.

"Don't worry, Everett," Goddess said, I think mistaking my trepidation. "You could survive much more damage than this as long as your amulet survives. As long as it exists, you are immortal."

That applied to her as much as me. No matter what schemes Jack and I came up with to escape, she'd be chasing behind us. Relentless. Yet, no one knew how to destroy the amulet.

The PCA's material was too degraded. The book Lady Ann had gotten the immortality spell from was missing, if it even had the amulet destruction spell in it. The only one who might possibly know how to destroy it was Goddess, the person least likely to share that secret with me... unless she didn't have a choice.

I suddenly knew what I had to do. Bolstered by two vampires' worth of blood, I lunged for her as fast as I could. Her eyes widened and she jerked back away from me, but I was faster. I sunk my fang into the side of her leg, just above the ankle.

Unlike the spicy tingle of the vampire blood, the taste of her on my tongue made me numb. As I swallowed the numbness spread out down my throat to my stomach.

"Everett, stop!" Goddess yelled an order.

I sat up, licking my lips. That was alright; I think I had enough for what I needed to do anyway. Goddess's blood, Goddess's memories.

As I sat up, Goddess backhanded me across the face. The force snapped my neck and sent me rolling away. I landed on my back, staring up at the stars whirling above me. My neck reset with a crack, but I barely felt it over the tingling numbness in my throat.

Jack growled and jumped between us as I tried to get back up, but he was slow, already hurt, and couldn't dodge Goddess's kick. Her foot hit him right in the stomach, sending him flying back into my chest. My vision blurred as I hugged him. My plan was doomed from the start if Goddess didn't give me a chance to work.

Goddess stood in front of me, her face a mask of fury as she stalked towards me. I cowered, trying to cover Jack's body with my own. A furry form leapt over my head, landing between me and Goddess.

Brun in warrior form, half-human, half-jackal. They towered over Goddess, foam dripping from their peeled back lips. The choke collar was gone. Goddess looked up at him scowling.

"Brun, sit. Change." She pointed to her side.

"No," Brun snarled, gravelly voice going even deeper. They pounced and I winced as their fangs tore into Goddess' arm.

"Jack," I grabbed the tip of one of Jack's over-sized ears and whispered in it. "I saw in your memories that the PCA doesn't know how to destroy the amulet, so I bit Goddess to learn the ceremony."

Jack yelped but then their eyes widened and he bobbed his head in understanding. "I understand. I'll help Brun keep her distracted." Jack licked my chin and dashed off. By the time he reached Brun and Goddess he was grown into his warrior form, standing on two legs, claws extended. He slashed at Goddess' side.

The numbness was spreading down my arms and legs now. I had to hurry. I didn't think it would kill me, not with my amulet still intact, but if it knocked me out too long, I'd lose access to Goddess' memories.

Trusting that Brun and Jack could keep her occupied, I stood, snatching up a discarded pocket knife that lay nearby. I could smell the blood on the blade. It was small, but better protection than nothing if anyone tried to stop me.

Stunned vampires had started stumbling in the direction of the new fighting. Avery and a few of the less hurt shifters like the bear were blocking them. Kurt looked up at me with wide eyes as I ran by.

"I order you not to help Goddess," I snapped at them before running off again. I didn't think they'd listen, but I couldn't stay to make sure. At least I might sow a little doubt and confusion enough to slow them down.

I could feel Goddess amulet nearby. Odd that I could suddenly feel it now. Perhaps Goddess had taken it out of hiding after Jack had taken me.

But no, when I followed the siren's lure of her amulet, I found it in the pocket of Jack's discarded and ripped pants, inside a bloody ziplock bag. I'd have to ask Jack what had happened later.

Dropping to my knees in the dirt, I sat back and closed my eyes. Rather than focusing on what I wanted to know, I tried as I'd been taught and let my mind drift. I'm Goddess, and I want to destroy the amulet of my troublesome high priest.

I opened my eyes and let Goddess's memories take over. I used my finger to draw a line in the dirt around me, calling a bit of magic to the circle as I went, closing it with a spell word. I felt it snap in place, and a hazy film formed between me and everything outside of the circle.

Next, I needed the amulet. The bag was so slick with blood that it took me a few tries to open the bag and dump the amulet out into my hands. The numbness was almost to my wrists now and my eyesight was turning black at the edges. I had to hurry.

I set the amulet on the dirt and picked up the pocket knife, raising it high above my head in a two-handed grip, blade painted down. I let myself sink back into the fugue state and yelled out the words to the spell that would sever the connection between the Goddess and the piece of her soul trapped in the amulet.

I also suddenly knew that the traumatic loss of a large portion of the soul might very well kill her. She'd been living through the amulet for so long and been awake for such a short period of time that there might not be anything left outside the amulet. I remembered the soul deep pain that had torn at me when Isabella had magically separated me from the amulet.

A surge of guilt made me lower the knife and twist to look at her. Jack and Brun were losing. Goddess' hands were bloody all the way up to her elbow and both jackals were covered in gashes, their fur matted with blood.

My shoulders slumped, but it had to be done. Besides, it wasn't like I hadn't killed before.

I lifted the knife again, and finished reciting the spell. At the final word, I drove the knife down into the grinning vampire face of the amulet. The knife, aided by magic, slid in all the way to the hilt. The blade grew hot, burning my hands, but I kept them in place, channeling magic into the spell. The amulet split in half with a loud crack.

A piece of me felt torn asunder. I fell back, gasping, losing the magic I'd gathered. My magic in the circle vanished as I fell backwards.

I couldn't move, I couldn't breathe, and I felt only half of myself. Lessened. Hollowed out.

"Goddess!" Kurt screamed behind me.

Jack darted to my side and put his paws on my chest, shoving his muzzle into my face. He was back as a jackal, blood dripping from his wounds even after changing. I felt like that was bad, but I couldn't seem to summon any emotion. All I could do was blink up at him. Jack licked my face, whining.

It took me a few moments to pull myself together enough to sit upright. The world swam and I leaned heavily on Jack's furry side. My vision had constricted to a pinprick and my fingers tingled as the Goddess' poison blood moved through me.

"Is she...?" I couldn't finish. My tongue weighed a thousand pounds. My lips were numb, and the few words I'd gotten out were slurred.

"She collapsed. I'm not sure if she's dead." Jack made his best effort at a shrug, the fur of his shoulder rippling under my hands. "I don't know how to tell on a vampire."

Jack pawed at my pocket. My amulet slipped out and landed on the dirt next to me. Right, I needed to destroy it too.

If I destroyed my amulet, I'd lose the magical protection. The blood I'd ingested from Goddess was poison to me, like the vampires had said their blood was to other vampires. If I destroyed it, would it kill me? How much was too much? But if I didn't, I'd lose the memory of the spell and be unable to destroy it.

I reached out a shaking hand to place it over my amulet with the wobbly letters of my chosen name. I closed my eyes and a tear rolled down my cheek. I had to destroy it. These were evil. The lure spell placed on it had already killed Nate and Oakley. If I kept it, how many more would have to die?

"Lean on me," Jack said. His fur was warm against my side.

Jack had broken the circle when he'd run over to me. I tried to reach for it to fix it, but fell on my face. My head spun.

"What do you need?" Jack asked.

"Circle. Fix." I managed to spit out.

I could feel when he'd put it back into place and sent a pulse of magic to it from my outstretched fingers. Then I got an arm around Jack and he pushed me back upright.

The knife was wedged deep in the dirt and it took me a few moments of tugging and wiggling the blade to pull it free. Then I stopped and looked down at Jack. His sandy-furred tail wagged and his muzzle pulled back into a smile. "Do it," Jack barked.

I don't think he realized what he was asking of me. Still, I smiled down at him and took a precious moment to kiss the top of his head between his comically large ears. "I love you, Jack," I whispered, then closed my eyes and recited the spell a second time.

My numb lips stumbled over the words, and I had to repeat myself several times. The second time, channeling the energy was almost easier, rushing in to fill the hollowed-out center of me where Goddess's amulet had burrowed deep inside my soul. I remembered her name now that the amulet's hold over me was gone. All her orders had been destroyed with it.

None of the assembled vampires gathered around the fallen Goddess, noticed what I was doing as I lifted the knife above my head with one hand, the other still gripping the fur of Jack's ruff, grounding me. I drove the knife down into the center of my carved name. Or tried to. My numb fingers lost their grip on the handle and the point hit the very edge of the golden disc. The tip of the blade barely penetrated, but it was enough. My amulet split into four pieces with a loud crack.

As the amulet shattered, I shattered with it, and the hollowness I'd felt before was nothing compared to this. With the breaking of Goddess's amulet, it was like the center of my chest had been scooped out; when my amulet broke it was like my entire being vanished, leaving me a paper-thin shell of self. I collapsed onto Jack and knew no more.

WHEN EVERETT'S AMULET SHATTERED into four pieces, he collapsed like a puppet whose strings had been cut, slumping over onto me, his eyes wide and staring at nothing. I barked for help, so upset I couldn't even form words for several long moments. Avery padded over and nosed at Everett's side then sat down next to me.

"The ancient one over there." He bobbed his muzzle in the direction of the knot of vampires. "Is in the same state. I assume these are the cause?" He pointed a huge paw at the gold pieces of both broken amulets that were scattered around Everett.

I nodded, whining again, and licked Everett's cheek. He lay on his side, head resting on my flank. His skin had turned a dark, ashen gray and his lips were purple. He didn't even twitch at the feel of my tongue, but Avery's warm presence next to me was calming and kept me from panicking.

I rested my head near Everett's so I could keep an eye on him for signs of life, such as they were.

Eventually, the vampires noticed that Everett was down as well when they came looking to their 'high priest' to tell them what to do. Tawaret was in the same state as Everett-catatonic and unresponsive.

The vampires seemed at a loss, wandering back and forth between Tawaret and Everett, as if one or the other might suddenly recover.

Avery freed Xander from his bonds, and he joined me and Everett. Rowan limped over as well, carrying Annabelle. I could smell the rot on Annebelle already; she was dead.

At a loss for what else to do, we gathered up the vampires and the injured shapeshifters and shuttled everyone in carpools back to Tawaret's mansion and their houses to recover. Everyone except Everett and Tawaret, who we took to the Las Vegas PCA office.

Stacy's eyes widened when she saw Everett. "Blood poisoning!"

She shuttled him into a different room and started barking orders at the other vampires. "How did this happen, Jack!" Stacy yelled at me as she got his limp body settled into one of the care rooms.

"He bit Tawaret." I refused to leave the room, but kept hold of his hand sitting near the head of the bed as out of the way as I could get.

"Shit. He must not be able to handle the blood of his own clan." She put a hand on her hip. "How long ago? And how much?"

"Two hours, I think?" It had taken us a while to get things organized and to coax the distraught vampires to let us take Tawaret and Everett away. "And not much. She ordered him to stop almost immediately."

"He might live then."

I tightened my grip on his hand. They pumped his stomach to be safe, but got nothing. Then they tried to get him to eat some bottled blood without success. He didn't respond to either Stacy or my cut arm in his mouth. They had to hook him up to an IV to get fresh blood into his system.

I sat at Everett's bedside all day until Avery dragged me back to his house to sleep in a real bed. Xander took my place, promising to call if there were any changes. But there weren't, not for another three days.

He woke up during one of Xander's shifts. When I came in, I found Xander with a bandage on the side of his neck and Everett sleepy-eyed, but awake, lying in a half-reclined bed.

I dropped down to my knees and scooped up his hand. "How you feeling?" I asked him, gently squeezing his hand. Some color was back in his cheeks but his skin was still a waxy gray.

"Okay," he said after a brief pause while he took a breath to speak. He blew the word out like it took a lot of effort to even do that.

"I'm so glad you're awake." I kissed his hand.

"Jack, we need to talk." Stacy's voice startled me. I gave his hand another squeeze, then followed her into the hall.

"What is it?" I folded my arms and glared at her; a bit miffed that I'd barely seen Everett before she pulled me away.

"I heard you were planning to take him back to Portland?"

I frowned. "Yeah, why?"

Stacy rubbed her arms, and I realized she was nervous. "Look, the vampires they bit..." She trailed off into silence, not meeting my gaze.

"I assumed that the addiction would have worn off when the amulets were destroyed."

She shook her head. "I think the amulet just amplified the effect. There are a few hundred vampires here in Las Vegas that would be pretty distraught if Everett left. Just these last few days when we didn't know if either of them would wake up, they've been panicking. I've been trying to keep them calm, but it's been a near thing."

"What else was the amulet doing that we didn't know about?" I hit the back of my head on the wall.

Stacy let out a shaky laugh. "Guess we'll find out in the next few months."

"What about my house? My job?"

"You'll need to decide which is more important to you. But I'm *not* letting Everett leave Las Vegas." Stacy stalked away.

I chased after her. "Wait, Stacy! Why was he unconscious for so long?"

She stopped abruptly and whirled on me. "He didn't tell you?"

"Tell me what?"

"The amulets kept them alive by storing parts of their souls. When Everett destroyed them, he severed that connection."

"His soul!" I covered my mouth in horror.

"Souls aren't finite things, Jack." Stacy touched my shoulder. "It's not like your body. Souls grow, change. The portion lost can be regrown, but in its absence, until it does, Everett still hurts. He'll need your support if you can offer it."

Could I? That was the question. Was I ready to uproot my entire life, again, for him? I hugged myself. "But he'll be alright?"

"Eventually, yes. The fact that he woke up... it's a very good sign. Tawaret, the Goddess, still hasn't."

EPILOGUE

Four Months Later

I'd been confined for the last few months while the vampire elders debated what to do with Goddess—Tawaret, I still struggled to call her that—and me. Each day they let a couple of vampires in for me to feed off of. Like a sedate version of the sunrise ceremony.

Tawaret still hadn't woken up. At this point, the elders agreed with me that she might have had too much of herself in the amulet. Goddess had been trapped, living through the amulet while her body was confined, for thousands and thousands of years. Most of her soul was probably inside it when it had shattered. She might never wake up.

For now, she was confined and restrained, being fed by IV drip like I had been for those first few days.

I barely remembered my first month at the facility except for Xander and Jack's constant presence, and snapshots of time. Jack had refused to leave my side, I was told, and had recruited Xander to be there when he couldn't.

Gradually I clawed my way out of the pit of despair that the loss of my amulet had left in me. It was like all my emotions had been sucked out when I'd broken the amulet. Even when I looked at Jack,

I remembered loving him, but he felt like a stranger to me. I still struggled with falling back into that feeling from time to time.

"How you doing?" Xander asked, glancing at me in the rearview mirror. He'd volunteered to drive me back to the mansion so that I didn't have to take a cab.

I picked at the seam of my jeans and shrugged, staring out at the flashing lights of Vegas. Halloween decorations fluttered from the displays, ghosts and fake graves stuck into the grass. It might have been October, but the oppressive heat hadn't let up at all. I felt betrayed, somehow, that it wasn't Jack driving. "Where's Jack?"

"He had an errand to run. Don't worry, he'll meet us at the house."

I hoped Xander wasn't lying, but I'd also seen Jack's plane ticket to Portland in Xander's memory the last time I'd bitten him.

With Nate and Oakley dead, ownership of the mansion Tawaret and I had been staying in had been signed over to Tawaret. As her progeny, vampire law made it mine now.

At Jack's suggestion, I'd opened the house up, letting in any vampire who needed a place to stay. About a dozen had taken me up on the offer, including Kurt and Stacy, and they had been maintaining it in my absence.

As for me, I was on a sort of permanent probation. PCA officers would be keeping a close watch on me, and reporting my every move back to the elders. Tawaret was being kept in Las Vegas under watch and guard. There'd been talk of destroying her, but it had been put on hold because the PCA didn't want to destroy one of only two vampires remaining in our bloodline.

Especially after the viral video. I already had a backlog of a dozen applications of humans wanting to have me as their maker; not that I planned on ever taking any of them up on it. Maybe Xander, if he ever changed his mind again. But we'd see.

After living on nothing but fresh vampire blood for weeks in Vegas, I still found human and shapeshifter blood disgusting. As part of my probation, I was only allowed to bite vampires who'd given permission.

Not that that would be a problem. Every vampire Goddess and I had bitten during the sunrise ceremony had already come to see me while I'd been under lock and key, and all had planned to stop by and visit later. There were so many in fact that Stacy had maintained the ceremony's reservation system, converting it into a bite schedule.

When we arrived, the mansion was lit up. A dozen vampires waited on the front lawn to greet me with large hand-written signs.

Avery stood on the porch, bounding down as I got out of the car to pull me into a hug.

"Woah there," I said after a moment, gently pushing away. "I thought you didn't like vampires."

He laughed and slapped me on the back. "I'm willing to admit when I'm wrong. Here let me get your bags."

Avery had come to see me while I'd been confined and sobbed into my arms, thanking me for being willing to jump off a building to save Xander from being turned. He'd even over-looked the fact that I'd bit Xander, and I planned to try attending some trans meetups again with him soon.

He moved towards the trunk but I stopped him with an out-stretched arm. "Don't have any."

I barely looked up from my feet as Avery led Xander and me inside. Music played from the living room and a big 'Welcome Home' banner had been hung above the back door, and streamers and balloons hung in little groupings around the room. Kurt was there, along with many familiar faces.

But not the one I cared about.

I dropped my backpack on the floor and turned to flee upstairs when I saw Jack, who'd been coming from the bathroom down the hall. He wore a silly party hat and a matching pink and blue striped shirt. I dashed for him and flung my arms around him. "Jack!"

Jack caught me in his arms and swung me around in circle before setting me back on the floor and leaning down to kiss me. I groaned, kissing him back and reaching up to twist my fingers through his hair, knocking off his party hat. It was good to be home and free.

He pulled away with a laugh.

"I thought you left me for Portland." I burst into tears, hugging him close.

"Sorry! I had to fly back to pack up my things and arrange a renter for my house. I thought you'd never even notice I was gone. Who ratted me out?"

"Xander," I said, sniffing.

"I didn't tell him!" Xander protested, coming up behind us.

"Not on purpose." I stuck my tongue out at him.

"Still biting him?" He ruffled my hair. "Dang, I should have known not to tell him."

"Where's Brun?" They would have been hard to miss even in the crowd, as tall as they were.

"They moved away as soon as they got out of the hospital. I think they went with the Montana jackal," Avery said.

"The who?" I glanced around blankly.

"Guess she didn't tell you about those plans." Jack hugged me. "She'd started sending out vampires to kidnap jackals for her. Only one she'd gotten so far was the one from Montana, who was found in the basement."

"Oh." I leaned into Jack, stricken by how isolated I'd been. "I'd had no idea."

Kurt appeared in a flash next to us. All four of us jumped.

"I've fixed up the barn so you can use it as a workshop. Stacy mentioned that you used to work at the museum, restoring artifacts. I've been spreading the word, and I already have you a whole waiting list of clients."

"You..." I blinked at him. "Who told you to do that?" I'd never seen Kurt take initiative on anything before.

Kurt looked contrite, another new thing. "No one, but I thought... I know you were unhappy here. I wanted to do something to apologize for what I did while under Godd— I mean Tawaret's influence."

"Thank you," I said softly, disentangling myself from Jack to put a hand on his arm and craned my neck to look up at his face. "But I know she hurt you too... Your partner..."

He shook his head, but I noticed he didn't shake off my hand. "Not your fault."

"It's not yours, either. You have nothing to apologize for."

He gave me a smile and now moved away. I let my hand drop. "It didn't take much work on my part. Vampires live a long time, and a lot of them have old things that need care."

With that he inclined his head to me again and moved away to mingle with the rest of the party guests.

In the former chapel, a DJ had been set up at the far end by the doors outside. The rest of the space was being used as a dance floor. Jack spun me onto the dance floor and we danced together for a few songs, until one came on that sent me back to the night I'd met Nate and Oakley, grinding at the club. I pulled him back into the living room, where the vampires on the couch all shifted to make room for us.

I sat on Jack's lap on the couch running my fingers through his short beard. "If you rented your house, where are you going to live?"

He chuckled and grabbed my hand, pulling it up to his lips. "I'd hoped here, with you."

Jack hesitated a moment then shifted me over so he could get something out of his pocket. He flashed me a smile. "I was going to wait until later, when we were alone, but... I'm impatient."

I giggled. "Hey, I'm the impatient one."

"Must be catching." Jack flicked open the little black box to reveal two men's gold wedding bands. "Everett, will you marry me?"

"Yes!" I squealed and threw my arms around his neck. The vampires around us burst into spontaneous applause.

I didn't know what the future held for me, or us, or if Tawaret would ever wake up, but for now I was happy and free. And that was enough for now.

Also by Roan Rosser

The Changing Bodies Series

Book 1 - Ritual of the Ancients
Book 2 - Bloodline of the Ancients
Book 3 - Goddess of the Ancients
Prequel - Jackal of Hearts – Newsletter Freebie

The Chaos Menagerie Series

Book 1 - Red Pandamonium
Book 1.5 - Diamond in the Rat – Newsletter Freebie
Book 2 – Phoenix Flambé – Coming Soon
Book 3 – Pandora's Fox – Coming Soon

Other Books

Almost Magic (#minithology)

Ink Stained and Spellbound (#minithology)

About the Author

ROAN ROSSER

My urban fantasy novels mainly feature the trans and queer protagonists grappling with things like identity and found families that I wished I could have read about growing up.

I escaped from the bowels of Utah (namely Provo) and now live in the sunny Pacific Northwest of the United States.

When not writing, you can probably find me beating up pixel baddies or in front of one of my sewing machines adding to my overstuffed closet or my army of homemade plush dolls.

If you find yourself blinded by the vivid colors and loud patterns of my homemade shirts, know that I'm only trying to warn you that I may be poisonous. Or venomous? Or both? Probably both.

f facebook.com/roanrosser

BB bookbub.com/profile/roan-rosser

🐦 twitter.com/roanrosser